Arwen Jayne

In the Unknown Everything Awaits

The Multidimensional Travellers. Book 1

Arwen Jayne

Disclaimer

While reference has been made to some real locations all other names, characters and places are fictional; the product of the author's overly imaginative mind. Any resemblance to actual persons, living or dead, businesses or places is purely coincidental.

This is a piece of fiction, enjoy it but if you're looking for scientific facts you might find it lacking. The story is purely a creation of my imagination.

Acknowledgements

Thanks to all my fans, friends and family who support my work with their ongoing help and encouragement. To Jen for her valuable feedback on the first draft.

In the unknown Everything Awaits

Cover Photo Credit

Photo by Jeremy Bishop on Unsplash, "view of the barrel wave",
Jeremy Bishop, Published on June 25, 2017,
https://unsplash.com/photos/iftBhUFfecE

Author Note

The metaphysical side of this book grew out of a short story I wrote in 2021 called "Finding Eden." For the curious, that story provides background on Deman, Rachael, Lydia and Vladimir, who all make appearances in this novel. Oddly it was the celebration of the life of a family friend that captured my interest in what life aboard a cargo ship might be like. Knowing nothing of that lifestyle, curiosity had me diving deep into research for the plot of the story. It led me into reading "The Outlaw Ocean" by Ian Urbina which was truly an eye opener. Given a previous life in the media I opted for writing the main character as a journalist and then plonked her down in a war torn country where people have no rights to a life of their choosing, keeping details vague so that it could mean quite a few places. And so the story begins…

1

Stepping out of the air conditioned car was like stepping into an oven. The air scorched my throat. The heat sapped my energy. On the up side, wearing a face veil to hide the fact I was a westerner did save me from the suffocating dust that blew around us in small skirmishes. It had me wondering if they were in fact demons.

I'd parked our faded green Land Rover in a little used side alley and locked it. Then I studied the hand drawn map I'd been given. "This way Jared."

"Can I at least bring a tripod?" My cameraman and longtime friend Jared brushed the choking dust from the fake black beard that gave him the slight appearance of being a local.

"No. We can't afford to stand out. If anyone sees you carrying that they're going to know that we're media and get curious. We promised her we'd do all in our power not to lead her enemies to her. She wants her message to get out but would rather keep her life. Can't really blame her."

Jared sighed in resignation, "I'll just bring the hand cam then. Hopefully she'll have a table or something equally solid I can use to get a steady shot. It would be a pain to do the entire interview handheld."

Being careful to keep to the shadows of the alleyways, for the cool and for concealment, we made our way to the faded blue unmarked door. I counted from the corner to be sure. Definitely the place. I knocked.

A single eye came to the peephole, reminding me to throw back my veil so she could see my face. The eye surveyed us then Adeela opened the door. "Are you Rylee Jackson?"

"Please call me Ry. And this is my cameraman Jared Petersen." Jared, tall, thin and gangly, gave her a friendly nod but said little. He was happily busy removing the fake beard.

"Very pleased to meet you both. Welcome to my home such as it is. Come in and make yourselves comfortable while I make some tea."

It was on the tip of my tongue to tell her not to worry on our behalf but I knew that ceremony was important in this part of the world.

Adeela returned with an ornate vintage silver platter that belied the spartan nature of her home. The best for the guests I assumed, accepting the fine porcelain cup of aromatic tea she passed to me. "Thank you." I waited while she passed a cup to Jared before I disturbed her with questions. I made use of the short time by sipping my tea, grateful to quench my thirst. It tasted sweet and smelled of cardamom. It was a style of tea I'd become accustomed to during my two years in this strife-worn country.

Adeela served herself then sat in a well worn but immaculately clean armchair. "I appreciate you taking the risk of coming to see me."

"I think the risk is yours," I noted.

"Perhaps the risk is to both of us."

Jared frowned but quietly watched the two of us banter as he sipped his tea. He was used to letting me take the lead, at least when it came to work.

"How can I help?" I wasn't one to beat around.

"Simply by covering the plight of women in my country."

"I think most of my viewers are familiar with their problems already."

"Yes, but can they put faces to those problems? I want to make the situation real for them."

"What do you hope to achieve by that?" I needed to know her hopes. I didn't want to give her any false ones. "Honestly, I can't do this interview as a news item as sadly there's nothing newsworthy in it, not enough for the television companies to pick it up and run with it. We could do an online article with an embedded video. You couldn't be sure how many would press play on that but it might be a start. For a feature I would need to do an in depth interview, heartfelt and emotional, with breakaway grabs of real life related to what we're discussing. I could try and sell that to my agent who might on-sell it to the internationals as a current affairs piece but it would need to cover an angle of the problem that hasn't been done before. I'm sorry if all this sounds non-committal but that's the nature of the industry I work for."

Adeela winced, clearly she'd hoped for more. "I want some way to get people out in the wider world to see the atrocities and injustices my people live with. I know I'm an idealist, Ry, but I hope that a groundswell of support for our cause might influence international politicians and decision makers to intervene and bring pressure to bear on those who abuse their positions of power in my own country. Somewhere governments must serve the people, surely." She paused to sip her tea, considering. "I can do heartfelt and emotional if that's what's required."

"Great," I loved co-operative and willing talent who would work to my needs. Though her hopes were indeed idealistic I'd do what I could. "Perhaps Jared, you could start by taking some cut away shots of Adeela's home. No offence Adeela but I want the viewers to see how you live, spartan yet elegant when it counts." I nodded towards the tea tray.

"No offence taken. You're the expert in this. I trust you."

Good grief. "I'm honoured, but really I wouldn't get into the habit of trusting media people. The story often comes before anything else. Ratings, that's what television companies care about and that drives what stories they will buy."

"I've seen some of your work. I believe you to be more compassionate than most, that's why I sent my message to you. I'm happy to work with you to make sure it's worth your while."

Hmm, "It would be easy to make this a feminist piece. About a place where it's illegal to even do what you're doing now, living on your own without a man in charge of you. But if you want a wider audience we need to make sure it doesn't turn off the men in our potential audience." I had an idea. Yes, it might actually work. "Does how you're treated have repercussions for the men in your society?"

Adeela's eyes widened in surprise and then she grinned. "Ah, I see where you're going. Clever. Well yes it does because the men are forced into accepting only certain roles, such as protector, warrior, financial provider and disciplinarian, that for some of them goes against their true natures. Some want to be caregivers, helping the sick and poor and helping to raise their children. Some don't want to wage war but are made to take sides and take up arms. They end up broken by what they're forced to do. Others would like to pursue lives that didn't involve marriage and a large family. Free of those responsibilities they could take up careers that don't always pay well but yet feed their heart and soul rather than their wallet."

"Excellent, let's take that slant. Not women's rights but equal opportunity for everyone to be themselves. To lead authentic fulfilling lives."

"I like it," Adeela readily agreed. "And it's removed blinkers I didn't know I was wearing. It's not a female problem. It's a human problem."

I could see I was going to love working with Adeela. "Jared, when you're finished with the house shots I think we'll set up and have a first run at the interview." It didn't matter if we didn't get it all on the first take. I could re-ask questions and do cut-aways. We'd piece it all together in the makeshift editing suite back in our hotel room.

A loud boom outside reverberated through the house and had the wall shedding dust. We all looked nervously at each other.

"Fighting sounds close," I noted, none too sure of our safety.

Adeela was on alert too. "I think it might be best for all of us if we leave the area. There's a back way out of my house."

I grabbed my notebook and Jared grabbed his camera. Dismissing any thoughts of making a run out the front and back to our vehicle we followed Adeela through the kitchen and out past the bedrooms. At the back door Adeela exited and held the heavy wooden door open for us. Jared was behind me, fear shone in his eyes. I was almost out the door when the missile hit the house.

2

I woke up briefly, in snatches of consciousness. I could feel Adeela tying something around my left arm. I had a vague sensation of being dragged on a sheet of something. Soft reassuring words caressed me as I drifted back into the blackness of an unknown void.

The next time my eyes dared to open I was lying in a bed, staring at the ceiling of a simple mud brick room. My body ached like it had been thrown against a wall, which it had. Vaguely I remembered the explosive blast slamming me against Adeela's neighbour's house. "Jared!" I called out, fearing the worst.

Adeela rose from the chair beside my bed. I hadn't even been aware of her presence. "He's not here. I'm sorry Ry. This is all my fault. I should never have called you."

"So you're single handedly to blame for those who destroyed your house. You're to blame for the strife in your country and to blame for those who rule it."

She sighed, "No, none of that."

"Then you're not to blame. Where's Jared?"

"He's dead Ry."

"Fuck." My heart constricted.

"I'm sorry."

Hot tears threatened to flow but I clenched whatever muscles still worked in my battered body and forced them back. "Not your fault. Not my fault. Jared and I both knew the risks coming here."

"Why did you come?"

"To fast track our careers." A fool's game in hindsight. "You don't get anywhere in our profession covering village fairs or dead donkeys."

Adeela choked, "Dead donkeys?"

"Not really, it's a euphemism for really boring stories you run as filler when nothing noteworthy is happening. Can I have a drink of water?"

Adeela passed me a glass, "Here, I should have asked you first up. I was just so happy to see you awake."

"And you?" I forced myself to think past my own searing pain.

"A busted rib. I was really lucky it didn't rupture my spleen. Bruising of course. I lost consciousness but thankfully only briefly. I was able to drag you away before any insurgents came to check on the hit."

"You think it was aimed at you."

"Don't you?"

"Maybe," I felt more lucid now. And while I knew Adeela was a target for the rebels her house could have just as easily been collateral damage. "I need to sit up."

"I'll give you a hand."

"No nurse?" I didn't want her straining her busted rib but there was a curious lack of medical staff.

Adeela seemed to understand my raised eyebrow, "We're not in a hospital Ry. I couldn't risk it. I brought you to my friend's place. He's a doctor. But he's not keen on me being here, because of the target on my back. I need to leave."

"And go where? We'll leave together." I felt resolved to save this woman, the woman who'd saved my life.

"You need a proper hospital, Ry."

"Why?" Fear gnawed at the edges of my mind. What wasn't she telling me?

She winced.

But when she helped me to sit up I saw the reason clearly enough. Horrifically clearly. " Oh - my - god!" There was a stump where my left forearm had been. "Your friend did this?" God help me, my arm had been amputated. Not that I was religious but at that moment I felt the need for something to yell at.

"No Ry, he just sewed you up. Your arm was in pieces all over my back patio. There was nothing to reattach. There's severe bruising on your left hip and possibly a crack in the bone. Your left foot's pretty mangled too. Karim's not sure it can be saved."

Reeling from what I now faced I yelled at my inner self to shut the fuck up and get it's shit together. "We both need to get out of here. I need a phone."

Adeela went and rummaged in a large bag on the bench. Finding what she wanted she passed it to me, "I salvaged as much as I could. I hope it still works."

I realised then just how much she had done. She could have run and left me but somehow this resourceful woman had used guts and determination to gather up what she could, patch me on site and get me here. "I owe you more than I can say."

Adeela blinked back tears, "You owe me nothing."

"That's not for you to decide." I fumbled with the phone and swore. Bloody hell, doing things with only one hand was an ask. Adeela reached over and supported the phone for me while I punched a number on my sat phone, wondering as I did what time it was on the other side of the world. I did the math and with relief decided it would be daylight there. "Deman."

"Ry, is that you?"

"What's left of me."

"What?"

"Long story. I'm in a really bad way, Deman. Jared's dead. I need out of this hell hole, fast, and I need an out too for the woman who just saved my life."

"Shit, how bad are you?"

"Might manage crutches," I hoped.

"Give me a moment to see what I have in the vicinity."

I listened to the furious typing on the other end of the phone.

"I have it. The Merkwood II's moored in the port near you. Can you get to it?"

"I'll ask." I looked to Adeela. "We need transport to the port."

Adeela paled, shaking her head, "Even if you could manage crutches, and I doubt that. You've lost a lot of blood Ry. You're in no fit state."

Hmm, "Did you hear that Deman."

"Leave it with me, I'll see what I can do."

"You don't even know where I am."

Deman laughed at that, "Keep your phone with you and keep it switched on. We'll find your location off of that. .I'll go and arrange a pick up. Don't be too shocked in the meantime if you see an apparition." He hung up.

I frowned, an apparition?

"Who was that man?" Adeela asked.

"A god-zillionaire shipping magnate I happened to go to school with. Hey, don't look at me like that. It's nothing romantic. We're just good friends. I personally wouldn't have it any other way. Deman's a ladies man, if you know my meaning."

"He's a confirmed bachelor."

"He is that." Or at least he was the last I remembered. But having organised our pick-up the seriousness of my situation hit me again with a vengeance. My career was rooted. Damned if I wouldn't get one final story out of it though. "You said you wanted media coverage Adeela. Sadly it isn't the damage to your house that might get it for you but the damage to an international reporter might. I don't suppose you managed to salvage Jared's handycam too?"

"You mean this?" Miraculously Adeela fished it out of the cavernous tote bag.

"Excellent," It's casing was badly scratched and beat up, almost as bad as me, but it still worked when I switched it on. "Now let me show you how to use it. If you'll accept the temporary job, you're now my cameraman."

"Don't you mean camerawoman?"

I rolled my eyes towards the cobweb laden ceiling, "Have it your way. Here," I pointed with my one good remaining hand. "That switches it on."

Adeela proved an able student. Once she was confident she went off to practise with the camera, going off to film Karim's wife working in the kitchen while I wrote a script for what I wanted to say.

I checked her footage, offering some suggestions around framing. I pointed out the need to be aware of stray objects in frame that might detract from the point of focus. Then we set up and recorded my report on what had happened to me and the why.

"This is Ry Jackson, reporting from my makeshift hospital bed. My cameraman Jared Petersen is dead. Both of us were caught in a bomb blast that targeted our interviewee's home. I sustained a number of injuries including the loss of my left arm. Why? Because this country leaders are scared of its ordinary citizens demanding basic human rights and they bombed one of those citizens in order to silence her.

They're scared of people who don't believe in their particular ideology. It's as if their very existence will threaten the survival of all they believe. Ideology is not a living entity to be defended from harm. It should be able to stand up to scrutiny or evolve. Yet in the name of their ideology, which they claim to be the only one that is moral and just, they're prepared to harm, even kill, dissenters."

I delivered a measured and informed rant about what they did to those dissenters and how it harmed their society as a whole. That they held a limited vision which didn't allow for the needs of the individual or indeed the different communities that made up their society.

"The truth is there is little hope for societies like this one until they progress past authoritarian ideologies that allow no room for difference. By imposing their model of what is right on their citizens they hamstring their economy and their development. Without difference there is no change. Without change there is no progress. Without progress there is no hope for a better life for their people.

According to Don Beck and Christopher Cowan's spiral dynamics model it could be said their society was stuck somewhere between being tribal and authoritarian with a few narcissistic abusers thrown in. To evolve past that they'd need to start investing in their economy, in infrastructure and in research and development rather than spending most of their budget on armaments as they do now. Encourage small business innovation and start dealing with community level issues such as environmental degradation and water quality.

Before I sign off for good and go to learn how to live with my new limitations I have this one plea. Let's, all of us, stop dividing the world into those who do and don't believe in our favourite brand ideology. Whether that ideology be political, religious, economic, tribal or even the sporting team we barrack for. Let's stop seeing the divisions and see the people instead. Humans, just like us." We saw ourselves as separate from plants, animals and minerals too, I thought to myself, but I didn't want to complicate my message. I ended the piece there.

Whoever edited could cut it down. And I suspected they'd cut a lot. My rant would be seen as political and not all media outlets would dare to go there. Hell, I'd done what I could. I'd given them the meat of the situation and they could take what they would of it. I only hoped it helped to get Adeela's message out, as we'd originally planned.

I'd give my agent, George, instructions to add in a retrospective on Jared work and to contact his next of kin before the footage was aired. I didn't have a clue how your registered someone as dead when you didn't have the body parts but George might know.

Then we set about convincing Adeela's friend, the reluctant Karim, to send our unedited piece to camera to George, using a VPN and the heaviest encryption I knew he could access. Having done that both Adeela and I drifted back off to sleep, her in her chair beside my bed and me, well, in the bed. I hoped no one saw my tears of self pity. I was a physical wreck and, though I hid it well enough, an emotional wreck as well. How could I come out the other side of this debacle? But fatigue dragged me into a reluctant rest, my body's need to heal itself over-riding my mind's worries about my future and the damage to my vanity and ego.

I woke, some time towards three in the morning, suddenly aware of a strange sensation in my mangled and heavily bandaged foot. My eyes ventured open but my brain did not compute. It couldn't be real. Deman had made a passing comment about expecting an apparition but I'd assumed I'd mis-heard or it had been some kind of weird joke that meant something only to him because it surely hadn't made any sense to me. He'd hung up before I could ask him what he meant.

But here she was. An apparition indeed. I could see through her to the other side of the wall.

She put a finger to her lips and shook her head, urging me to keep silent, then she went back to her work. She held her hands over my foot and I could literally see light passing from them into my foot. For the first time in hours I could feel my foot.

When she finished there she made a hand motion which I took to mean I should turn onto my right side. What the hell, she, whoever she was, seemed to be here to help so I obliged.

I felt the same strange tingling in my damaged hip. It wasn't like sciatica. Almost an electrical kind of energy that pulsed within the depth of the joint, followed by a pleasant, warm sensation that radiated out from that one point. When the apparition had finished there she moved her attention to my other bruises and lacerations.

I pointed frantically to where my arm had been but she just shook her head sadly. Damn.

The apparition floated over to where Adeela slept. Once again I could see the light pouring from the woman's hands, this time into Adeela's ribcage. Then the ghost evaporated.

I was alert, stunned, my heart pounding furiously as I tried to process what I'd just seen. Was I in a waking dream? But I felt a push on my mind, like I was being told to sleep and I did.

The next time my eyes ventured open the pale rays of dawn's light shafted through the only window in the simple mudbrick room. The world looked real. No angels, ghosts or whatever. It had been a dream. I was sure of that now.

Karim's wife brought us breakfast while her husband checked my foot. Carefully he unwrapped the bandages then he froze and stared.

"What?" Panic seized my gut. I had no idea if he knew English but someone had better damned well tell me what was going on. "You're not cutting off my foot." I declared adamantly.

Adeela stirred and yawned. "What's going on?" She rose from the decrepit cloth covered armchair where she'd been sleeping

There was a rapid fire exchange between Adeela and Karim in their own language, way too fast for me to follow with what little I knew.

"Someone better start talking to me in English. It's my bloody foot." I swore. "Is it infected? Dropping off? What?"

Adeela shook her head, "Actually no. It's healing remarkably well."

"Well that's a good thing isn't it?" I relaxed, somewhat.

"It is but Karim's never seen healing this rapid. Come to think of it, I don't feel so bad either." She poked at where I knew her bandages were. She didn't wince. She looked up in wonder at Karim and just shrugged her shoulders.

Karim hustled her to another room, I assumed to examine her. They returned, again in deep discussion in their language. Karim was praising his god, I picked that much out. I was guessing, given the religion of the country, it might not be a good idea to start talking about an otherworldly woman who poured light from her hands.

"So what's the verdict?" I wasn't too sure of Adeela's doctor friend but to use a cliche, which always griped me, beggars couldn't be choosers.

"Karim thinks it's a miracle. I'm hesitant to dissuade him as he now feels honoured that he was chosen to help us. But he's still keen to see us gone, because of the risk our presence poses to his family."

"I'm keen to be gone too." I dug into my breakfast, feeling somewhat safer now the threat of them cutting off my foot seemed to have gone away. I munched on the freshly baked bread, liberally spread with sour cherry jam, savoured the heavily sugared black tea and then dug into the tasty tomato omelette. It wasn't my usual breakfast but it tasted good. At least it hadn't been the local delicacy of sheep's hooves boiled in water. I said my thanks to Karim's wife as she went to take the tray away.

My phone vibrated on the bedside table. I looked at the number and then picked it up. "Deman. Any news?" I didn't switch the call to speaker mode in case he said anything about my night time visitor. No need to spook, ha, the locals.

"How're you feeling this morning?"

"I've got company, but yes, many thanks." I answered his query cryptically but as succinctly as I could.

"Understood. The captain of the ship is sending two guys around to pick you up and drive you to the port. Jeff Felly and Mike McNee. They'll have ID with them. They have your location and should be there very soon."

"I owe you." I knew he wouldn't like it but I had to say it.

"Stuff off. I'm just sorry we couldn't do anything more."

I assumed he meant my arm. "And Adeela?" I wasn't about to tell the man his job but I still wondered how we were going to ship her out of this country and get her into mine.

"Ah, yes, your camerawoman. Don't worry about that for now. Just get on board that ship, both of you."

"Of that we have every intention. Go back to your no doubt busy day, Deman. I'll give you a call when we're safely at sea."

"See that you do," he hung up. Deman wasn't one for frivolous chatter.

Karim left us but returned to let us know our pick-up had arrived and that they were waiting out in the foyer.

Adeela helped me dress, covering up in the usual concealing garb that was common to her people. No doubt the clothes had been donated by Karim's wife. Adeela grabbed the tote bag containing what was left of my possessions. None of us were too sure how much I should test out my newly healed foot and hip so I leaned on Adeela for support and we went out to meet our greeting party.

"G'day ladies. Howzit goin'?" one of the guys extended his hand for a shake.

I cringed at the over-the-top accent as I shook his hand. My intuition was telling me something was definitely off about the pair. "Nice to meet you and you are?"

"This is Jeff. Me, I'm Iron Man Mike," he laughed somewhat nervously I thought. "Bonza day don't ya think?"

And there it was again, the tension between my shoulder blades increasing as I listened to his outdated slang. Added to that was the fact that the supposed Jeff was strangely silent. "I haven't been outside yet so I couldn't say. I don't mean to be rude but can I see your IDs?"

They handed them over and I studied them carefully. No photos but the details looked legit. "They seem to be in order," but.

Mike looked pleased, though I noted the pleasure had a sly tinge to it, "The car:s outside, if you'll come with us."

I casually patted down my garment as if checking for something. "Oh, just a moment, I think a bandage has come loose. Adeela, could you help me with it?" I went to return to my 'hospital' room.

"No probs," Mike hadn't twigged that I was onto him. "Youz sheilas do what ya need and we'll wait out here."

When we got back into the bedroom Adeela was instantly onto me, "You haven't got a bandage there. What's up?"

"They're not who they say they are. No-one speaks Australian like that these days. Not unless they're comedians or something. Certainly not seasoned sailors in the merchant navy. I suspect the real Jeff and Mike are down some alley by now with their throats cut."

Adeela swore quietly in the local tongue then looked around the room. She found a scalpel and wrapped it in bandages before handing it to me. "Are you going to be okay to walk?"

I put a little more weight on my left foot and tested it, "Seems good but let's at least pretend I'm an invalid. They'll underestimate us then." I suggested, not too loudly as I didn't want us to be heard from the other room.

"Good thinking."

Karim must have sensed something was up to as he came in to check on us. Adeela spoke to him quietly and urgently.

He nodded and went to a cupboard. Pulling out a black doctor's bag he retrieved a vial of something and drew up a syringe. He placed that and a spare vial into Adeela's waiting hand. She pocketed both.

"We'd best go before they get wary," I suggested. "We want them both away from Karim's home before we attack."

"You're so sure they're not who they say they are?" Adeela asked.

"Oh, I'm sure. But I'll know more once we get into that car. We know which direction the port's in. Let's see where they head and what else they say."

I could clearly see the worry on her brow, "We might get in the car but will we get out?"

Karim eyed us with worry too, but he wanted us gone. He wished us a 'go in peace' and then opened the door to hussle us out.

The guys were still waiting. Mike smiled, as if relieved. "This way then." He opened the passenger door for me. Adeela got into the back of the car next to the so called Jeff.

"Beaut day isn't it?" Mike made light conversation with his fake Australian banter while I fumbled one handed with the seat belt. So many things were going to be awkward in my future but now was not the time for self pity. I made sure I could feel the knife in my pocket.

"So where're you from Mike?" I asked, trying to guess which location he would attribute to his fictitious persona.

"Up near the Gold Coast."

"I know it well. Whereabouts? I might know some of your people."

Mike frowned. That stumped him. "Er, right in the centre of it," he fudged.

"Guess you hate the rainy season in July."

"Oh yeah, gross."

"Yeah, so much drier in December."

"You could say that."

His lack of knowledge of when the tropical wet season hit that part of Queensland confirmed my suspicions. Now how did I let Adeela know. I had to hope Mike's English wasn't as good as I knew Adeela's was. "It's just a pity the precipitation starts in November, not July." I was gambling on Adeela, who seemed highly educated, knowing the meteorological term while hoping fake Mike didn't.

Mike's brow furrowed even deeper as he tried to process that but Adeela took my cue. I didn't see her do it but we all heard the supposed Jeff swear as he started patting his hip, as if looking for a spider or something that had just bitten him. His eyes started to droop and his head dropped forward.

I unclipped my seatbelt and peered over my seat, "Er, Mike, I think something nasty just bit Jeff. He doesn't look so well. Maybe you should pull over so we can check him out. We might need to call an ambulance."

Mike fell out of character, swearing in the local language. As he looked around for a place to pull off I used the distraction to pull out the razor sharp knife and placed it against his jugular.

His eyes widened

"Now do as I say Mikey and you can live another day. Take that exit over there, the one that says port. If you don't take it you're dead."

"You're a woman. Women don't kill."

"Says you. Personally given the choices of being killed, raped or tortured or killing you, I pick the last option."

"We only wanted the other woman. You can go."

"Nice try, take the turn. In three, two, one…"

He took the turn.

"Good choice Mike."

"What gave me away?" Mike muttered, a small trickle of blood seeping down his neck from where I might have pressed a little too hard.

"Well let me see, it might have been the over-the-top 1970s comedic slang. Now brake carefully at that set of lights. This thing in my hand slices awfully easily. Sorry for the mess on your collar. Now what did you do with the two whose IDs you took?"

"They're dead, in an alley near where you were staying. We couldn't risk them contacting your people."

"So you took two innocent people's lives. Bastard."

"I'm a dead man myself now I've failed," Mike bemoaned as he carefully paused at the stop sign then very carefully took off again. "We were supposed to return with the other woman. She's on a list of people the decision makers want silenced. They're afraid she might stir up a rebellion. Well more than the one we've currently got. The big boss doesn't take failure."

"None of them do," I readily agreed. "You'd best get out of the country Mike, if you know what's good for you."

"Can I come with you?" he asked pleadingly.

Of all the gall! Though a tiny vestige of compassion stirred for the man who was soon to be on a death list himself, I couldn't risk it. "You know we can't trust you. You're going to have to find your own ship."

With the knife still at his throat he wasn't about to argue. He carefully drove us to the international port area. I could see the Merkwood II in the distance. "Stop the car. You can let us off here." I didn't need him to know which ship we were boarding. "Adeela, come and check this one's pockets for weapons. I don't want him shooting us in the back as we get out and my one hand is kind of busy holding this knife."

"Sure thing." Adeela got out and went around to open the driver's door. With an amused smirk she patted him down. I guess it wasn't often a female in her country got to touch a male that way. She found his commandeered ID, two hand guns, a stunner and a knife in his boot. Adeela wasn't smiling now as she pocketed the weapons within her cavernous, one size fits all cover garment.

"Take the keys," I suggested, "We don't want him running us down either."

"Hey, what hell hole do you live in lady?"

"This one."

"I could just tranq him," Adeela offered.

I sighed, against my better judgement, "Nah, he's been co-operative. If he keeps that way we won't shoot him as we leave. That a fair enough deal Mike? Are you going to start walking in that direction?" I pointed opposite to where we were going.

"You've got a deal, lady."

"Don't turn around once you start walking. I have the second highest ranking at my local gun range back home. I don't miss." I took the knife back from his neck. "Out!"

We watched him depart. When he was far enough away Adeela whispered in my ear. "So you're a good shot."

"Couldn't hit the side of a barn, but he believed me, that's all that matters. Did you get the other man's ID?"

She stared at me a moment then shook her head in wonder, "Yeah, I got it. You're good at the bluff."

"I'm a journalist."

We found the ship and had a lot of explaining to do.

"I'm awfully sorry captain," I handed the IDs over. "They were killed by the two thugs hired to kidnap us."

Captain Jefferson Wilcher looked between us and I knew what he saw, a heavily bandaged one armed injured woman and a local, kitted out in nothing but the local garb, "Tell me how you escaped."

So we told him.

"You let him go?" he asked, astonished.

"He won't live long. Not if he's silly enough to return to his boss empty handed."

The captain didn't seem so sure about that and obviously wasn't taking any chances. He looked around at the crew in his vicinity, "Chief Officer Pertwie, advise the port authorities that we need to make an unscheduled early departure. Bribe them if you have to."

"Yes, Captain."

"Second Officer Wellard, take these ladies to medical. Check them and then find them some accommodation."

The captain then apologised to us, "I'm sorry ladies, you're going to have to share a cabin."

"That's not a problem Captain," I assured him. "We're truly sorry for the loss of your crewmen and grateful for all the help you're giving us."

"Hmph," I wasn't sure he liked us. At the very least he didn't like the imposition. "I'll advise the owner that you're safely aboard." Then he left us in the capable hands of the Second Officer.

After our checkup Wellard showed us to our cabin.

"I don't think the captain likes us," I couldn't help but bring the subject up.

"He's just lost two valuable crewmen and now he has the painful duty of notifying their relatives" Wellard explained.

"And he's exchanged them for two liabilities. Is there any way we can help out on the ship rather than be dead weight?"

The Second Officer blinked, reassessing us. "I'll ask. You're not trained for maritime duties but there might be some menial work, if you're willing."

I shrugged nonchalantly, "I'm a bit limited with one arm but I could dust and clean, maybe scrub the loos."

"And I'm quite handy in the kitchen," Adeela offered. "Peeling spuds, washing dishes, whatever."

Wellard smiled at us, "The captain might not like you at the moment but you may yet earn his respect. I'll get back to you with your duties once they're assigned. In the meantime make yourselves comfortable. Lunch will be served at midday. Someone will collect you and show you where to go. Your cabin is equipped with most you'll need including spare pillows, blankets, drinking water and tea making facilities. You'll be expected to keep everything stowed away when not in use and make your own beds. The captain runs a tight ship," he warned. "We'll be leaving port shortly and our new heading will take us to the Seychelles before we start making the homeward journey. Welcome aboard ladies." He gave a curt nod then left us to ourselves.

"Bunk bed." I noticed.

"I can't see you clambering up top one armed. You'd best take the bottom."

"Yeah," I grunted, "thanks. Don't wet the bed."

Adeela spat out a shocked laugh. "Promise not to. You know you're refreshingly frank and direct."

"That's because I loathe manipulation and subterfuge, unless there's a very good reason for it." I'd come across too many tricky people in my life. "I like direct."

"I think I do too." Adeela mused. "I've spent too much of my life worrying about upsetting those who hold the power in our society. All the time self-editing what I say. It gets wearing."

Though I knew, sadly, that some lies and subterfuge are necessary. "How the hell are we going to get you into my country? Deman didn't baulk at me bringing you so I assume he has a plan." I tried my phone but had no joy with it. Likely I wasn't getting a signal inside the ship and I wasn't game to go wandering up on deck without permission. I already had a feeling that discipline on the cargo ship was in some ways not dissimilar to a naval vessel. At least the captain had said he'd tell Deman we'd gotten on board. I cursed now that we'd done a runner before putting together a viable plan. Getting to safety had seemed the most important thing at the time. Keeping Adeela from decades inside some immigration prison had now moved to the top of the priority list.

There was a knock at the door.

"Who is it?" I asked, even on board cautious. Spend too long in a hell hole of a country and you get like that.

"Purser Williams. I have some work clothes for you."

I opened the door and accepted the pile of garments, mostly black trousers and white shirts, from a jovial man who sported a neat beard and a balding head. It was the first real smile I'd had since coming on board. I smiled back. "Thanks so much."

"Something in that lot should fit you. I'll come back later and pick up your dirty clothes and have them laundered for you. Just leave them in a neat pile outside your door."

"That would be wonderful," Adeela piped up. "If I can be of any help with that let me know."

Williams looked super impressed, "Wellard said you were willing to pull your weight around here. He'll give you your duties at lunch. I'll be back to escort you to that." He warmed us with his smile again and left.

Adeela took her share of the clothes and studied them with no small amount of fascination. "I've haven't worn pants since I was a child in England. Won't the men focus, you know, on where my legs join my torso?"

An interesting thought. "Most of the men I've ever come across fall into two categories. Tits or bums. That's where they'll look and imagine."

"They'll look at the shape of my arse?" she asked, somewhat horrified.

"I wouldn't worry. Yours is quite nice."

"And why did you notice?" Clearly her mind didn't compute that statement.

"I'm a girl. I'm self conscious. Pays to know how you compare."

Adeela shook her head in amazement. "See, I've never had to worry about all that."

"So don't worry. Learn to strut yourself. Be proud of your figure. Stand straight and tall. Boobs out, belly in and swing those hips. Like this," I demonstrated.

Adeela broke into fits of laughter.

"So not helping my ego," I grumbled. I glared at the buttons on the shirt I'd just been given. There was something else that was going to hurt my ego. I wondered if the ship's supplies ran to velcro? Ah, welcome to my new world.

Williams dutifully returned at midday and took us towards the mess hall. There was no mistaking the clamour of voices, the clang of cutlery and plates and the aroma of tasty morsels. As we entered the room a hush descended. Heads turned. A few looked inquisitive. Others scowled or quickly looked away. It was obvious we were being held to blame for the loss of their two colleagues. I doubted there was a solid argument against that. We were just going to have to work to convince them we weren't so bad.

We took our allotted trays and queued at the serving counter.

"Steak, chicken or vegetable frittata," the server curtly outlined our options

Given I didn't see myself cutting up a steak anytime soon, if ever again, and no way was I going to suffer the indignity of someone else doing it for me, I opted for the frittata and a side serve of well cooked vegetables. Whether from choice or for moral support Adeela chose the same.

We didn't get to sit at the captain's table. Instead Wellard and Williams welcomed us to a table at the back of the room. Wellard held out my chair for me and helped me get seated. My inner feminist cringed but my equally vocal inner pragmatist reminded me I was going to have to get used to some assistance and not rebuff those who wanted to help. "Thank you Wellard." I wasn't used to the surnames thing, it seemed unnaturally formal, but I guessed it was how the ship ran.

"Salt and pepper, Ms Jackson?" Williams asked.

"Thank you." He kindly ground some over my frittata. What the hell, live dangerously. I was kind of addicted to the taste of both. I figured it was the hot weather. I needed the electrolytes. Yeah, that's my excuse. I savoured a mouthful of frittata.

"Wellard says you're both interested in helping out while on board." Williams commented, as he had previously. I guessed he was using it as a way to start the conversation.

Adeela saved me from having to quickly swallow my food and answered for both of us. "We are. I imagine this journey will take some time. I for one can't imagine sitting inside our cabin the whole time, doing nothing. We've imposed ourselves on your good will. We want to pitch in and do our bit."

"If that's the case," Wellard flattened out a computer printout "I've been having a look at the roster. As you know we're short staffed by two and I don't say that by way of blame, just fact. If I put you, Ms Shirazi, in the kitchens that would be an immense help as I could move Seaman Jones out of there onto other duties. Now Ms Jackson, I know you're learning to cope with your recent injury. The captain and I put our heads together and thought that since you're a journalist it might be worthwhile you using the duration of the trip to learn to type and use computers one handed." He looked to me to see how I would respond.

"I do wish you'd just call me Ry."

He grinned at that but shook his head, "Off duty perhaps, but not while you're working for us. So what do you think?" he prompted me to respond.

"I think you and the captain are right. I'm going to have to learn to cope. Now's as good as ever. What did you have in mind?"

"The captain voice records his logs. It would save his senior staff a great deal of time if we didn't have to type them up ourselves."

Both Wellard and Williams looked at me hopefully. The challenge had been offered. Would I accept?

"Consider it done. When do you want me to make a start?"

Wellard pushed a contract at me. "I've run a background check on you. We've decided to trust you with this work but I must point out that you must consider the contents of the log confidential. This contract outlines our expectations and also ramifications if you don't meet them. Have a read over it while you eat." He passed another contract to Adeela. "Yours is a straightforward contract Ms Shirazi. Though until we can arrange some identity for you I'm afraid we can't pay you. We'll backpay you once you're legit."

"We weren't expecting to get paid," Adeela was somewhat taken aback.

I was more curious about what Wellard had just said about getting an identity f

or Adeela. "Just how are we going to fix Adeela's little problem?" Okay, actually a really big problem but…Wellard winced, "That's on a need to know basis for now. You're going to have to trust us as much as we're going to have to trust you."

The captain's office was small but cosy. I'd kind've imagined walls of dark green and a mahogany desk but it was nothing like that. Just another room on the ship and the desk little more than a bench that could be wound up and down to suit a person's height. The seat was fixed to the floor, but equally adjustable. I guess if the seas got rough they didn't want furniture roaming around the room. The computer was embedded in the wall but appeared to be state of the art. Wellard had assured me that a satellite link meant that an internet connection was possible but he sternly warned me against using the captain's equipment for my own purposes. He showed me what needed to be done, gave me a communicator so I could ask him questions if I got stuck, and then left me to it. I was on a leash but trust was being offered.

As I listened to the captain's notes and began the painstaking process of typing them one handed I began to wonder if there wasn't a better way. Yes I needed to cope with my limitations but what about when I left. It was just crazy in this day and age to be doing this double handling. So I dared to access the ship's internet and, as was my strength, I researched the options for voice recognition programs. Not cheap but I was prepared to pay, by way of a thankyou, so I did. Not that I had any cash on me but I could access my electronic funds. I downloaded the program and then set about training it to recognise the captain's voice.

Wellard came, at what the locals called fifteen hundred hours, with a pot of tea and some bickies. "How's it going?"

"Almost done."

He quirked a brow, "What do you mean done?"

"I've got all of this week's backlog into the system. I'm just spelling and grammar checking."

His jaw dropped, "That was fast. Can I see?" He asked slightly disbelieving.

I didn't take offence at his doubt but I think my eyes twinkled with concealed mirth as he frowned at my expression. He took a seat at the computer and scanned through what I had done. "How?"

Here went nothing. I was either about to be in a serious load of shit for using my initiative or … well, I didn't really know how he would react. "Voice recognition. Software paid for by me. My gift to you guys and the captain. Let me show you how it works."

When I'd finished showing him Wellard sat back in his chair and stared at me a moment. Then he grinned. "That's bloody brilliant. Well then," he scratched his head as if considering possibilities, "finish up with your checking and give me a call when you're ready to log off." He meandered off seemingly rather pleased.

My shoulders relaxed. "Well that went okay." Though I wondered since I'd caught up on their work, what would they have me doing tomorrow?

3

I heard footsteps behind me as I strolled the corridor back to my cabin but since it was a busy ship I thought nothing of it until I was spun around and thrust up against the wall.

"My friends are dead because of ya," the man's angry face was close enough I could smell his recent coffee.

I steeled my nerves and met his startling emerald green eyes. "I'll admit there's a connection between me asking a friend for help and your captain sending two of his staff to collect us but I'm hardly to blame for a bastard of a country that blows up a woman's house because she wants some basic rights. Like the right to education, work and the choice of whether to marry and who to. I'm not to blame for them blowing up said house when I was in it with her. Nor am I to blame for the two thugs sent to abduct her and no doubt kill both of us. Those that sent the thugs being utter cowards who shake in fear that a woman might drive a movement demanding basic human rights. You think you can lay a guilt trip on me for the problems of an entire country, you've got brains for mush buster."

The man stared, taken aback, "My name's not buster."

"Officer O'Reilly, take your hands off of that woman. Now!" yelled the Captain who'd come along at just that moment, thankfully.

O'Reilly released me and backed away, "My apologies Ma'am"

God I hated that term. It sounded like madam which to my mind was someone who ran a brothel. But I'd just had an apology so it was time to be graceful. "Apology accepted"

"O'Reilly," Captain Wilcher addressed the now at attention seaman, "Do you have a problem with the fact I sent Seamen Felly and McNee to collect Jackson and Shirazi?"

"No Sir."

"Do you hold me personally responsible for their deaths?"

"No Sir, ya couldn't have known what would happen to them."

"But you think, somehow, that Jackson should have predicted what would happen to them."

"No Sir, she couldn't have known either."

"Then why are you harassing her?"

O'Reilly sighed a sigh of defeat, "Someone to blame, Sir."

The Captain hmphed, "Well at least that's an honest answer but I think Jackson is facing enough challenges as it is. She doesn't need you adding to her woes. Nor does Shirazi, who's just been ripped from her home and her country, such as it was."

"It was wrong of me Sir."

"But understandable. We're all grieving O'Reilly."

You could see O'Reilly's sudden realisation that it wasn't just him feeling the way he was. "Still," he turned to me, "I apologise, Ms Jackson." Though I could see the apology grated him.

Wilcher sighed, "I know how the crew feels about our unexpected cargo. I'm not reprimanding you this time O'Reilly but see that it doesn't happen again."

Cargo? Hmph. But I kept my peace as I watched their altercation.

"I'll make amends by watching out for her and Shirazi, Sir."

"Excellent." The captain returned his attention to me. "By the way, Jackson, good work on my files. Wellard briefed me. Be on the bridge at the morning watch changeover tomorrow at 0750. I'll have more work for you if you are willing."

"Certainly Captain." I smiled and nodded my thanks, for everything.

He hmphed, as seemed his habit, but I caught the slight twitch of a smile. He might be a hard ass but it appeared I'd come up in his estimations. Life on board would be far easier with his support than without it.

After the captain had disappeared well and truly out of sight O'Reilly swore, "Bollocks and buggerations."

"Colourful." Nearly as colourful as his frizzled ginger red hair and beard. Piercing green eyes peered out of that uber macho mass of hair and took my measure. Since I was thinking of hair and he'd claimed a willingness to look out for me I wondered if he might be useful. "I don't suppose you know where I could find someone around here to cut my hair?"

He looked at said long blonde tresses, assessingly, "Why would ya want to cut that? Yer hair is, dare I say, annoyingly beautiful."

I dismissed the unexpected compliment and shrugged my more lightweight shoulder as a hint to my plight. I really didn't like talking about it. "I'm just trying to adapt." Misery momentarily washed over me like a wave but I shoved it back. I refused to tear up in front of this crap of a man, well in front of anyone, preferably. The first person who called me a victim was going to get thumped. Ah yes, that thought brought my smile back.

If O'reilly sensed my inner turmoil he didn't say. He just grunted. "I might know someone. Follow me."

I did, but, "Do you have a first name?"

"Reilly, as in Reilly O'Reilly. Reilly being my dad and me being Reilly, the son of said Reilly. But around here ya call me O'Reilly, Officer O'Reilly or sir."

Well, I guess there was a certain naming simplicity in that. "Ok," I quickened my pace to keep up with him. "So you're from Ireland then?"

"Belfast. Not that it's any business of yer's."

Rude bastard. "Damn, and there I hoped you might charm me with your Irish brogue."

"Ya do rabbit on, don't ya,"

"Charmed, I'm sure," but I took the hint that I was talking too much and kept my peace as we continued on down the corridor to one of the many similar cabins that lined it.

He pounded on the door. "Open up Northey."

Northey did just that, greeting me with an unrestrained smile. "One of our two visiting beauties. Please come in." His West Coast American accent flowed over me like a Rocky Mountain stream. His sandy coloured hair rippled over his shoulders. Eyes of slate grey, verging on blue, sparkled with inquisitiveness.

Northey's cabin wasn't spartan. Walking into it after the starkness of the rest of the ship was like walking into an Aladdin's cave of delights. Colourful rugs, cushions, wall hangings. Not cluttered. Not even opulent but definitely as unrestrained as his smile. "Pleased to meet you Northey, I'm Rylee Jackson. My friends call me Ry."

"Then while we're in the confines of my palace I'll call you that. And, in here, you can call me Jim. Can I get you something to drink Ry?"

"Love a green tea if you've got one Jim." Anything other than the standard shipboard swill they called tea, I hoped.

"Of course. Plain or flavoured? I've got mint, chai or lemon," he thumbed through his selection in his compact kitchenette.

"Lemon would be great." I'd had a hunch Jim wouldn't disappoint.

"Your usual Reilly?"

"Black and strong thanks Jim. I need to clear the cobwebs. Landed myself in the shit with tha captain. Ended up promisin' to keep an eye out for our guests."

"Well aren't you a lucky guy?"

"Hmph."

"Grunt like that too often and you'll start sounding like the captain," I mused. "And may I point out that I didn't ask you to watch out for me."

Jim's eyes flicked between us, amused. "So Reilly and Rylee. It's got a ring to it."

"Don't you start Jim," Reilly growled. "I just brought her here because she asked if anyone could give her a haircut. Ya do a pretty good job on mine, when I need."

"Hmm," Jim passed me my tea then circled me, "It's in good condition. Just a trim then?"

"No, I was hoping for a bit more. Something shorter, more wash and wear." I nodded towards my unsaid missing arm. "Something easy to manage. Doesn't have to be fancy."

"Oh but it does." Jim countered. "Do you know how few opportunities I get to play with a head of hair like this?" He frowned as he took a closer look at my scalp. "Why on earth would you dye your hair? Your roots are the colour of burnished walnut."

"One word. Television. When the world's going to shit audiences want a pretty leggy blonde breaking the bad news."

"But there are male reporters," Reilly butted in.

"And they can look any shape and size they like, the more rugged and battle weary the better. The authoritative look I'm told. Not that it matters to me any more. Seen any one armed news reporters lately?"

"Manky bastards," Reilly swore.

Manky? I'd google it later but it sounded about right. "Them's the breaks. I'll go job hunting when I get home." Maybe I could transition sideways into radio or the papers. Something to worry about it later. "Here's where I am now. I need to adapt to my current situation."

"Well you're a brave lass," Jim decided as he went to find his tools of trade. He wrapped a large bath towel around my shoulders and went to it.

"My 'shadow' walked ahead of me as we made our way to the mess hall for the evening meal. Thankfully, curiosity had dimmed and only a few terse looks came my way as we entered. Reilly seated me at Wellard and Williams' table and then went to sit with his mates, though I continued to feel his eyes on me.

"Ms Jackson," Wellard greeted me. "A new look then. I must say you have the appearance of a warrior woman who shouldn't be trifled with.

Which was what I'd thought too but hadn't been sure if I'd been kidding myself, "It's very kind of you to say so Wellard."

"Roast pork and veg, chicken casserole or vegetable lasagna tonight," Williams rattled off the limited menu. "You're seated already, let me get something for you."

I didn't want to be waited on hand and foot but I knew to be gracious. "The lasagna, that would be great Williams. Thank you."

Adeela surprised me by wandering over with her own tray in hand. "Wow, look at you."

I smiled my pleasure at the praise, "Thanks. And you, I thought you'd still be working." Her own hair was uncovered and tied back in a neat ponytail. It looked like Adeela was doing her own share of adapting.

"Finished my shift. Have to say I haven't enjoyed myself so much in years. The cook tries to be an ogre, what with striding around and yelling out orders but actually he's a real sweetie."

Williams choked.

"Cook took me under his wing and helped me whenever I was unsure. The other kitchen hand was a bit standoffish at first but by the end of the shift we were all trading friendly barbs. I think they kind've forgot the whole I'm a girl thing. It was like visiting an entirely new planet. Certainly a whole new language."

Wellard chuckled, "I bet. I'm glad to see you ladies settling in. Ms Shirazi, you mentioned you like reading. I rounded up a few novels for you and left them at your cabin door. They're only in English I'm afraid."

"That's wonderful, Thank you," Adeela was easy to please. "Actually English is my first language. I went to a grammar school in England when my father was stationed there. I would have liked to have gone to university at Cambridge but, " she shrugged, dismissing the obvious regrets, "at least I got the bulk of my schooling over there."

"Your father must have been a truly enlightened man," I observed. Educating daughters not exactly being common for her part of the world.

"He was. He was attached to the embassy in London for a while.

That's where he met my mum, Pamela Rose. His family, of course, didn't approve of the match but by that time dad had grown accustomed to the rights common in the West so he married her anyway."

"What happened to her?" Wellard asked as he mopped the gravy from his plate.

"She came with him when he returned home but she found it hard to fit in. She loved us both dearly but I know she suffered from the culture shock, the loss of rights, the lack of acceptance. Yet she never caved to the enormous pressures placed on her. I guess I'm the way I am, in large part, because of both of them. Unfortunately my uncle saw her as a bad influence and had her killed. Dad died of a broken heart a couple of years later."

"Manky bastards," I swore.

Williams eyed me, somewhat surprised by my turn of phrase. "Indeed." then he had another thought "So, Ms Shirazi, would I be right in assuming then that you're a British citizen?"

"I am," Adeela agreed, "I have dual citizenship, Dad made sure of it. Sadly I don't have those documents with me and even if I did I don't think they'd help me get into Australia."

"No, but having British citizenship may certainly simplify things. We'll need to apply for a visa for you. And you Jackson?"

"Born and bred Aussie. And no, I don't have my documents with me either. I had them hidden in a safe spot in my Jeep which was blown to smithereens in the missile strike that took out Adeela's house."

"I'll let the captain know."

After dinner Wellard checked me out in medical again, making sure there was no infection in what remained of my left arm. He seemed more than pleased with my progress. "Someone should study your genetics, Jackson. I got onto Shirazi's doctor friend and he sent me a copy of his treatment notes. If I didn't know otherwise I'd swear this injury was weeks old. You heal remarkably well."

"Yeah," what else could I say.

My 'shadow' followed Adeela and me back to our cabin, swearing when he saw the graffiti on the door.

"Die bitches, not very inventive is it?" I sighed. "I could just find a white board marker, cross out 'die' and put 'rule' underneath the 'bitches'."

But Adeela didn't see the joke. She'd gone a shade of pale green and it wasn't from the ocean swell.

O'Reilly tested the paint with a finger swipe and then brought it to his nose to smell. "Turps based," He decided. "I'll be back with some turpentine and some rags. I'll have to report this in."

We'd just about finished cleaning the mess when the captain came to inspect it. He frowned, none too pleased. "I've stored the photo you sent me, O'Reilly. I'll keep the evidence in case there's any more attacks of this nature."

"More," Adeela moaned.

"It's a concern Ms Shirazi but I keep a tight ship. Any victimisation is completely unacceptable and will be dealt with. At the moment we can't be sure who's targeting you but we can keep the evidence. I'll address the crew tomorrow. Third Officer O'Reilly is in charge of ship security and crew safety. He'll keep me apprised. O'Reilly, is there anyone we can rule out as suspects at this stage?"

"ETO Northey was friendly and welcoming to Jackson when he cut her hair. I'd trust him, sir."

I had no idea what an ETO was but I'd ask Jim what it was he did later. Yeah, I know, I should have asked before but I was more interested in a haircut at the time. "I don't think Wellard or Williams have it in for us, they've been very supportive," I put in.

"And the chef has been very patient with me, when no one's looking," Adeela added.

The captain laughed at that, "The chef? Good grief. Well it sounds like we can rule out some of my key staff. O'Reilly, talk to the Bosun. Together you should be able to draw up a list for me of Seamen Felly and McNee's closest friends and workmates. I'll see you and our new probationary Deck Cadet in the morning. Shirazi, good work today, consider yourself appointed as trainee Steward." He dismissed us and continued on his way.

I held the garbage bag open for the cleaning rags Reilly had finished with but I was wondering, "Deck Cadet? Did he mean me?"

"Don't let it get to your head Jackson. You're what we call a general purpose rating. Basically you do whatever jobs we ask."

Hmm, some titbit of knowledge scratched at my brain. I had a vague feeling a Deck Cadet was a bit more than that but, "I thought I was already doing that, whatever was asked."

"So far." unsaid was his doubt that I would continue to do so.

"Cook really does like me," Adeela had her colour back. Her appointment as a trainee steward having made an impact.

"I wouldn't say that too loud. I think he likes his image as a tyrant. And if the Captain's putting you on as crew then we'd best get you some basic training." Reilly decided, knowing he was the one that would have to make sure all their paperwork was in order. But of course the Captain knew that. Wilcher wasn't known for teaching anyone to suck eggs. He expected his staff to think and work things out for themselves, unless it was something that potentially impacted on others or the ship's cargo.

"Why do I need training to peel spuds?" Adeela wondered.

"Do you know where the lifeboats are or the first aid kits? How to use them? Can you put an electrical fire out? If an emergency siren sounds does it mean there's a person overboard, there's a fire or that you should abandon ship? What is the procedure for abandoning the ship?"

"Er. Okay, maybe a bit more than peeling spuds," she agreed.

"I've done some first aid before," I vaguely remembered some of it.

"Good, then it shouldn't take you too long to work through the online component for that bit. Then you can help Ms Shirazi do the same. I'll bring you both a laptop to share. You can make a start."

"Doesn't sound like I'll be reading any of Wellard's novels tonight," Adeela bemoaned.

"And who's going to teach us firefighting?" I wondered if they had an onboard instructor for that.

O'Reilly pulled a face, not relishing the prospect, "That would be me."

As the grumpy sod walked away I wondered if he'd put himself on his list of suspects.

4

O'Reilly had been right. It didn't take me long to do the theory part of my first aid online since the knowledge was only a couple of years old in my head. The CPR sign off would have to wait until we got to the Seychelles where I could do a practical exam.

It was starting to sound like we wouldn't get much sightseeing in but I could hope. As I drifted off to sleep I imagined white sand beaches, palm trees, giant tortoises and coral reefs. And anyway, why were they reefs and not reeves? Roof became rooves, at least in informal speech, so surely that applied. Words fascinated my journalistic mind, but not for long as sleep drew me under.

A tingle in my foot woke me and once again I eyeballed my personal visiting apparition. I judged her to be a woman in her late forties or early fifties. A distinct patch of white hair amongst the shoulder length auburn hair made her seem quite magical, though without the flowing robes and magic wand. Shit. I'd happily convinced myself I hadn't seen her. Though there was really no other explanation for my healing. Who the hell was she? I wondered.

Lydia Greenfell, the name flashed through my mind. *A friend of Deman's. We work together.*

Was I really hearing her or was I delusional? Talk now, worry later, I told myself. *I can hear you.*

Lydia finished her work and sat on the edge of my bunk. *And I you,* She nodded. *I'm only here in my etheric form but I think because of all the healing work I've been doing on you I've made some kind of connection that's helping you to hear me.*

Etheric? Did she mean she really was some kind of heavenly visitation?

Her laughter filled my mind. *Hardly. I'm flesh and blood like you.*

Lying on my bed back in Australia. I'm having what some might call an out-of-body experience but in truth I'm well anchored to my body and simply projecting myself to your location. I'm not really here.

You don't say. I sat up and used my good hand to try and touch her but there was nothing.

Lydia patiently waited for me to digest all this. *I can help you to understand Ry, if you'll give me permission.*

To do what? I was ever suspicious and cautious, two years in a war zone had honed those inbuilt traits.

I believe if I could touch your forehead I could enhance your ability to see me, to see even your own etheric field.

Curiosity waged war with my doubts and won, *Okay.*

She reached forward and gently touched a spot slightly above the midpoint of my eyebrows. I felt a tingle and then it was like a door popped open. The world took on a new dimension I would never have believed unless I'd seen it. An ovoid area of pink light surrounded Lydia. That pink was tinged with purple. I stretched out my good arm and looked at it with new eyes. I was bathed in a deep blue.

It means you have a strong mind and strive for truth, Lydia explained.

And you? I wondered.

A soft heart and an open mind. A healer and wielder of magicks.

I'd normally have dismissed her claim to magical ability but it was hard to dismiss the fact that she was here or the degree to which she had healed me. *But there's nothing you can do with my other arm?* I nodded to what was no longer there then gasped. I could see a complete arm, made of light.

Etherically it's still there. Unfortunately on the physical level there was nothing left for me to heal except to seal the wound.

Damn, I'd thought that might be the case. But I flexed my etheric arm, utterly fascinated. *Is this why some amputees can still feel their limbs?*

Partly. There is also the fact that the brain is wired in a way that it expects and still believes the arm should be there.

Damn well should be, I agreed.

That you can see it may mean you can work with it and empower it in ways that others couldn't. I could strengthen it for you but I think you should see if you can do that yourself.

Do what?

Send love and gratitude to your etheric arm. Acknowledge its existence so that it doesn't fade.

Fade? I asked in panic.

If you truly wish to understand you could research the ancient Egyptian knowledge of the subtle bodies. What you can see can exist separate from the physical body while you are still alive but without the body part to anchor it I'm not sure what would happen to it over time. I'm not all knowing. You would do well to nurture it with love. There are other levels of your subtle being that you carry from lifetime to lifetime, the soul's container of memories, personalities and inherent traits but this is not it.

Double shit. I didn't want to lose this last vestige of my arm. I closed my eyes and sent it thoughts of need and gratitude. *Be strong, be whole*, I encouraged it. *Know that I see you and damn well love you.*

When I reopened my eyes my etheric arm was glowing, a clearer, bluer light and Lydia had gone.

I did go back to sleep, eventually, but when Adeela woke she found me at the laptop.

"Studying hard?"

"No, not really, just something that piqued my curiosity."

Adeela looked over my shoulder. "Egyptian metaphysics? A dream you had?"

"More like a ghost, but she said she wasn't."

Wide awake now Adeela stared at me, "What ghost?"

I cleared my throat, none too sure that I should be admitting any of this to anyone but Lydia had said truth was my thing. If I couldn't trust the woman who'd saved my life, who could I trust? "The apparition who first visited me the night we were at Karim's. She healed me. Healed your ribs too."

Adeela sat down on the bunk, next to me, "And?"

"And last night she came back. I, um, spoke with her telepathically. Look I know this is far out…"

"No, go on," Adeela urged, utterly fascinated. "What did you talk about?"

So I told her.

"Oh, my god, that's so amazing."

My eyes widened, "You believe me?"

"Well it explains the instant healing. No-one heals that quickly."

"There is that. But, I'm not admitting this to anyone else."

"Wise."

"Now, can I sell you a condominium in the Bahamas," I joked, to lighten the mood.

Adeela frowned, "Don't. I believe you. Why would you try to make me doubt you?"

"Because I'm not sure I believe it myself."

"But you can still see the etheric double of your missing arm."

"Yes I can."

"Well then, let's go and have some breakfast."

Once washed, I stubbornly fumbled with dressing myself in regulation black and white then we went to leave our cabin, only to find someone outside of it. "Who are you?"

"Able Seaman Merryman, Ms Jackson."

"Have you been out here all night?"

"No ma'am, but I was on night watch so I put your cabin on my rounds. I figured you'd be getting up about now. May I escort you to the mess?"

Adeela and I already knew the way but I was guessing someone was either keeping an eye out for us, or on us. "After you."

If the menu of an evening before was limited to the dishes of the day, breakfast was not. It appeared everyone got their favourite brand of cereal, yoghurt and fruit or cooked breakfast. I settled for raisin bread, a greek yoghurt and a fruit compote. Using my hip to balance the tray I carted that, including a pot of tea back to my table but it appeared that I wasn't to eat yet as the captain stood and everyone stopped in their tracks.

"If I could have your attention I have several matters to table. First, as some of you are already aware, we are adjusting our route home and will be making a detour to the Seychelles. If you're due shore leave and wish to take it there please inform your immediate supervisor before the end of the day so that we can adjust the roster accordingly.

The next matter I wish to discuss is less pleasant. Late yesterday graffiti was discovered on the door of our guests Jackson and Shirazi. The graffiti was of an offensive nature and when the culprit or culprits are found they will be summarily dismissed. Personally I'd like to make them walk the plank but modern day regulations preclude me from doing so. Shirazi and Jackson have proven themselves by working hard since they came on board. In reward for their efforts I have appointed them as trainee crew, subject to them meeting basic training requirements. I ask for your patience and help in getting them up to speed on their new roles. Shirazi will be working as a trainee steward, supervised by our chief chef and Jackson has been assigned as a Deck Cadet, under the supervision of the deck officers on watch."

A rumble of chatter rolled through the room like a wave.

The captain continued to stand, indicating he hadn't finished yet. He cleared his throat and the room went deathly silent.

"Finally there is the matter of the Bosun's missing pet. His tarantula, Horatio Nelson, has escaped his quarters."

A few quick snickers of mirth ensured.

"Which is a concern because we can't have rogue wildlife disembarking when we return to Australia. However, as Bosun is very fond of his pet, I ask you to keep an eye out for the spider and if sighted contain it by placing a bowl or glass over him and calling someone from the watch to attend to him. Bosun has asked me to point out that Horatio is not aggressive unless threatened. He may give a painful bite but that bite won't kill you. However if stressed he may shed hairs and those hairs can cause severe irritation. So, if you can't contain him, leave him be and call someone else. That is all." The captain sat down and went about pouring himself his tea.

A clamour of voices filled the room.

Williams, at our table, laughed heartily, "Well that last bit will give them something to focus on rather than our new crew."

Yes, but...a spider is loose? Though I was wise enough not to voice my fear. I'd never been comfortable around those critters. Not since camping as a kid and I'd seen a huge dark shape on the roof of the tent. It had been the shadow of my father's hand near the lantern but I'd screamed the whole campsite down before I'd realised that. Then there was the time I'd picked up a bunch of shells at the beach and while I was carrying my treasures back to the car a huntsman spider had come out of one of those shells and run up my arm. Huntsmen are harmless but the memory of the sensation of one running on my skin still gave me the shivers.

5

After breakfast the shift change, or the changing of the watch as they called it, gathered on the bridge for handover. Watches apparently lasted four hours. The officers of the watch doing at least two shifts a day unless otherwise scheduled. Though overtime seemed common and popular with the crew who had little else to do. Two people had to be on the bridge at all times, or so I'd been informed. Whoever of the crew had a watch certificate could be called on to assist during the watch. This shift would have Chief Officer Pertwie in charge, assisted by Able Seaman Merryman. I didn't count.

Pertwie studied me and frowned, "You're missing a button on your shirt Jackson."

I shrugged, it couldn't be helped, "It popped off when I was trying to practice dressing myself one handed."

It was the captain's turn to frown, "Williams, see if we can find some polo shirts for Jackson."

"And some elasticised pants," while I was on a roll I had to try.

"Very well. Now if we've finished redesigning your uniform Jackson, I'm assigning you today to O'Reilly."

I tried not to make a face but the captain saw my grimace and chuckled. "It is the Third Officer's role to supervise new deck crew while they're learning basic safety and security procedures but I suppose we might, since it's your first day on the job, let Pertwie give you an overview of what we do up here. You can assist O'Reilly this afternoon."

Oh joy, "Thank you Captain."

Having dealt with me Captain Wilcher moved on to other matters. "Pertwie, I'll relieve you at midday."

"Very good Sir. I've adjusted our heading to take us to the port in

Victoria on Mahé island in the Seychelles."

"Excellent."

O'Reilly frowned. "Sir, won't that route take us perilously close to Somali waters?"

"There haven't been any attacks on large vessels of late. It's still a risk. Though I think we have adequate defences to deter them. Ask the Bosun to deploy the razor wire and make sure the water cannons are operational. We want to avoid the use of deadly force and the inevitable mess in the international courts that that would bring but check what we have in the armoury just in case. Jackson can give you some help with your inventory of our safety equipment, after lunch. Then you've got the 4 til 8 watch."

"Yes sir" O'Reilly dutifully ignored me as he left.

Wilcher nodded to Pertwie, "I'll see you at changeover."

"Yes sir."

Wellard had had control of the bridge during our meeting, and was finishing his watch . He patted me on my back as he left. "Pertwie has his coffee black, no sugar. You'd best keep him supplied or he gets grumpy."

Pertwie rolled his eyes. "You can make one for yourself and Able Seaman Merryman, while you're at it." Pertwie decided. "Then we'll see if you're as adept at learning to read navigation charts and taking weather readings as you were at digitising the captain's log."

Damn! I'd labelled myself as a smart ass hadn't I? Hopefully these two were professional enough not to try and take me down a notch or two for it. Though I doubted I could have the same hopes of O'Reilly.

As I made the coffees I took a moment to take in the full extent of the bridge. It was certainly no starship but there was an impressive array of screens, gadgets and communications devices. Pertwie stood at the helm, at a wheel much smaller than I'd imagined. He was surrounded by an aura of deep red. I had no idea yet on what any of the colours I was seeing meant but my intuition suggested it meant command. It was probably no coincidence then that it was the same colour that I'd seen around the captain. Both seemed to be grounded individuals, not fazed by much.

Merryman had the binoculars to his eyes and was peering out at the horizon. The colour around him was a lighter blue than my own aura. What did I know about the man that could tell me what it meant? He seemed friendly enough.

I was guessing hierarchy was important so I made Pertwie's cup first and passed it to him before making Merryman's. I wondered what it was like to stare so long, out at the ocean. "Anything out there?"

He lowered his binoculars, "Nothing, and that's the way we like it. Want a look?" He passed me the binoculars. "Focus is here, if you need."

"What am I looking for?"

"Storms on the horizon, vessels where they shouldn't be, pods of whales, freak waves, floating containers...anything that might cause the vessel harm or obstruct its progress. Though we try to avoid the whales for their benefit as much as ours. The occasional albatross is sheer magic to watch."

I could hear it in his voice, he loved his job. "What about the things you can't see?"

"That's what we have radar for. Though we're still unlikely to detect a military sub in stealth mode. Meteorological readings help us to get a sense of the weather before we see it on the horizon."

"I guess there's no weather forecast for this far out," I mused.

"No taxpayers to pay for the service. Though we do get notifications about the big stuff, the hurricanes, cyclones and typhoons. Out here in the Indian Ocean we call them tropical cyclones."

"Which," Pertwie interrupted, "is why you'll bring your drink and come over here so I can show you how to take some basic weather readings."

And so I spent an insightful and mind-stretching morning getting a high level view of what they did on the bridge. Frankly nothing was left to chance. When you're this far out, help could be a long way away. Everything had a backup alternative. Navigation maps on the computers for sure. But if the power went out they still had the old paper based ones stashed away flat in drawers. There was VHF communication, satellite and internet but also a plain old wire connected phone system that connected the bridge to the engine room. And if that failed? Well then it would be the job of the deck cadet, me, to run a message.

Information was the stuff of trade on the bridge; depth soundings, temperature, humidity, direction...anything that told us the ship was safe and on course.

Two people at all times were required to be on the bridge, I guess in case one suddenly had a heart attack or a mental breakdown. As the trainee it was my job to stand in as relief if one officer left the room. Not that I understood much yet but I followed instruction and recorded what readings I'd been shown how to take. The morning passed quickly. Only another hour and the morning watch would be over.

With my head overloaded with so much new information 0I nearly missed the movement out of the corner of my eye. Something very quick, very large and very black ran over the console and disappeared into a gap between the desk panels. It took all my control not to scream, "Fuck!"

Pertwie turned to glare at me, "No swearing on the bridge Jackson, I expected better of you."

"I'm sorry Sir, but a very large spider just ran across the bench. I think we've found Horatio."

Pertwie pursed his lips in an effort not to laugh at me, "In that case, we'll let you off without a reprimand." He went to the intercom. "Bosun, you're damn spider's up here on the bridge."

"Understood, were you able to capture him Chief?"

"No, but we have his rough location."

"Do you want me to come up there, sir?"

Pertwie decided no, "Might not be any point unless he comes out again. Do you have anything we can draw him out with?"

"I've got some live crickets chilled in my bar fridge. They're his favourite food. You could tether one of those."

Pertwie pulled a face, obviously revolted by either the cruel and unusual torture of the crickets or the fact they were kept in the fridge. He sighed heavily, "I'll send Jackson down for them. She'll meet you where you're working."

Pertwie drew me a rough map of where to find the Bosun, "He's scheduled to have a work detail there. Take this ladderway, down the corridor then the one to your right. They're working on the starboard side. Don't get into any trouble on the way and don't dally. I expect you back in fifteen or I'll send a search party."

Ladderway? I hoped that didn't mean I'd be holding on with my one hand to some ladder. "One lot of doomed crickets coming right up," I tried to make light of it but the whole idea of pegging out any creature for another to eat had shades of old stories about feeding the maiden to the dragon. Though I guessed Horatio was hungry by now. Shit, was I feeling for the spider too?" Fortunately 'ladderway' turned out to just be another bit of jargon, for a fairly ordinary stairwell.

It took a firm push with my good shoulder to open the door out onto the deck where the maintenance crew were working. I found them, by following the sound of electric grinders and hammers, working away at the rust. While some of the team did that others were onto painting surfaces that had already been cleaned.

Some glanced at me as I neared but most kept on with their work. So which one was the Bosun?

Bosun Devender Singh turned out to be the one with the bright clear orange aura, a smiling Sikh, complete with turban. At the moment he was dressed in an orange boiler suit, nearly the same colour as his aura. He still managed to wear a small ceremonial knife or kirpan on his belt and a steel bangle on his right wrist, signifying his faith. I'd done an in depth feature documentary on a group of Sikhs once and though I didn't personally much go on organised religion I'd admired their ethics.

"Cadet Jackson, did you really see Horatio?" Devender asked, keen to hear that his beloved spider was okay.

"If you mean something about eight inches across with a large hairy bum and hairy legs, like hairy black velvet."

Singh clapped his hands together in delight, "Hairy black velvet, Yes!" He was clearly as delighted by that as I had been spooked.

"I had no idea tarantulas could be so fast."

"Ah yes, the Brazilian Black is very fast. But also very docile. He's probably very scared right now, being in such new surroundings. I don't know what made him roam so far or how he got out of his enclosure, let alone my cabin. I let him roam inside my cabin when I'm in but the rest of the time he has his home."

I was mindful that Pertwie didn't want me to dally. "You'll have to tell me more about him later. Right now, though, I must get back. First day on the job and all that. You understand?" I hoped he did because I got the impression he could talk long and lovingly about his pet.

"Of course, I'm sorry, let me just get the crickets."

"Uh, yeah, sure." The sacrificial offerings. Poor sods.

I followed him to his cabin where he went in and retrieved a small carry bag, more than I'd expected. "There's a plastic bowl in there that you can use for putting over him. Some cardboard too, big enough to fit under the bowl. Do you know how to use those to catch a spider, Jackson?"

"I've seen it done." Usually by other people who I'd cajoled into catching my unwelcome house spiders.

"Just remember he's fragile. He's a bit like you really."

I didn't know what he meant but accepted the bag. "We may not catch him today, he's hiding in the equipment."

"I know, he's more likely to come out at night, but I'm greatly cheered that he's okay and that he has a champion like you to look out for him."

"I …" hell I hoped I kept a blank face. "I'll do my best. Got to go. I'll let you know if we see him again."

But we didn't see him again on that shift. The captain and a Seaman Santos turned up at ten to twelve for the handover.

"So it appears we'll have some extra company," Captain Wilcher mused. "Has he been seen since, Jackson?"

"No Captain, he hasn't taken the cricket we put out for him. The Bosun said Horatio's a night hunter so you may not see him."

"Leave your spider catching kit here just in case. Go have some lunch Cadet. O'Reilly should be finishing his break now. You can report to him after you've eaten."

"Thank you Captain," I left fearing the real reason they wanted me gone was to talk about how I'd gone with everything this morning. Whether I had an aptitude for the job or not. But I reminded myself that not everything in life was about me and they probably had more important things to discuss than the first day of a not so able-bodied seaman.

As I walked to the mess I felt a shiver down my spine. A distinct feeling that I was being watched or followed. But I put it down to performance nerves from the morning and went to find out what was on the menu."

Since the 'fish of the day' was a well cooked tuna mornay with no bones for me to maul one handed I settled for that, avoiding O'Reilly until I had to.

I'd just wiped my plate with the bread they gave us when he wandered over, "Finish up Jackson, we've got work to do."

I guessed that meant the black forest gateau on the dessert menu for the day was out of the question. I took my plates to the sideboard and followed his backside which was already disappearing out of the mess. I swore at myself for even noticing his backside, reminding myself that while his physique begged to be noticed his attitude did not.

He shoved a clipboard at me. The topsheet showed a layout of the deck with various points marked. "Yer job is to direct me to the various pieces of gear we're checkin' on. I expect ya to use the correct terms to direct me. Starboard" He pointed to the right. "Port," he pointed to the left. "Bow," he pointed to the front. "And Stern," he pointed to the back. "Got that 'av ya?"

"Yes."

"That's 'Yes sir' or 'Yes O'Reilly'."

"Yes sir."

"Now the ship is divided into six areas. The middle bit is called the beam made up of two parts, the port beam and the starboard beam. The bow is divided the same. And for some reason I can't fathom some eejit named the back bits the port and starboard quarters instead of sixths."

"Got it sir."

"Hmph. Now look at the legend. See the symbols for lifeboats, lifebuoys, antipiracy gear etc. I don't want to have to back track so we'll do them in the order we find them. What's first, on the starboard quarter."

"Er," I studied the legend.

"Quickly Jackson, we haven't got all day."

Bastard. "Lifeboat, sir."

The lifeboat turned out to be quite different from anything I could have imagined. It was like an orange blob. A very large fully enclosed capsule with a hatch on the side. After checking that the release mechanisms were in good condition O'Reilly urged me to follow him inside.

Did I really want to go inside of a large plastic or fibreglass shell, I couldn't tell which, hanging on the side of the ship like a tomb in waiting? Not really, but I did. It was spartan inside. A raised seat for whoever steered it, a helm in miniature. The rest were rock hard benches. No cushions. No creature comforts at all. If you were in this thing you were strapped into the equivalent of a seatbelt.

O'Reilly did a count of the food and water rations, batteries, the sea sickness tablets, sick bags in case the former didn't work, oxygen in case the vessel was closed up to long, various distress and locator beacons, smoke signallers and flares. He did a test of the communications, calling back to the bridge to make sure everything worked. After a thorough check of absolutely everything we exited the mini-vessel and crossed it off our to do list.

"Ya should already be tellin' me what's next," he chided.

I hurriedly studied my plan again. "Starboard bow fire extinguishers, sir." Hell, I hated calling him sir. It seemed like a term that should be used on someone you respected. But while I didn't like the man he did seem to know his job. And, grudgingly, I had to admit he was a damned good trainer as he was putting me in a situation where I had to quickly learn not only shipboard terminology but also what were the key safety features of the ship. I was sure there'd be a test later.

Determined not to give him cause to grumble, I did my best to observe everything he showed me and engrave it in my brain. Not that I cared about pleasing him but if I could start to anticipate him maybe the afternoon would go easier. No doubt such a response was part of his devious plan but I went along with it.

After a while we did kind've got into a routine, though he still griped at me some. He looked at his watch and swore, "I've got to get going. We'll pick this up tomorrow. I need to get to the handover for the next watch on the bridge. Ya'll have to find your own way back to yer cabin."

"I'll be fine," thank you for asking, not.

He ignored my comment, "Ya've got an hour and half before dinner. I want ya to see what ya can find out online about firefightin' on ships, the different extinguishers and their uses and under what circumstances fire doors can be opened. Now give me that." He took the clipboard from me and hurried away without so much as a see you later. What was his problem? He was obviously efficient and hard working. He was a good trainer, proven by how much he'd pumped into my brain during the afternoon. He even seemed to have people skills, being mostly civil, courteous and respectful with other crew … except me.

I meandered my way through the labyrinth of corridors , delighted when I did manage to find my way back to my cabin. Getting out the computer tablet I thought I'd contact Deman first. I knew the Captain had been reporting to him and Lydia, whoever she was, probably kept him up to date as well but I had promised to contact him. I didn't know what the ship's internet capacity was so I thought it wise to avoid a video call and opted for a simple email instead.

Hi Dem,

All's well. Adeela and I are settling in. We're enjoying the work they've thrown our way. You're paying me a salary by the way :) Thanks for sending Lydia, though my brain's still spinning as to how. I'd be lying if I said I was in a great way so I won't. Frankly I'm trying my best not to be a victim, what with losing Jared and my arm. No point, can't change what's happened. But I don't have to like it. Adeela's been a great support. She seems to have taken the upheaval in her life really well. A born adapter I think. Hoping she'll keep in touch with me when we get back home. Looking forward to our stop in the Seychelles.

Many many thanks for the rescue. I owe you, like forever.

Ry

I hit send and settled in to do a bit of study. O'Reilly seemed determined that I meet the basic requirements for being one of the ship's crew. He had sneaky ways of forcing me to learn by putting me in situations where I had to. He wasn't one to spoon feed you. He'd show you something once and you'd better damn well take note because a little while later you'd be expected to apply it. So if he wanted me studying up on fire extinguishers I could just bet I'd be expected to know by tomorrow. I determined that I wouldn't embarrass myself.

6

After dinner a few volunteers offered to clear away the plates and wash up in the kitchen. Apparently the cook was bringing out his guitar. I did my bit to wipe down the tables and waited to see if he was any good. I'd sneak away if he wasn't.

I started getting curious when he took the quickly setup stage, carting in a worn but much loved Gibson guitar. The equipment at least was good then. As to the person, he presented a formidable profile. His skin was so dark I'd be surprised if it didn't suck in all surrounding light like some galactic black hole. His eyes watched and took in all. I suspect he was both gauging the audience as well as watching to make sure the cleanup of the galley really happened.

My real surprise came when Adeela came to stand beside him. What was she going to do? Hold his music for him?

But it turned out she could sing. Pure, effortless melody leapt forth from her lungs, filling the room while the chef accompanied her. We all quietly took our seats and listened, spellbound.

One of the seamen who I didn't yet know broke my trance, tapping me on the shoulder and whispering in my ear. "The third officer says you're to come to the bridge and, I quote, 'feed the damned spider'."

I rolled my eyes, why me? Surely the bosun could feed his pet. Damn O'Reilly. I gave the musos a well deserved round of applause as they finished a set and quietly left.

I knew I could use the pass card I'd been issued with to access the bridge but I also knew that protocol required that I seek permission before I entered so I pressed the button on the intercom outside of it. "Deck Cadet Jackson."

"Well don't stuff around Jackson, get in here." I knew that voice.

He was still grumbling when I entered. "Damned thing must be hungry, it keeps runnin' all over the place."

Of course he wouldn't think to feed it himself. It was almost like he had a sixth sense that I had, if not a phobia, a certain amount of discomfort when it came to spiders. I went to the kitchenette and retrieved a cricket from the bar fridge where I'd stored them. Here spider, nice spider. I went over to the console where I'd seen him before.

The spider raced out, stared at me for a moment, grabbed the cricket and just as rapidly disappeared again.

"Did you get it Jackson?"

"It was too damned quick," and I'd been transfixed by its stare. "It took the cricket though. I'm guessing he's gone somewhere nice to munch on it."

"Hmph," was all I got out of O'Reilly. "Dismissed then," and he turned his back.

I rolled my eyes, shook my head in frustration at the man and left.

But I didn't get very far. As I reached the bottom of the ladderway that led up to the bridge I found myself surrounded by three men in balaclavas. As soon as I saw them I tried to make a run back up the stairs but one grabbed me by the leg and dragged me back down, not caring that I bumped down the stairs on the way.

I started to scream at the top of my lungs but a swift hand clamped over my mouth as another landed a kick.

Silently and ruthlessly they pummelled me then left me there at the bottom of the stairwell. They'd said nothing. Just drifted back into the depths of the corridor from whence they'd come.

Trying to stay conscious, I crawled painfully bit by bit back up the stairs and banged on the entrance door to the bridge. Not exactly standard procedure but at that moment I didn't really care.

The seaman assisting on the bridge opened the door and gasped. "Jackson, my god."

But I was already drifting into black. It was starting to be a habit of mine.

My mind found its escape in some kind of nether world. And I became aware that I wasn't alone. "Lydia?"

"You're truly going through a bad patch aren't you Ry?"

"Better me than Adeela. She's been through enough."

"And you haven't?"

Probably, maybe. I looked around at my surroundings. "Where am I? How'd we both get here?"

"You're subconscious called me to you. Do you remember what I told you about the subtle bodies a human possesses?"

"Yeah, I read up a bit about it."

"Well the world is the same. It has its own subtle bodies. You're not in the physical one right now."

Er, I didn't like the sound of that. "I'm dead then. That sucks."

"No, not dead, but you found a way to escape your pain. You must go back Ry."

"So I will die if I stay here?"

"No, but you'll stay in a coma and your body will weaken. Eventually death but it would be a slow one. That's not to say you can't visit this layer of existence. In fact I would recommend you explore your etheric body and its potential further. When you've recovered I'll help you learn to project yourself anywhere you will but for now, tschau." And with that she touched me on my forehead and sent me back into my aching body which was now lying in the ship's infirmary with all sorts of people looking on worriedly.

Wellard shone a torch in my eyes. Talk about blinding.

"Hey, can you not do that?"

"Jackson, you're back with us." He seemed immensely pleased. "What happened to you?"

"Do we have to interrogate her now?" A certain grumpy voice asked from the back of the room.

O'Reilly was here? I had a moment's thought to be polite as well as curious, "Sir, I thought you were on the bridge." Why wasn't he on the bridge?

"I broke protocol and carried ya here. Santos had the bridge. Ya could be grateful, ya know. Ya weigh a ton."

"Do not," but I wasn't in a fit state to argue.

"It's alright Jackson," the Captain interceded before the two of us could get into a jousting match, one I wasn't up to. "Bosun came up to relieve O'Reilly. And he's right. Questions can wait until morning."

"No sir."

"No sir? You're not in a fit state to be insubordinate, Jackson."

"I'll be alright by morning. You'll see. Anyway, while I can still think…" and I told them what had happened.

The captain frowned, "Three masked men who kept silent. It's going to be hard to identify them."

I had one thing I could identify them by but it wasn't anything anyone in the room was going to take seriously. I'd seen their auras. Now how was I going to finger the bad guys in a believable way. One other thing concerned me. "Where's Adeela? Is she safe?"

Wilcher snorted, "As soon as we heard you'd been attacked Chef took it upon himself to protect her. No-one takes on our cook. She can come and see you in the morning but for now no-one comes into the infirmary except for myself or one of my officers. Wellard will be staying here to make sure you haven't got a concussion. I've stationed two seamen outside the door to protect you both. Get some sleep Jackson. I'll come and see you in the morning. We'll have to decide what's to be done to protect you and Adeela. I can't afford full time guards for you both. We might be able to get you airlifted off to the Seychelles if the owner will front the cost."

I'd be damned if that was happening, especially as I meant to be about making my assailants pay. "No airlift, please, not unless Adeela wants it and, though I may be reading her wrong, I don't think she will.

And I want to work tomorrow, Captain."

The captain laughed at that. "I doubt very much you'll be going anywhere tomorrow but if you make it to breakfast and can be at the 07:50 meeting on the bridge you can work. If not, rest."

It didn't take a psychic to know he didn't think I would be getting out of the bed any time soon.

"You wake me every hour and I'm hitting you Wellard," I warned as I snuggled under the sheets, as much as you could snuggle under hospital bed sheets.

"Adding threats to insubordination. Your rap sheet's getting longer Jackson," Wellard chuckled good naturedly. "How about this? You give me your would to wake me up if you wake up even briefly during the night. I'll check your obs then. I've given you an injection to relieve the pain but if you start hurting you give me a yell. Deal?"

What did he mean 'if' I started hurting. I could feel every kick they'd landed but I guessed the pain wasn't as sharp as it could be. "Deal. Where're you sleeping?"

"Here, in the chair. Anyone gets past the guards outside, they're going to have to get past me too. Get some sleep."

I didn't know how I felt about all these people caring about me. It wasn't a situation I was familiar with. "Thanks." Just don't get used to it, I warned myself.

I slept solidly at first. Bombed out, you could say. When I stirred Wellard popped an eye open and quietly took my pulse and looked in my eyes without engaging in conversation. Neither of us were keen to be jarred fully awake. He noted down the obs and we both went back to sleep.

It was in that boundary between dream and dreamless sleep that I heard Lydia's voice. "Sleepy head. I wondered when I could get through to you. Take my hand." She offered her etheric arm and as I took it I was instantly whizzed across a sea of nothingness, landing in what I vaguely remembered as Deman's office. Speak of the Devil. There he was, not a day different than I remembered. I guess he hadn't spent the last two years in a war zone.

"No I haven't," he answered, evidently hearing me as easily as Lydia did. "And you still seem to be battling. You know you could have picked up the damn phone Ry. I've only been getting condensed reports from Wilcher."

"There's no phone service on the ship. I was going to look at doing something online."

"I know you're quite capable of tethering your phone to the ship's internet."

Hmm, "That would work." I kicked myself for not having thought of it.

"You were putting it off because you were ashamed of your new physical condition," Lydia interrupted. "You weren't ready for someone who knew you from before to offer sympathy for the situation you find yourself in now."

Fuck, was I that transparent? Oh, that's right, I was in my etheric body. I was transparent. "You a damned psychologist or something Lydia?"

"No, I run an orphanage."

"Oh," well that I hadn't expected of her but somehow it fit. "I suppose you're right. I guess I've been trying to find my feet before I face the life I've left behind."

"Wilcher says you and Adeela are both fitting in well."

"Yeah, apart from those who hate our guts."

Deman sighed, "They're scapegoating you."

"Well duh. The trouble is protecting us is placing a strain on the ship's human resources."

"That's why I'm suggesting to Wilcher that you get some self defence training."

"If you're already talking to the captain you didn't call me here for that." though I had to wonder how they thought someone missing an arm was going to defend herself against the likes of three burly masked men.

"No we didn't. We called you because you show potential."

"For what?"

"For a bit of snooping of course. Here you are in your etheric form, a long way away from where your body is lying on a bed in the Indian Ocean. And here am I with Lydia in my office, even though we're both in trance back at Rache's place."

"Rache?"

Deman dismissed my query with a wave of the hand, "We'll tell you that story later. Suffice to say that since you've developed the ability to consciously co-exist in both physical and etheric forms you're quite capable of going anywhere you want doing what journos do best. Snoop."

"Oh," my etheric eyes warmed at the thought. "I suppose I could. But why am I snooping?"

"Just a suspicion I have that someone's using my ships for a smuggling operation."

"I don't know Deman. Wilcher keeps a good eye on the ship's operations. I can't see how anyone would get away with that for long."

"Humour me. Just keep an eye out for anything odd."

"But first, heal yourself," Lydia chipped at me, "or do you need me to do it for you?"

I knew when I was being goaded but, "Hell no. Ah, but I might need you to take me back."

"Shift your focus back to your physical body and you should find yourself there," Lydia advised.

Shift focus? Hmm. I tried picturing my physical self as it lay in bed. In a flash I was back in it. I looked across to see Wellard still sleeping in the chair so I determined not to wake him. Instead I set about doing what I'd told Lydia I was capable of, healing myself. I focused on each bruise and bump and sent it love and gratitude along with visions of strength and wholeness.

That done I shifted my focus back to the etheric and went on a snoop around the ship but it was as quiet as you would expect of a ship at two in the morning. Except for a seaman on watch in the engine room, two officers on watch on the bridge and an errant spider scurrying unnoticed across the ceiling of the bridge. Though the spider did seem to notice me. Stopping to stare into my eyes, as if to say hello. I surprised myself by saying hello back.

I listened to the conversation of the two bridge officers but they were only discussing the ship's current heading and their hope for some shore leave.

"You got anything lined up in the Seychelles, Fernandez?" the taller of the two asked

"Got a girl, Keisha, I sometimes see there. Works at one of the local travel agencies. I met her when I booked a diving trip last time we were through. She's not keen on the fact I'm hardly ever around. I'm working on convincing her of the advantages."

The taller seaman laughed heartily "And what would those be?"

Fernandez straightened his shoulders, "Well the leave's good, when I get it. And the pay's good. She'll get enough time on her own to appreciate me when I return."

"She'll need to trust that you don't have a girl in every port."

"Hmph, the trust will have to go both ways. Have you seen some of those Seychelles guys?"

It was an insight to listen to them. I hadn't really thought about how a seaman's work impacted his social life. At least satellite internet could keep them in touch with their families these days although I didn't know if all boats had that. What if something happened to one of their family while they were out at sea? You couldn't exactly duck home to sort things out. I was left hoping Fernadez's girlfriend could be convinced, for his sake. Maybe love would make it work.

Having gotten nothing from my first foray other than practice I decided sleep was the best I could do and returned to my already healing body.

7

"You can't be serious Jackson," Wellard complained as I got out of bed. "You're still sporting some healthy bruises and that's just the surface stuff I can see. I know you told the captain you'd work today but, honestly, no-one expects you to."

"I'm better than I look," and the bruises were already fading so fast I doubted I'd have any by the end of the day. "I won't give those bastards the satisfaction of knowing they did me over properly. And I'm not going to sit in bed bored all day. Let me see. Hmm. Boredom versus putting up with O'Reilly's grumpy tuition. I'll take the later thankyou."

Wellard shook his head in amazement. "Well you'd better get dressed then. We'll go together to breakfast. See how you feel after that." He was obviously hoping I'd back down by then. "Williams found a couple of polo shirts and some elasticized pull on pants for you yesterday. I'll go and get you a change of clothes and be back. Don't go anywhere without me."

He was being reasonable so I'd stay put, "I'll be showering."

The mess had its usual clamour of noise. A few looked up to see us enter then went back to pouring coffee, chatting with friends, buttering toast and everything else that went along with a full and hearty breakfast.

My body cried out for protein as a reward for all the healing it had been doing. I often opted for whatever was the vegetarian option, though not always. Today I helped myself to a double helping of crumbed sea bream, sweet potato mash and a side dish of yoghurt and fruit. I ate heartily and washed it all down with a pear juice I'd zapped in the servery microwave.

Wellard watched me, utterly fascinated, "Eating for two I see."

"Need it," I muttered as I took another bite of food.

He considered that, "I'm guessing the speed with which you heal uses up a few calories."

I shrugged my shoulders, "I suppose." I didn't really worry about it. If I was hungry I ate, if I wasn't I didn't.

Our musing on my body's need for fuel was interrupted when Adeela came charging over. "Ry. You're alright?"

"A few bruises still but I'm up and moving."

"Against medical advice," Wellard muttered.

"I'm fine," I assured everyone. I surreptitiously blinked at Adeela, hoping she'd get the hint.

She did, "Ah. You, um," she glanced at Wellard then thought of what to say, "you consulted with Lydia?"

"Did it myself this time. Lydia thinks I'm capable."

"Who's Lydia?" Wellard looked between us and had to ask.

"A healer," well she'd healed me so I guessed I could call her that, even if it had turned out she was the manager of an orphanage. "A friend of Deman's. She's been teaching me to," hmm, I couldn't exactly talk about the etheric stuff, "heal fast."

"How?" Wellard was genuinely interested.

"There's no magic to it, Wellard. It's just good old fashioned love, gratitude and appreciation directed into my body parts."

"I don't know about the no magic. The way you heal is nothing short of amazing."

I shrugged my shoulders. Even I didn't know how come it worked so well, "Guess I'm a natural." But I frowned as a group of men entered the mess and went to sit at a table at the end of the room. If they saw me at all it was out of the corner of their eyes. It was as if they were determined not to see me. "Who are those men?" I whispered to Wellard.

He noticed my look and frowned. "Engineering. You recognise them? I thought you said those who attacked you last night were masked."

"They were." Shit, how to explain.

But Adeela beat me to it. "She sees auras," she quietly told Wellard. "Got to go. Cook will wonder where I am." She escaped before I could growl at her for divulging my secret.

Wellard raised his eyebrows, "Auras?"

"I know, I know. That's not for general knowledge, okay. O'Reilly would make liver pate out of me if you gave him that ammo. Not to mention I'm trying to get taken seriously as crew. Please, just don't."

Wellard patted my hand, "I won't make gossip of it but I may need to tell the captain. Though it's going to be difficult fingering crew based on it. We're going to need more evidence than that."

Did I tell him I could go out of my body to snoop. Maybe not. He was taking me seriously for now. Perhaps because he'd seen the extent of my ability to heal. But there was no need to test his belief further. "I'll keep my ear to the ground."

"Stay away from them," Wellard warned. He looked at his watch. "We'd best get moving."

The captain's eyes widened in surprise and admiration as I followed Wellard onto the deck of the bridge."Jackson, you seem to be moving okay."

"Getting there, captain."

"Excellent."

"Sir," Wellard interrupted, "If Jackson and I could have a quiet word with you for a moment."

Wilcher frowned but noticed Wellard's eyes flick towards the others who were just now stepping onto the bridge. "Very well. Pertwie. We won't be a moment."

"Very good, sir."

We stepped outside onto an observation deck.

"Captain," Wellard gave me a look to shut up while he explained. I was cool with that. "Jackson and I were down in the mess this morning when three men entered. There was something about them that set her on edge. Perhaps it was their size or the way they moved. She's not sure."

The captain eyed me, as if expecting more of an explanation.

I couldn't really give one. "Just, the hair on the back of my neck. You know the sensation."

"I do but unfortunately it doesn't give me enough reason for me to detain them."

"I understand sir. I just thought you should know."

"Did you recognize them, Wellard?"

"All from engineering sir. De Silva, Sharma and Lasseter."

"Hmm, all comrades of Felly and McGee. Okay, I'll take it under advisement. Let's get this handover done."

The captain looked thoughtful as we re-entered the deck, tapping a forefinger to his lips as he thought. Our curious eyes watched him. "Okay, change of schedule. O'Reilly, you were an engineer before you changed track to become a deck officer. I want your ears down there. See if there's any talk about Jackson."

O'Reilly's glance flicked to me. Frowning, he looked back at the captain. "You suspect somethin' sir?"

"It may be nothing. But Takemoto's been complaining she's short staffed down there. If you wouldn't mind."

"No problem but who's goin' to continue with the safety audit?"

"What do you think of Jackson continuing it, if she has someone to offside her? Is she up to it?"

O'Reilly eyed me, considering. "Possibly, she's a quick study."

My god, had that been praise that just came out of his mouth?

The captain's eyes gleamed with mirth when he saw my mouth drop, "That she is. Okay Jackson. That's your job today. If your injuries start to slow you down, report back to Wellard. I'll have Bosun assign you one of his crew, one he trusts, to offside you. Make sure you take your lunch break. If I get time I or one of my officers will come down to check on how you're going. We're putting a lot of trust in you Jackson, are you up to it?"

"Yes sir, I won't let you down."

"Make sure you don't. If you're unsure of anything use your handheld to contact O'Reilly. There are no stupid questions."

I'd rather hell froze over before I had to ask O'Reilly anything but the lives of everyone on board depended on all the safety gear being functional so I would if I had to. "Thank you sir." Though I had no doubt O'Reilly would check my work.

"Don't thank me Jackson, I just threw you in the deep end. Okay moving on. Pertwie, take a break and get some sleep. Wellard, since Jackson's back on her feet and you've slept, I take it, you can take this watch with Seaman Merryman. Santos and I will come and relieve you at midday. I know that's all a bit jumbled up at the moment due to last night's events and us being down in crew numbers. We'll sort it all out once we get to the Seychelles. Dismissed."

Once O'Reilly had loaded me up with my map of the ship's fire fighting apparatus, aka FFA, and safety equipment, checklists and an order to present myself at the ship's gym at 4pm I went in search of the Bosun.

I found him and his work crew not far from where they'd been working the day before. They were busy attaching a perimeter of razor wire to the side of the boat.

"Sir, sorry to interrupt."

"Goodness, I'm not sure I'm used to being called sir. Just Singh or Bosun will do."

"Sorry Bosun. The captain wants me to continue the safety audit O'Reilly and I started yesterday. O'Reilly's helping out down in engineering. The captain ..."

"Already spoke to me on the communicator. Seaman Patel's the man you want to help you." He called him over.

"Patel, you're well versed in the ship's safety equipment." It wasn't a question.

"Yes sir."

"Have you any objection to working with Jackson?" Unsaid were the various factors someone might object to, not least of which was me being one of the women two of their crew had died because of. "She'll be needing not only help but protection."

"I heard what happened, Bosun." He turned politely to me, "I'm more than happy to protect and assist you Cadet Jackson. Though, given what I know of O'Reilly, perhaps it will be both of us needing protection if we don't make a start." He laughed, so obviously he didn't mean that in a bad way. Probably.

"Um, great," I had a vision of O'Reilly, with his flaming orange hair, framing his angry face. Yeah, we'd better do a damned good job. "Ah, just one thing before we go, Bosun. I meant to let you know Horatio ate last night. He seems well enough though too quick for us to catch yet."

Bosun smiled, greatly pleased by the news, "Excellent. Look after my spider's friend Patel."

Patel chuckled again, he seemed an amiable sort. "I will."

Patel and I actually made quite a good team. He knew I was on a learning curve so he expected me to think things through, only prompting when he thought I was truly lost. We checked expiry dates on equipment, noted any wear in fire hydrant hoses and found one fire extinguisher missing a pin. Mostly we were slowed down by the checks on the lifeboats and life rafts. So much went into each vessel. We checked everything from the expiry dates on rations, the charge on batteries, numbers of flares to whether locator beacons still worked. Hinges and release mechanisms were oiled and greased as appropriate. Catches checked to make sure they closed. Water bottles refreshed. We worked methodically down our check lists. Did O'Reilly really have those checklists embedded in his brain? I guessed he'd done it so many times he did.

We stopped for lunch and I had a chance to share a quick sandwich with Adeela while Patel went off to talk to some of his friends.

Then we were back at it. We'd made some good progress but of course there was still much of the ship to cover. It was that immense. A kind of floating city. Patel told me the ship was 60 metres wide. That was twice as wide as the house block I'd grown up on. It was hard to imagine. How long it was I had no idea but I knew the deck was covered in literally hundreds of containers stacked up to six layers high. It was like a towering giant, floating around the sea.

The part that held the bridge, the galley and the crew accommodation was like the ship's equivalent of a high rise, the 'superstructure', or so Patel informed me. He did much to educate me about the parts of the ship and enough jargon to have my head swimming by the time our shift ended. It was like I was learning to speak an entirely new language.

"Thanks so much for your help today, Patel."

The compliment appeared to please him, "No, thank you. I spend most of my days chipping rust off the ship or greasing working parts. It's been a welcome change. I hope we can continue this tomorrow."

"Me too." I wondered if he yearned for a promotion but I didn't feel I knew him enough yet to go prying. Honestly some of the work on board seemed pretty gruelling. Dirt, noise, grease, yep that just about summed it up. At least as far as what I'd seen among the maintenance crews. I was told the engineering section was worse. Where ear protection was mandatory and temperatures in the main engine room routinely exceeded 45 degrees celsius. I wondered, idly, how O'Reilly was doing.

"I'll walk you to the gym then." Patel offered, drawing me from my thoughts.

8

What was I doing at the gym anyway? Did Deman really expect me to defend myself? Though perhaps it was a good way to get fit for the kind of work I was now doing. I figured I'd work with some light hand weights. Maybe do a bit on an exercise bike. I was still in recovery wasn't I?

When I opened the door to the gym I started to wonder. O'Reilly was on a bench heaving some pretty heavy weights above his head. "'Bout time. You're two minutes late Jackson."

"I'm off shift," I gleefully pointed out.

"Not till I've finished with you you're not. Captain's orders. I'm to teach you some MMA."

Did he mean mixed martial arts? Surely not. "Uh, hello, missing an arm, remember."

"Yer got a perfectly good arm still and two legs." He eased the weights done, wiped down the bench and then wiped his hands. "So. Here's the chance ya've been waiting for, I'm sure. Ya get to hit me."

"What do you take me for, some bitch?"

"I take ya for a woman with spirit, a woman with a surprising amount of resilience." He picked up a pad, moving to a matted area, positioned it in front of him. "Make sure your thumb's on the outside of your fist to avoid getting it broken. Now hit this. I want to see ya move me backwards."

Well, he asked for it. I drew back my right hand and punched.

"Didn't move me. Harder. What are you, spineless?'

He was goading me but I'd be damned if anyone called me spineless. I threw a punch and drove him back, oh, maybe an inch.

"Better. What about a kick?"

"If I kick an opponent they're only going to grab my ankle and floor me," I griped.

"Humour me."

"Hmph," I kicked.

"Not like that," he whinged. He dropped the pad. "Like this. It's harder for them to guard against an inside leg kick. Ya can also use a full body kick or a kick to the upper body. I'll show ya on the dummy over here."

The poor dummy got walloped. Ouch that would have hurt the ribs.

"Now you try."

I didn't get anywhere near the height of the ribs.

"Hmm. Okay we'll shelve that until we get ya stronger and more flexible but put the inner leg kick into yer arsenal. Now, falls."

"You mean like fall down. That's painfully easy."

"That's the thing, it shouldn't be painful. A good breakfall can do a number of things. Breakin' ya fall, obviously, but also settin' ya up to flee or into a better position to fight. Always flee if ya can. It's not cowardice, it's self preservation and that's what we're about. Now come at me, to push me over.

I pushed. He fell and rolled in a fluid motion that gave him the momentum to spring back up and grab me in an arm lock that forced me hard against his surprisingly toned body. My own body heated in a traitorous upwelling of desire, savouring his hot breath on my neck.

He must have felt it too as he broke his hold on me quickly and stepped away, averting his eyes but not before I saw the heat in them. Damn.

"Shouldn't Adeela, sorry, Shirazi, be in on this lesson?" Hell she could chaperone us.

"Shirazi hasn't got a mean streak in her body. Cook's going to teach her how to escape various choke holds and evasive manoeuvres. Defence only."

"Oh, so I have a mean streak." The jibe was more like his normal opinion of me.

He turned to face me again and gave a long exasperating sigh. "What ya 'ave is the spirit of a warrior. An ability to bounce back from crises like a duck shakin' water from its feathers. You're resilient, cocky and intelligent. I wouldn't be wastin' my time on ya if ya weren't."

It hadn't been the response I'd expected from him. "Well aside from you having to waste your time on me I guess that sounds, well, pretty good actually."

"Ya don't say," he smirked. "So when ya'v finished bathin' in that warm glow maybe we could get ya doing some breakfalls. Let's go through the steps."

We spent a good twenty minutes on that and then finished with some weights, both leg raises and one handed with some light hand weights. He finished off by showing me how to do one handed pushups. Now there was a thing. Though when I tried I only managed to raise my torso off the ground, not my whole body.

At least the earlier awkward moment had passed, though it still ran replays in the back of my mind.

"That'll do for the day." Reilly announced. "I'll walk ya to the mess."

"I think I need a shower first," we both did.

He threw me a towel from the bench and pointed to the changing room, "One in there. Thought you might want one so I've put you a change of clothes in there. Don't take too long. I'll do the same and meet you back out here."

Under the shower, soap in hand I was sorely tempted to attend to the aroused nub of my clitoris. Damn. He'd said not to be long. And since I seemed to be in my tormentor's good books for once I thought it best not to rile the O'Reilly, pun to myself intended. Regrettably I finished showering and quickly dressed. I bagged the used clothes, taking them with me to deal with later.

Fresh and clean O'Reilly was waiting for me. I blushed when I wondered if he'd had the same dilemma in the shower I'd had.

"What was that thought?"

"Nothing, absolutely nothing. It was a good hot shower."

His lips twitched, "Yes, it was."

There was a bang on the outside of the gym door, "Shift your asses."

O'Reilly rolled his eyes and opened the door. "All yours Takemoto."

"Hmph, took your time."

O' Reilly turned to me, "Cadet Jackson, meet our chief engineer Takemoto."

The woman looked anything but Japanese, well maybe. "Ah nice to meet you." She was huge. Almost as formidable looking as the cook. Certainly not petite. Elaborate tattoos covered what I could see of her arms, extending down onto the backs of her hands. Her almost pitch black hair was drawn back in a short ponytail. The hair matched the colour of her eyes.

"And you're wondering what the hell am I? I can see the question in your eyes. Had it a time or two. My grandfather was a Hawaiian. He married my grandmother, a Japanese worker on the sugar plantations of the time."

"Well I think I'd want you on my side if I was cornered in a fight."

Takemoto barked out a laugh. "Heard you were lacking in guile. Like it. Now if you'll excuse me. I've got some weights calling me." She left us to go into the gym.

"She looks formidably strong, " I noted, out loud.

"Has to be. I'll take you down to engineerin' sometime so ya can see what they work on. It's not a place for the faint hearted."

"I'm sorry you got sent down there on my behalf."

"Hush, we won't speak of the why of it. Too many places for ears on the ship. An' anyway. I started out as a marine engineer. I like workin' out how stuff works and fixin' it. Machinery, like what runs this ship, has a soul."

"But you changed career paths."

"Figured, even with ear protection, I'd likely end up deaf in old age if

I stayed workin' in that department. That and it's as hot as hell itself down there. It's a much better life up here. I just had to go back to school and learn all the navigation stuff. The rest I learned on the job."

"Any easy to understand books on navigation?"

He gave me an appraising look, "Yer truly interested?"

I shrugged my shoulders. "It's kind've my way to dive into any situation I find myself in. I spent two years in a war torn country but while I was there I made time to learn the customs, the politics and a bit of the history. Even a few words of the language. It made for a more enriching experience."

"And a safer one, I'd dare say."

"That too. Look, I've never been on a ship before. Never even really thought about it. But it's like it's its own world. A complete system."

"One that needs constant maintenance to keep goin'," O'Reilly muttered.

"Yeah we don't want it dissolving into a pile of rust. But back to navigation. It looks complex because you have to be able to fall back on using the older ways if the newer ones like the global positioning system fall over. Or the computers suddenly die and you can't get a digital map up on the screen. But it's interesting."

"Yeah, It is. Look Jackson," He checked over his shoulder to make sure no-one was in the vicinity, "I know I've been an ass but when people are around I'm goin' to have to keep bein' that way. At least until we know who you're up against."

"I understand." Frankly I'd kind've come to expect it of him. This new more polite side to him would take a bit of getting used to. But if he was going to try and find out who in Engineering were after me he couldn't be seen to be my friend.

"Good," He pushed through the doors into the mess and left me to catch the door before it closed in my face.

My mind did a one eighty at his sudden flip of character, adjusted and then went to find some well earned food. Hmm, the vegetarian offering for the night was eggplant and yellow pea stew served with flatbread. Was it just my imagination or was some of Adeela's local cuisine getting into the menu?

I sat down at my usual table, on my own, but was soon joined by the purser. "Williams," I politely acknowledged him with a smile. He had such an affable nature he was an easy man to like but I guess given his service role he had to be. Actually I didn't really know much about his role on the ship. "Have a seat and tell me more about what you do."

William's laughed, "You truly have a journalist's curiosity. Few have ever bothered to ask me that. They're usually more interested in the chief engineer or the captain."

"Well that's just plain rude, and elitist of them."

"I guess so, I hadn't thought of it that way."

"From what I've observed, everyone on the ship has a vital role to play and we rely on each other to do our duties. It's a system. One bit's missing or goes down, the rest suffers."

"Which actually gives me a lead into why I'm here, apart from to enjoy your refreshing company. Merryman's twisted his ankle and Fernandez's got a boil on the foot."

"Ouch."

"Yes, I imagine Fernandez is limping as badly as Merryman. But since they're down for the count as you put it we're short of crew on the bridge roster. The captain wondered if you were up for a bit of overtime. You got pretty roughed up last night. How are you feeling?"

I rotated my good shoulder to be sure. "Good I think. A bit of muscle fatigue from my workout session with O'Reilly but the bruising from earlier isn't bothering me. When do you want me up there?"

"Now, actually. If you could finish Merryman's four to eight shift. Pertwie's up there with the captain filling in until I can find someone. That just leaves me to find someone to help with the eight to midnight."

I had a thought, "What about Seaman Patel, I think he would be interested. He's efficient and has a quick mind."

"Ah yes, you worked with him this afternoon. I'll accompany you to the bridge and suggest it to Wilcher."

I eyed the desserts on the sideboard with regret but Williams noticed. "Get a doggy bag. I've got to get something for Pertwie anyway."

While he organised a takeaway for Pertwie I grabbed some walnut stuffed dates and waved down Adeela for a container to put them in.

"I hope you like them," Adeela sounded uncertain. "They were kind of an experiment. Cook wasn't sure how the crew would go with a few international oddities on the menu but by the looks of those who've gone back for seconds of the stew I've done alright."

"Going to have to kick a bit more confidence into you girl." I noticed Williams heading out of the kitchen with Pertwie's meal. "Look, got to go. Doing some overtime. Make sure you lock our cabin door. I'll be back a bit after eight."

"You stay safe too. I want all the details, on everything, when you get back."

Since we hadn't really caught up since the day before I guessed it really was time to download, though there was so much spinning in my head I wasn't sure where I'd start. "It's a deal." I went to catch up with Williams who was grinning at me but nevertheless giving me the eye to hurry up.

"So, what is it you do, Williams?"

My question amused him, "You're tenacious, I'll give you that. Well I suppose you would say I'm in charge of administration. If this was the navy I'd probably be considered a warrant officer. I'm responsible for currency exchange, ordering supplies of food, drink, bedding, clothing and essential stores. Even making sure we have enough candles and batteries in case the power goes out."

"So you make sure we don't run out of stuff."

"Essentially. And the cook and stewards report to me. I report directly to the captain. But at the end of the day I'm the one who ultimately gets the blame if the crew don't like the onboard food and living conditions. Though the crew are responsible for the cleanliness of their cabins and doing their own laundry."

Hang on. "But you've been doing mine and Shirazi's"

"Well, you're kind of guests, though you seem to both be cementing yourselves into the crew quite well. Despite your enemies."

"So tell me where to find the crew laundry. You've got too much to do without having to do my laundry."

"It's really no bother. I have to do my own anyway."

"And I really appreciate that but if Shirazi and I get special favours it won't help our case with the rest of the crew."

"Hmm, I see your point."

9

I wasn't sure if it was the sight of the food or me that brightened Pertwie when we turned up. I was guessing the food.

Williams left me to discuss with the captain my suggestion of having Patel as the assistant on the next shift.

Pertwie found a patch of bench space to eat out. "I don't see a cup of coffee in my hand."

"Sorry sir. Black, no sugar" Thankfully I remembered that.

I made it and placed it in front of him, "Meteorological readings sir?"

"Not while I'm eating. Grab the binoculars and keep a good look out in all directions. Navigation's on autopilot. Yell if anything worries you." With that he went back to eating.

It seemed like a casual dismissal but I took it as I saw it. Trust. I took the binoculars and went to keep watch, nonplussed when Horatio ran over the wall to where I was to say hello. "I'll feed you shortly," I whispered.

Once Pertwie had eaten his meal I handed back the binoculars and went to do the hourly readings. Only then did I retrieve one of the hibernating crickets from the fridge.

I wondered if spiders could smell. Apparently they did. "Sir, if you could get the spider catching bowl I think I can entice Horatio onto the bench."

"Damned spider," Pertwie swore. "How am I supposed to maintain a lookout if I'm catching spiders? Can't you catch him while you feed him."

"Um, only one hand here," did I really need to point that out?

Pertwie looked duly chastised. "Okay one second." He did a quick 360 with the binoculars just to make sure the coast was clear then made for the bowl as Horatio slowly and tentatively approached my hand, as if sensing with his legs. "Okay, on the count of three release the cricket and back away."

I did but Horatio was quicker than either of us. In a flash both he and the cricket were gone. "Well, I'll be damned. He's only got seven legs."

"Hence the name. Though I think Bosun should have called him Speedy Gonzales instead", with a certain amount of resignation he put down the spider catching bowl and picked up the binoculars. "Nothing out there, but damned if I don't have an itch between my shoulder blades."

A blip on the radar suddenly had both our attentions. "Something's out there." That much was clear. "Coming from behind on the port side." I gulped. Whatever it was was heading to intercept us.

"Damn it," Pertwie swore. "Jackson, call the captain. Tell him it's urgent. I'll try to raise the vessel on the radio."

I hit the intercom, "Captain to the bridge ASAP. Unidentified vessel approaching, rapidly."

Wilcher responded immediately. "I'm on my way. Any contact with the vessel?"

Pertwie shook his head forlornly.

"No sir," I answered the captain.

"Sound the general alarm. It may be nothing but we'll be sorry if it's not."

I hit the appropriate button. A repeating stream of seven short and one long warning tone ensued.

Wilcher burst through the door and grabbed the binoculars off of Pertwie.

"Still can't see them," Pertwie commented, "but we have them on the radar."

The captain studied the errant blip and frowned. "They know exactly where we are and they're coming for us."

"Sir, if they are pirates what of the women on board?" he glanced at me worryingly.

Wilcher looked at me thoughtfully too, "No offence Jackson."

"None taken sir. I'm the least of your concerns right now."

"No, you're not." He went to the intercom and pressed the button to go ship wide. "Attention all crew. We have a possible pirate vessel closing in on our position. Estimated time for them to intercept us is ten minutes. Pirate defence team report to the Bosun. Safety and security team report to Third Officer O'Reilly. Hopefully this is nothing more than a drill. Takemoto and Shirazi to the bridge."

Wilcher turned to me. "I want you and Shirazi to go with Takemoto. She knows a few hidey holes on this ship. Might be dark and cramped but better than being sold off as a slave or worse."

I couldn't agree more. I just wished I could've been more useful, rather than someone's worry. "Thank you captain. Good luck."

"Sir, seven minutes out and closing," Pertwie warned.

"Go, Jackson."

I met Takemoto and Adeela at the bottom of the ladderway. Takemoto didn't hesitate. "This way!"

"Where are we going?" Adeela was pale with fright but wanting information.

Takemoto explained as she hurried and we followed her down into the bowels of the ship. "When they build ships physics dictates the shape. It's not like building a square box. There's a lot of curves. A lot of unused space. Some we call void spaces." She stopped at an unassuming patch of wall and proceeded to undo the fastenings that held a panel in place. "I've modified this hatch so I can close it from the other side. Well, don't dally. Get in."

We all clambered into the hole. Takemoto passed me and Adeela some spare torches she'd brought with her in a small backpack, then proceeded to secure the hatch behind us. "I've got enough rations in my go bag to last us a couple of days. There ain't no toilet facilities in here so you're just going to have to go over there if you need and the rest of us will look away. I have toilet paper, sanitizer and hand wipes though," she explained. "We'll need to keep as quiet as mice. Noise can carry through the structure. So only talk if you have to."

"How will we know if it's safe to come out of here," Adeela worried.

Takemoto pointed to her earpiece. "I can listen in on the intercom and if that fails the captain or O'Reilly, who both know my hidey hole will come down and rap on the outside, seven loud bangs and one soft."

"The reverse of the general alarm," I figured. "Clever."

"Well, make yourselves comfortable," Takemoto suggested. "We could be here a while."

"I found a patch of cold steel 'floor' and claimed it as my own. That's when I had an idea. "Adeela," I whispered. I doubted that any of the pirates, if they were pirates, were on board yet but thought it best to get myself some practice. "Can you watch my body for a bit while I go on a scouting mission."

"Oh," Adeela perked at my idea. "Yes of course."

"What?" Takemoto wondered.

"She's going to go out of her body into the etheric."

The chief engineer's eyes widened in surprise and disbelief.

I left Adeela to do the explaining. I was already shifting my awareness as Lydia had taught me.

Given we had a couple of moments until the other ship arrived I made my first call to Deman. Six hours ahead of us he was fast asleep with one arm around whoever he had in bed with him. The mysterious Rache perhaps.

Deman sensed me and woke me up. "It's four in the morning Ry. This better be bloody good."

I summarised our situation.

"I can't go to the Seychelles coast guard with that. I need to know for sure. Get up there and snoop."

I huffed, "I was about to. I just thought I'd give you a heads up first."

I willed myself away from him and up onto the bridge. Pertwie and Wilcher were watching, with no small horror, the helicopter that had launched itself from the ship that was now tracking beside the Merkwood II. Those on the unmarked vessel were endeavouring, despite our razor wire fences, to attach their vessel to the side of ours.

The helicopter didn't attempt to land. Instead two heavily armed men lowered themselves onto the ship's forecastle, aka the front of the ship's deck.

A jet of water from a well aimed water cannon being manned by O'Reilly nearly succeeded in washing them overboard. They were only saved by the safety harnesses that still attached them to the helicopter. In a well practised manoeuvre they rolled in different directions, out of the path of the water cannon's stream, releasing their harnesses as they did. In a rapidly orchestrated pincer movement they advanced on the cannon, one grappling with O'Reilly who was finally taken down with a blow from behind by the other.

Having secured their prisoner, they moved to the razor wire on the forecastle, armed with heavy duty cutters.

The helicopter, which had been hovering, now headed to the other end of the ship, dropping two more men onto the roof of the bridge.

I took a moment to check on O'Reilly. He had a pulse. I sent him a quick burst of healing energy. I didn't think there was anything my etheric body could do about his restraints so I willed myself to the bridge to assess their situation.

Already more pirates were clambering up a rope ladder the two with wire cutters had thrown down to the other ship.

I was momentarily spooked when I realised Deman and others in etheric form were beside me. "Deman! I thought it was only Lydia who could project herself."

He patted my good shoulder. "Think again. Look sorry for being pissy before. I've no real excuse except that it was 4 in the morning and I was having a really good dream. Let me introduce the team. This is Vladimir Petrov, Rachel Bashandi and Lydia you've met."

"Well it's nice to meet you all but this is going to help how?"

"Trust me," Deman disappeared.

"How's disappearing help?" Our situation was dire and now all these people showing up. I truly didn't know what to do next.

Fortunately Lydia took charge of the situation. "Deman's just hopped back to brief his assistant with an update. Mr Whiting's already got the Coast Guard on standby. They're just waiting on Deman's report."

"And how are they going to believe how he got the information?"

"Why, you rang him of course," she winked, "on your sat phone."

"Well of course I did," it was a good cover story. In fact if I'd thought about it I could've gotten my phone from my cabin and done just that, since I'd finally gotten around to hooking it up with the ship's internet."

"You didn't have time," Lydia consoled me. "Now let me properly introduce you. This is my daughter Rachel and this is Protector Vladimir Petrov who often works with us."

"Works with you? What are you? A bunch of troubleshooters?"

"You'll see."

The pirates, unaware of the etheric presences in the room, tried to force the door to the bridge only to find it held, due to being a dual purpose fire and security door. They banged on it anyway. "We have your crew as hostages. If you don't want them to start dying, open up."

Pertwie and Wilcher knew they had no choice, despite the fact they could all be killed anyway. They had to try and save the crew.

"I'm disengaging the lock," Wilcher informed the pirates. Okay, you can come in now."

Two swarthy men armed with ubiquitous AK47 machine guns entered the bridge yelling loudly and threatenly waving their guns in Pertwie and Wilcher's direction. Both raised their hands and kneeled as instructed. The taller of the pirates stepped forward and announced himself. "My name is Ahmed Hassan. I am now captain of this ship. You," he pointed at Pertwie. "Contact the owner of this vessel and tell him we demand 100 million in ransom." He handed Pertwie a sat phone that he just happened to have on his person. He turned to one of the other pirates, "Axmed, take their captain. I want the rest of his crew rounded up. He's to order them to hand over all their belongings and items of value. If they fail to comply, shoot him. Also any women on board are to be brought directly to me. We could both do with a bride if any are fair of face."

Axmed saluted him, "Yes captain."

While all this was happening Deman returned. "Ry, you're a deck officer. In training anyway. Can you get this vessel back on course for the Seychelles?"

"How? I'm not here physically"

"Will power."

I looked at him uncomprehending, did he believe just thinking about something would make it happen.

"Allow me to show her Deman," Lydia offered. "Sometimes seeing is all you need. Watch that piece of paper", she nodded to some notes on the desk. In a moment they rose into the air, as if carried on a gust.

Our new captain looked momentarily surprised by this but then looked at the open door and ordered Pertwie to close it. He started issuing orders to Pertwie to set us on a heading towards the nearest Somali port.

Pertwie changed the bearing under the watchful eye of the pirate and then was ordered to kneel in the corner with his hands behind his head.

"Now's your chance," Lydia nudged me. "He can't blame Pertwie if you change it back now. Focus your mind to a pin point within your third eye. See the blue flame in your mind's eye. That's it. Say 'I am knowledge and will directed'. I find that mantra sometimes helps me direct my intent."

"I am knowledge and will directed." I murmured to myself, directing that will to the console.

Lydia placed a hand on my back, seemingly giving me a power charge. The map shifted as the bearing altered, back onto its original course.

Deman clapped me on my good shoulder. "Knew you could do it. Okay. I'm leaving you in charge of the bridge. Lydia if you could stay and help her. Vladimir, Rache and I will go and see what we can do."

"Do me a favour Deman and check on Third Officer Riley for me. He's on the forecastle. Alive when last I checked but they may think he's down for the count. If you could get him out of restraints it would be one to our side."

"Good thinking Ry. Rache, Vlad, with me."

"Don't call me Vlad. I'm not Dracula."

"Damn, and there I was hoping you were going to impale a few pirates." Deman, Rache and Vladimir willed themselves away.

"They've got swords," I stared in wonder at where they'd been. Though the girl with them had held a long fighting stick.

"Comes in handy from time to time. You never know what you might meet up with in the etheric."

"Like what?"

"Best not to name them. Let's just call them entities."

"Yeesh."

"Is that a spider?" Lydia started and swore.

"That's just Horatio. He won't hurt you. He's a speedy gonzales but very docile. Aren't you my friend." Still at the navigation console I stretched out my hand to the spider. Call it gut level inspiration but I had a feeling Horatio would sense me. He came right up to my etheric form and tasted with his legs. I leaned forward so I was eye level with him. "You know you could earn yourself an extra cricket if you shed a few of your hairs on that big mean man standing over there. Maybe even bite him. Just be careful. I don't want you to get hurt."

Lydia watched us both, entranced and horrified. "Do you really think he understands?"

"No idea. Worth a try though." I went back to minding the bridge, trusting what would be would be on that front.

"How do I turn off the damned alarm?" the officious pirate demanded of Pertwie.

"Console on your left. Red button"

"Hmph", he went over and switched it off.

I waited until the pirate started to walk away then used my will to switch the alarm back on.

Ahmed swore, "I turned it off." He walked over and did it again. It stopped for a moment and I got it going again. Well wasn't this a great way to distract him from the fact I'd put us back on course for the Seychelles?

"Be careful," Lydia warned. "He's starting to seethe."

She was right. I had to think of Pertwie who was the most at risk of us in the room. But Horatio took that moment to race out and bite Ahmed on his hand, just as he pressed the button off again. Fortunately the spider made as rapid an exit as his appearance as chaos ensued. Ahmed yelling and swearing in his language, something that no doubt meant 'my hand, my hand.'

Pertwie sprung into action, coming from behind the pirate to get him in a headlock. He and the distressed pirate brawled on the floor as Pertwie wrestled for his gun.

"How can we help him," I asked Lydia

"I'll give Pertwie an energy boost." She did and Pertwie instantly got the upperhand on the screaming pirate.

I used my will power to 'kick' the gun away from them. Grabbing it in midair I raised it and bopped the pirate on the head, rending him unconscious.

Pertwie was staring unbelieving in my direction as I was suddenly wrenched back into my physical body.

10

"I'm telling you she's in a coma." Adeela was pleading. I took that as a hint and played comatose.

"Why is she like that?" One of the pirates who'd found our hiding place demanded.

"She's terrified of confined spaces. Sent her into an apoplectic fit," Takemoto suggested. Sounded like a reasonable excuse to me.

"An apo what?" His English wasn't that great.

"A fit, a seizure. She freaked out. Got hysterical. Her mind shut down."

Finally they understood.

One pirate kicked me in the guts and it took all my will not to groan or flinch.

"Invalid anyway. Should just shoot her and put her out of her misery. She's of no use to us."

Hang on! My short life suddenly flashed before my eyes.

"No," Adeela threw herself on top of me. Okay, struggling to breathe here. "You can't kill her. She has vital knowledge about the ship's operations," Adeela fudged.

Silence. Doubt? Yeah, I'd probably doubt that too.

But. "Bring her," pirate A ordered pirate B. I felt myself thrown over someone's shoulder.

"How the hell did they find us?" I heard Adeela ask Takemoto.

Takemoto sighed, "O'Reilly told me you have enemies in my section. One of them must have guessed where I'd hide us and told them in return for who know's what reward. Those men have now made an enemy of me."

I heard a slap. "Women will be quiet."

I flopped along on the pirate's shoulder, my head on his chest, wondering what I could do. Could I will anything to happen in the physical as I had in the etheric? I allowed one eye to slit open just enough to spy my etheric arm, all that remained of my left arm. Hmm, what I really need right now was a weapon. Maybe my etheric hand was my weapon, since it was hanging strategically near his crotch. I'd have to be prepared to be thrown to the ground but I figured if I relaxed as I dropped then rolled, hmm. Might work but then what? I'd have one disgruntled pirate on my hands. Though it might be a distraction. If I could just word up the others. *Adeela, hear me.*

She gave no acknowledgement but Takemoto was staring in my direction. *Takemoto, I'm going to cause a distraction. Nod if you hear me.*

She gave a slight nod of her head.

Okay. Here went nothing. *In three, two, one…* I grabbed and twisted the man's balls with my etheric hand.

Clutching his private parts he screamed. I fell from his shoulder and rolled just far enough away I could scissor my legs around his feet and topple him.

In the midst of this Takemoto had elbowed our other pirate in the guts. She was now on him and bashing his head against the heavy steel floor.

Adeela froze momentarily, stunned, but then shook herself and grabbed the machine gun off the one Takemoto was subduing.

I was still struggling with my pirate but suddenly I had help. Vladimir appeared in the hallway, visible only to me. I caught the bag of plastic ties and the roll of gaffer tape he threw at me. "Thanks Valdimir." I secured my writhing pirate while Valdimir gave me an update.

"Pertwie's still got control of the bridge but we need to get back up there in case they try to retake it. They still have hostages so they could still use the same threat as before."

"Yes but Pertwie now has their boss as a counter hostage. Where's Deman?"

"Willing the restraints off your third officer. He should be rounding the corner about now."

"Ry, who are you talking to?" Adeela asked, flummoxed.

"Lydia's friends."

"Oh," as if that explained everything.

"I don't think your cabin mate has lost it," Takemoto reassured. "I can see the energy swirling around her. She has unseen allies."

"Then why can't I see them," Adeela was obviously peeved at being left out.

O'Reilly barrelling down the corridor towards us broke up our discussion. "You girls 're alright I see." He came to a stop, took in the sight of our disarmed pirates and smiled a smile of pure satisfaction.

"We're alright, How's your head?," I worried. "They knocked you out cold."

O'Reilly gave me a puzzled stare and then felt the back of his head, coming away with a little blood on his hands. "Is that what happened?"

I'd finished securing my pirate so I tossed the tape and the bag of ties to Takemoto and got up to walk over to O'Reilly. "Turn around. I can stop the bleeding."

He looked at me, doubtful.

I let out an exasperated huff, "Look would everyone stop asking me who, how and what. Questions and answers later." I directed my will through my good hand, into his scalp and stopped the bleeding. "Now set aside your disbelief, all of you. We've got four extra people on our side helping us but you can't see them. Suck it up and trust me for now. Vladimir, says we have to get back to the bridge. Pertwie regained control over the bridge just before I was flung back into my body. Last I looked I had the ship's heading back on course for the Seychelles. Pertwie will have checked that by now. Deman, the ship's owner, has notified the Seychelles coast guard of our situation. Help is on the way. We just need to stop the pirates causing harm to anyone before that help arrives. The greatest dangers at the moment are to Captain

Wilcher and to Pertwie on the bridge. Suggestions people."

Takemoto laughed, "You'll make a damned fine captain one day, Jackson. Okay I'll head up to the bridge and help Pertwie."

Where'd she get the idea of me ever being a captain, no matter. "Great. Lydia's there too. You won't see her but she may be able to assist. You heard me in your head so you might hear her. She can go anywhere on the ship and get you intel, keep you up to date. She can possibly talk to Horatio too. I could."

"Horatio, the spider?"

"Don't knock it. He's how we retook the bridge."

Takemoto shook her head, amazed, "Okay. I'm on it." She disappeared into a hatch which I assumed took her covertly into the direction she wanted to go.

"What can I do?" Adeela asked.

I turned to Vladimir. "Any ideas?"

He threw me some keys, which gave the appearance of mysteriously appearing and flying through the air. "I lifted these from a pirate. Whole heap of your crew is locked up in the mess hall. If she could get to them."

"Can you mind her back?"

"Do what I can." Vladimir nodded.

"Okay Adeela, you're a go." I passed her the keys, "Go and let our crew out of the mess. Get them to find whatever tools or anything else they can use as defensive weapons. Vladimir's got your back. If he sees any trouble he'll let me know."

Adeela nodded to the empty space that I'd been addressing. "Thanks Vladimir." She grabbed one of the pirate's machine guns and headed off.

"You know how to use that thing?"

Adeela just laughed. "Unlike some of us I'm actually not a bad shot."

"They'll have you up on murder charges if you kill anyone," I reminded her.

Adeela didn't bother turning around, "Can't exactly charge someone who doesn't officially exist."

"Shit," I realised then quite a few of us had taken Adeela's politeness as weakness. I made a note to stay on her good side. I turned to O'Reilly. "Let's go rescue Wilcher."

"And where do you think he might be 'Captain'?"

I reached out with my mind, "Deman," I said it outloud so O'Reilly would know what I was up to.

"They're doing a cabin to cabin search for valuables. They have the captain as their hostage, using him and his master key to gain access."

"Bastards are searching the accommodation area for anything of worth they can take," I muttered. I didn't want to lose my laptop or my battered camera. But those needs were my own. Wilcher's wellbeing was tantamount. "They have the captain with them."

"I know a quick way up there. You trust me to help you up a ladder? I know it's awkward for you."

Damn. "Yeah, I'll trust you, for this."

That amused O'Reilly, even as he bent down to pick up the other AK47. "I guess I deserve your reservations. Follow me." But not before I gave a passing kick at the nearest pirate. Neither pirate could complain. We'd gagged them with the gaffer tape. And wasn't that going to be ouchy when that came off. Oh dear, how sad. Invalid indeed.

O'Reilly frowned, "Was it really necessary to kick him?"

"Hell yeah, he wanted to put me out of my misery."

"He what? I'll kill him."

It took all the strength of my good arm to grab him before he could double back, "You'll do no such thing. We don't need you up on charges anymore than Adeela. I'm alive. Wilcher might not stay that way if we don't get to him. Where's this quick way of yours?"

O'Reilly gave the pirate in question one last look, as if etching his features into his brain, then started back on the way we'd been heading. "I know a service hatch, much like the one Takemoto just took towards the bridge. It's this way."

I looked at the ladder and wondered how the hell I was going to get up there.

"You go first," O'Reilly urged me. "I'll give you a boost up each rung and I'll catch you if you lose your grip. You said you'd trust me, for this," he reminded me.

Hmm. I stepped up onto the first rung and reached up with my right hand. Holding on with my hand I then raised my feet up to the next rung.

O'Reilly got behind me. Machine gun, with it's safety lock on, slung across his shoulder, "Now lean back against me while you let go with your hand and reach up to the next rung."

"Shit," this was like one of those team building exercises where you allowed yourself to fall backwards trusting the other person would catch you. Always figured that was a dumb thing to do. Trusting myself I was good with. Trusting others, well, they had to earn that trust. O'Reilly had yet to do that. Was there a compromise to be had? I reached out with my etheric arm to steady myself while I reached out with my physical one. And I started to climb.

"How are you doing that?" O'Reilly asked with no small amount of consternation and wonder.

"Need I remind you to leave the questions and the doubt until later. Just be ready to catch me. Tell me to slow down if I'm getting too far ahead of you."

"No, you're doing fine, showoff. Twenty more rungs and we should be at the accommodation deck," he whispered.

I took the unspoken hint and shut up. We didn't want the pirates hearing us. I concentrated on climbing.

When we reached the top I froze, "We need to see what's on the other side," I whispered. "Can you hold me for a second?"

"Sure?" He didn't sound sure.

"Look, I'm trusting you. Trust me. I can go out of my body and assess the situation."

"Okay."

"Okay, here goes," I went within, shifted focus and let go. And I was flying. I loved my physical body but this alternate reality was becoming like home too. I floated at ceiling height so I didn't have to deal with the weird concept of people walking through me. The pirates had made a fair bit of progress in their raid and were well past the hatch. I slid back into my body like an arm going into a sleeve. Okay maybe arms weren't a good analogy for me. But… "They're out of sight, down the corridor and to the right. Two pirates and Wilcher. If we don't make too much noise as we get out of here we should be alright," I whispered.

"Okay, you go out first then but as soon as you are stay put, I'll pass you the gun and come through."

"I'm a hopeless shot."

"Doesn't matter. Just look threatening. Put on that 'captain' persona you had going before. Did it for me."

As in made him shake in his boots or something else? I didn't want to ask. "Okay. How do I undo this hatch?"

"By letting me reach around you," he shoved the handle down with force. Barely a clunk. We both paused for a moment to listen. It was like we were suddenly on the same wavelength. Maybe life and death situations did that to you. Nothing moved. No sounds of yells or footsteps.

Tentatively I opened the hatch and stepped out.

O'Reilly passed me the AK47. He made a sign for me to take off the safety. If you were pointing at someone would they look at that? I wouldn't, I'd be thinking of where to run, but I took the safety off and took a stance that made me at least feel like I meant business. O'Reilly quietly clambered out and took the gun from me, signalling for me to stay behind him. I followed him.

We tippy toed to the corner of the corridor we knew they were last at. O'Reilly took out his mobile phone. I guess he carried one for more than making calls as he set it to camera and edged it past the wall. No-one appeared on the screen but we could hear voices. They were inside one of the cabins, rummaging. He put the phone back in his pocket.

As quickly and quietly as we could we made it to the outside of the cabin in question. O'Reilly made a sign for me to wait, then he dropped and rolled to the other side of the door. I guess if anyone had been looking out to shoot they would have been aiming too high. My estimations of O'Reilly went up a notch. More importantly they hadn't seen him.

He did the trick with his phone camera again and held up two fingers. I assumed that meant the two pirates I'd seen while out of the body. Then he charged in.

Commotion ensued. Shots fired. Screams. I held my breath, imagining the worst. O'Reilly came back out, blood splatter on his shirt. He was followed by Wilcher who was carrying two more AK47s and a selection of knives. When Wilcher noticed me outside he started then looked surprised. "I thought I sent you into hiding."

"Long story, they found us."

"Sir, " O'Reilly interrupted. "If you'll trust us, Jackson can get us intel on where to go next."

"This was the last of the cabins. I thought I was dead for sure once they got what they wanted. So I'm all ears right now. But we can't dally long. They may have heard the gun fire."

"I need somewhere to lie down to do my thing. We could go in the cabin there."

O'Reilly shook his head. "You don't want to do that."

"It was self defence Jackson." There was a strong hint, from the captain, not to argue. "They were going to shoot O'Reilly but he shot them first. And no, you don't need to see that. There's a linen cupboard over here." He used his master key to lock the cabin and went to go and unlock the large walk-in laundry storage. I hadn't even known it was there. We all got in and closed the door.

"Okay, do your thing, Jackson," O'Reilly nudged.

"I won't be long. I'll ask what the others know first." I connected my mind with first Lydia and then Deman. I saw what they saw. Adeela had released the crew who'd been locked in the mess and they were now an angry horde, wielding wrenches, hammers and anything else they could lay their hands on. Adeela was taking point, since she had the gun. And she was flanked by the cook and the bosun, both of whom had armed themselves with what they'd taken from some now bruised and battered pirates. But another group of pirates were outside the bridge, trying to batter the door down. Takemoto had made it up there. She and Pertwie had barricaded the door. Lydia had some kind of force field going that was holding but I could feel her tiring. My eyes sprang open. "Priority is the bridge. They're under attack."

"We retook the bridge?" Wilcher asked, surprised. "How'd we do that?"

But O'Reilly, by now, knew the correct response. "Later Captain. Right now we do as Jackson says."

"We do, do we?" Wilcher seemed amused by this but gestured for us to lead the way. "This is going to be one hell of an interesting debrief if we ever get out of this mess."

We gained the next level safely. Deman was waiting for us there. I held up my hand for the others with me to stop. "Getting intel," I explained. "What are we up against Deman? How are we going to do this?"

"Who's she talking to?" Wilcher whispered to O'Reilly.

"The ship's owner. He's here helping us. I know that sounds bizarre…"

The captain sighed. "We've made it this far. What does Deman say, Jackson?"

"There's five pirates at the top of the ladderway trying to break the door to the bridge down. We'll never make it up there alive. Plan B."

O'Reilly frowned "I didn't know we had a Plan B."

"We spook the Somalis."

"How?"

"Deman and Rache are on it. We wait. We should have the pirates fleeing down the ladderway very shortly."

"We can't handle five pirates," O'Reilly pointed out.

"You don't have to," Adeela announced, coming up behind us with her army.

"At least give me a damn knife, someone," I muttered. I realised I was no longer needed but I would damned well defend myself.

Cook handed me a vicious looking knife and gave me a look that probably said 'don't cut yourself on that thing and make sure you get it back to me later.

I nodded that I would.

Screams of fright and yells in rapidly spoken Somali Arabic came at us before the pirates did. They were running as if in fear of their lives and seemed to have lost all sense that they might be at danger of other risks. They skidded to a stop as they saw our small army. A few started to raise weapons but a howling wind that had followed them blasted them as icicles started to form on their weapons. Even more wondrously, snow started to fall, within the corridor.

While the seaman on our side were perplexed by this only a few seemed spooked, making the sign of the cross of saying prayers. "It's on our side," I yelled, hoping that would reassure them. Those who weren't spooked, like O'Reilly, Cook and Bosun, advanced on our foe and proceeded to disarm them.

Vladimir threw me some more gaffer tape and Jim some electrical ties which he'd no doubt pinched from Jim's supplies anyway. Though Jim couldn't see the thrower he still managed to deftly catch the bundle with one hand.

It gave me great pleasure to gag the pirates while Jim secured them, the rest of those on our side holding them down.

The snow had stopped falling and the icicles were starting to melt into large pools of water on the floor.

"I can hear helicopters," Adeela announced, still pointing a gun at our hostages.

Wilcher frowned, "Hell."

But Lydia told me the good news, "It's alright captain, it's the coast guard."

He stared at me a moment and then took my certainty at face value. He turned to O'Reilly, "Lend me your communicator." Then he spoke into it. "Pertwie, Takemoto, unbarricade the bridge. We have things in hand. Contact the coastguard before they land. Tell them we have prisoners and two dead pirates on the accommodation deck."

I had wondered if the captain would simply have thrown the bodies overboard. Maybe if they'd had time. But if I knew Wilcher, he would do things as much by the book as he could while protecting his ship and his crew.

11

The Seychelles police had been called on board to deal with the bodies. Wilcher, O'Reilly and I gave statements, leaving out all the difficult to believe stuff. There would be a hearing into the matter once we reached port but no-one seemed too worried. Deman, now back in his body back in Australia, had contacted the captain, by phone, and assured him he was sending his best international lawyer to the Seychelles, just to make sure everything went smoothly.

In the meantime Interpol had flown out in their own chopper, to take charge of Ahmed Hassan and his henchman Axmed. Apparently they had a long string of offences against their name and had been on their international wanted list for some time. The Seychelles Coast Guard took the rest of the pirates into custody, having sent out a high speed catamaran out to meet up with us.

All that remained were the explanations. The key players crammed around the small conference table.

"So," Wilcher looked pointedly at me, "What happened?"

Shit. No-one on board this ship was ever going to take me seriously again after I explained all this but I explained it anyway.

Silence and stares ensued when I finished.

It was the captain who asked, to be sure, "You're telling us that the ship owner's girlfriend Rachel called up a frost elemental."

"I wouldn't exactly call Rache his girlfriend. I think she'd object to that. She takes her independence quite seriously."

"Jackson!" O'Reilly intervened.

"Oh, right. Well apparently they befriended it when they were on another job, rescuing someone who'd been kidnapped by an evil man who styled himself as a sorcerer. The man had enslaved the frost elemental. Rachel set him free so he kind of likes her. Deman thought the pirates might think they were being attacked by an evil Djin. Some sort of arabic boggeyman. Don't ask me, I'm not up on their mythology."

Takemoto broke the tension in the room by laughing uproariously, "Well, whatever, that's some tale. Forgive us if we don't comprehend it all but I have to say that whatever happened, we're grateful, Jackson."

"Well said Takemoto," the captain readily agreed. "Though I won't be putting all of this in the ship's log. If anyone asks we'll say we just got lucky."

O'Reilly leaned back in his chair, to muse and to stare at me, "I'll take luck like that any day."

"On a more somber note," and Takemoto's look said just that. "We still have the issue of three malcontents in my section. I suspect at least one of them gave away our hiding place."

Wilcher looked grim, "We still have no evidence. As soon as we dock in the Seychelles I'm getting ETO Northey to buy and install some security cameras. One for outside Jackson and Shirazi's cabin, one near the mess and one near the entrance to the bridge. More than that would get the crew offside. They need their privacy. O'Reilly, have you had any conversations with any of the suspects?"

"Only of a casual nature."

"You need to be seen as Jackson's enemy."

"I know," and surprisingly he didn't look happy about it. "I'll do my best to bitch about her performance during this crisis. Few outside this room know what really happened so they don't need to know she was pivotal in saving the day."

I blushed, "It was my life on the line too."

"You took charge, Jackson. While your actions may appear to be out of a fantasy novel they were effective. Just remember I think that when you hear the gossip back that I'm putting you down."

"I won't hold it against you," and I wouldn't, even if I was still unsure of him, "but does this mean you can't train me in the gym?" If anyone had walked in on our moment the other day the ruse would have been up.

"She has a point, O'Reilly. Okay Jackson, co-ordinate your defence training with Cook so you can join in on the classes he's giving Shirazi."

"But make sure you don't neglect your weight training," O'Reilly demanded.

"I can assist her with that." Takemoto assured him. I might not be into mixed martial arts but I can make sure you toughen up, Jackson. If my crew don't like it, that's their problem. They're not exactly in my good books right now. Somali pirate bride indeed."

The captain's mouth twitched into a smile, "I think you would have started a revolution in Somalia before that happened."

"Why thank you captain," Takemoto took that for the compliment it was.

The captain rose from his chair, "Well I think that's all for now. Dismissed." He left to go back to the bridge. It was his shift.

I stood up as well but O'Reilly took me to one side. "I really do apologise for the ass I'm going to continue to be towards you. As a token of my good will," he took two books from behind his back and handed them to me.

I looked at the titles, immensely pleased, "You found me some stuff on navigation."

"Actually they cover a fair bit of bridge operations. These seem to read the easiest. I still use them for reference so I want them back when ya're finished."

I reached up and kissed him on the cheek. "Thanks."

Apparently it was someone else's turn to blush. I didn't think men could blush. I was wrong. I shifted topic. "O'Reilly"

"Yes?" he seemed pained now.

"What's an ETO?"

He smiled realising he was back on solid ground, "An Electrico-technical officer. Deals with all the stuff on the ship that has electricity running through it."

Well that explained why Northey would be the one installing the security cams. I headed back to my cabin, books in hand, humming quietly to myself. All in all a good day.

12

It took us a few more days to reach port. A few more days to attend to my duties, enjoy Adeela and Cook's food, feed and keep trying to catch Horatio, lift weights with Takemoto and practise my self defence. And more of O'Reilly giving me grief. Though honestly, knowing he hated doing it gave me a smile on the inside even if I played the game and looked peeved.

The roles Adeela and I had played during the crisis had certainly bought us some credibility amongst the crew. Though the superstitious kept their distance. Of the engineering crew, apart from Takemoto, I kept well clear which wasn't hard as I didn't fancy going down into the noise and heat of that section.

Off duty, when not in the gym, I studied, preparing for the practical training I'd undertake in the Seychelles. And I snuck in time to film the antics of the bird life that came to perch on the ship the closer we came to land. Horatio also featured in some of my wildlife docos. I was starting to mentally flesh out a storyline I could put the footage to. I kept hoping to see some whales but had had no luck yet, though some of the officers, knowing my interest, were being kind enough to keep a lookout for any pods.

I'd set up a video blog, as much to journal my transition to life on board the vessel and my adjustment to my physical constraints. I hadn't been expecting anyone to be interested in it. There were certainly plenty of life on the sea blogs out there. But I guess it was my unique circumstances that had some intrigued. My gender, my injuries, how I'd come to be on board and the few supernatural elements I decided weren't too over the top. So no I didn't mention frost elementals, telepathy or telekinesis but I did discuss bits of my out of body experiences, how I still related to my left arm, on an etheric level and detailed my research into the subtle bodies as a way to understand what I was experiencing. I tried to be disciplined to make a quick post daily, if I had something interesting to add, and that seemed to be keeping my small but growing fan base happy. It gave me an outlet for what was left of my old life.

I'd rung my mum and brought her up to date. Her confidence that I'd make a go of whatever I chose to do from here on gave me a much needed boost.

Then there'd been my discussions with my agent. George was sympathetic but frank about my chances of continuing to work on the international news front. He'd been the one to suggest I explore writing and filming wildlife. I was a journalist so the first came relatively easy. The camera work I'd have to learn. I knew what I wanted to see on the screen so that was a start but I'd need to buy some better equipment in the Seychelles, if any was to be had. The Seychelles, afterall, only had a population of around a hundred thousand but they did have tourists. Hopefully some of those tourists needed high end video gear. I could have bought some online and hoped that it got to the Seychelles in time for me to collect but that option seemed fraught given the current delivery delays plaguing the planet.

So I put the better camera, tripod and gear on my wish list and trusted the universe would provide. Sounded a bit new agey but given my life over the last little bit I was starting to have a different perspective of what might lie beyond the physical. Maybe the physical itself was more malleable to thought and intention than I'd once believed.

A bang on the door roused me from my thoughts.

"Get your ass into gear Jackson. You and Adeela are due at the trainin' school in 30. Your lift's a waitin' on the dock."

Minutes. Shit. Had we already docked while I'd been asleep? I rattled Adeela's top bunk urgently, "Wakeup. We're there. They've got a car waiting for us."

"What?" Adeela woke, sleepy and bleary eyed.

"I've already had O'Reilly around yelling at us."

"I haven't made breakfast yet."

"We're off our normal duties for a few days," I threw some clothes up to her. "Remember?"

More awake now Adeela sat up, "We're in the Seychelles, already?"

"Appears so. Don't suppose you have any muesli bars stashed in here," I asked hopefully.

"Behind the kettle," she clambered down.

I hurriedly washed under my arms. Not that in this climate I'd stay without sweat for long but it was a start. I chewed on a bit of muesli bar while I dressed then quickly scrubbed my teeth. That would have to do. Hmm, a pen for my pocket perhaps. I passed one to Adeela, "Just in case they haven't got anything decent for us to write with. Anything else they want they'd better be providing."

Adeela adjusted her shirt then quickly combed her hair, "So what's up first?"

"Safety training, firefighting, getting into a life raft, that sort of thing," I assumed.

"Grab a change of clothes then," Adeela suggested.

"Good thinking. And the bathers Takemoto loaned us." Fortunately they were one size fits all that could be adjusted at the sides. "A towel maybe" I threw my phone into my carry bag too. "Ready?"

"As I'm going to be. Glad it's not me doing all the extra stuff you're going to be doing. I just need a sign off on the basic crew stuff and then I'm out of there."

"Lucky sod," I swore. But I was actually looking forward to that extra stuff. We would only have a short while in the Seychelles while they cleared up the details around the pirate incident but I was determined to make the most of it. We locked the cabin and proceeded down the corridor, "Do you think there's any nightlife in the Seychelles?"

"Hell yeah, I researched that last night," Adeela looked slightly guilty as she admitted it. I was guessing she was about to break out. "But the first thing I'm going to try is the beach bazaar. Starts in the afternoon and goes to the evening. Food, music, arts and craft. It's on tonight."

"Okay, after they let us out let's go there."

"Deal."

We found the car waiting for us on the dock and we were both delighted to find ETO Northey driving it.

"Can I call you Jim now?" I wondered as we stepped into the rental. I let Adeela take the front.

"Sure can Ry. I'm heading into town to buy some security equipment."

"Fancy shopping for some video gear while you're at it?" I asked opportunistically. Though the logistics of him doing that worried me, "I'd lend you my credit card but I lost mine when I got blown up."

"Bank transfer?"

"Okay that'd work."

"What's my budget?"

I told him.

"Wow. You're after some serious gear. I think you just made my shopping day. Any preferences, what are you after? What do you want it to do."

I scribbled down a few suggestions and passed the note to Adeela. He glanced over, though mindful of the road. "Hmm."

"Or similar."

"Leave it with me. I'll try and swing a deal that we can return the stuff if it's not what you want. You girls coming back to the ship after your training?"

"We were hoping to go to the beach bazaar," Adeela admitted.

Jim's eyes lit. "Brilliant idea, I'll hit Takemoto up for some shore leave. We'll meet up and go there tonight. Permission to be your tour guide. I've been to these islands a few times."

"You're on." Adeela and I both agreed.

13

The training school was a white washed one story building with palm trees out the front, on the edge of a small private jetty. I guessed the boat moored there would be a training vessel.

We knocked on the door of the main office, hoping we were at the right place.

"Come in!" a gruff voice invited us.

The imposing Seychellois man was seated behind a plain wooden desk that was half covered with paperwork, books and a computer. He stood as we entered. His eyes gave us a quick assessing once over. Politely he extended a hand "Retired Captain Joseph Larue, And you would be?"

"Deck Cadet Rylee Jackson and Trainee Steward Adeela Shirazi, reporting for training sir." I thought an official approach was best. I could tone it down a bit if they were more casual.

"When Captain Wilcher enrolled you he didn't inform me that one of you might have difficulties with the training."

Adeela rolled her eyes, "I think Captain Larue means you Ry."

Yeah, I knew who he was studying with a certain amount of consternation. I greatly doubted it was because my hair roots were showing, making me look more like the brunette I was, with blonde tips. "I am more than capable of undertaking the required practical training, sir."

"So you can swim?'

"One armed freestyle sir. I swim with my right arm. I found a demonstration of it online and I've been practising in the crew's indoor pool."

He chewed on that. "CPR?"

"I can, admittedly with some difficulty, do one armed pushups. I think I have enough strength in my arm to do compressions."

Larue was starting to study me with more interest, "How are you going to go on the firefighting drills?"

"I'll use my legs to balance and hold the extinguisher, if that's what you're referring to. I can pull the release pin and aim the spray with my right arm."

"Sir," Adeela interrupted us. "During the recent pirate attack on our vessel Jackson led the rescue of the Captain and secured the bridge."

"Adeela," I complained, "It was a team effort. Captain Larue," I continued before Adeela could embarrass me further, "I may not have the usual capacities of most you train but that doesn't mean I can't do what's required, with some adjustments. I'm not dis-abled," I asserted adamantly, "I'm just unidextrous."

Larue laughed, "Well that's certainly the first time I've ever heard that term used. Your captain spoke highly of you both. The fact that he didn't mention your unidexterity can only mean he saw it as irrelevant. So," he studied a schedule he'd printed out, "I plan, over the next two days to put you both through your first aid practicals, firefighting, evacuation procedures and survival at sea. Then the captain has Shirazi enrolled at a local hospitality and culinary school for three days. You, Jackson, I'll bury under a ton of theory in the remaining three days, enough to give you a head start if you decide to take your training further. If you both survive that you'll get the weekend for sightseeing our beautiful islands before your ship leaves port on Monday. Wilcher's hoping all matters pertaining to your pirates will be ironed out by then. So let's go grab a cuppa, fill in some forms, and then put your through any first aid you didn't cover online."

"Shouldn't we wait until the other students get here?" Adeela wondered.

"You're it. The ship owner paid for you both to be put through an accelerated course. So you can expect that with that kind of teacher-student ratio you won't be slacking any time soon. Any other questions?"

"No, sir."

"Then let's get started, time's a wastin."

My cardiopulmonary resuscitation prac proved to be less problematic than bandaging. How to hold the bandage in place while I secured it? I had to lean against the dummie's wounded limb so I could stop the bandage falling straight back off while I wrapped it around. I could have used my etheric arm but Larue's eagle eyes didn't miss much. He smirked at my antics but seemed pleased enough with my efforts. "Adequate," he pronounced. "Hopefully you'll never have to do that as I doubt any patient would want you getting that close to them. That covers you both for your first aid. Let's move onto firefighting. Shirazi, what shouldn't you put on a kitchen fire?"

"Water, sir."

"What should you use?"

"Depends whether it's an electrical fire or an oil fueled fire. Dry powder would work on both. CO2 would work best on an electrical fire. There's also a type of wet chemical you can use on oil based fires."

"You've studied up, I see. Let's go and look at some equipment and see if you can tell me what's what."

Adeela and I grinned at each other then followed him. Our late night quizzing of each other was proving it's worth. Maybe this training business wouldn't be as gruelling as I first feared.

My cockiness dissipated when we progressed to putting out real fires. By the end of the day we were both sweaty and grimy and neither of us was a sight to behold. "I don't suppose you have some showers around here, Captain Larue?"

"I think we might. Okay, you're both starting to sag. Go and clean up, we're finished for the day. Be here at 0800 tomorrow. We have another full day ahead of us. Hopefully I won't drown you." Chuckling evilly to himself he showed us to the showers.

Somewhat less ragged, clean and sporting our change of clothes we went to meet Jim who was waiting out the front for us, head buried in a book as he bopped to whatever music was playing through his earbuds. I knocked on the side of the passenger door. He looked up and grinned, as if caught out, "You're earlier than I thought.

"I think he realised he'd worn us out," Adeela moaned.

"What comes of missing breakfast," I figured that hadn't helped. "The sandwiches we had for lunch filled a hole but that was it."

"Well if you ladies are hungry I know just the place. The Bazaar should just be getting into full swing. Let me go and show you the delights of the local market's cuisine."

I felt my being lighten, joyful at the prospect. "It's a done deal." I got into the back of the car with thoughts of snooping at his shopping but there didn't seem to be much. "No luck with the camera hunt?"

"Actually it went really well. I think you'll be pleased. I took it all back to the ship. Didn't want to leave it all in the car while we went out and about."

"Sensible," though my curiosity was mildly disappointed. "Are you going to tell me what?"

"Nup," he grinned. "It's a surprise. You'll have to wait until you get back to your cabin. Thought you might need an incentive to get an early night. The market can be a bit of a distraction."

Adeela laughed from the front seat, "He's wise to us Ry."

"Hmm."

But if I was peeved at having to wait to see my purchases all was forgiven when Jim handed us both a wallet, "Courtesy of the captain, He thought you might need a pay advance, now that you're both nearly bonafide crew."

"Brilliant."

"It won't get you far. Things tend to be exy on the island, especially in the tourist traps. Best to eat and buy like the locals."

"Figures," I wound the window down, breathing in the rich tropical air. The closer we got to Beau Vallon beach the more I could hear the beat of drums, the loud calls of street vendors selling their wares and the general rumble of the crowd.

We parked the car then ambled past the stalls, buying a well earned curry and for dessert, coconut cake.

Adeela did a pirouette to show off a colourful cotton top she'd just purchased, only to freeze mid turn when she spied our ship's cook looking her way with an appreciative smile.

"Go girl," I whispered in her ear.

Adeela blushed adorably, "Er, you wouldn't mind?"

"Hey, I've got Jim to keep me company." I gave her a little push on the back. "Go on!"

She did, leaving me to ask Jim, "Don't they need a cook on board tonight?"

"No, the captain was going to order in pizzas for the few not on shore leave."

I eyed Adeela's receding back, hoping I'd done the right thing. When the cook greeted her and they headed off on their own odyssey through the market I figured I'd done my bit. "What's his name anyway? I can't keep thinking of him as 'Cook'."

"Bhekizizwe WakwaDlabazane."

"Huh?"

"It's Zulu."

"I think I'll just call him 'Cook'."

Jim laughed, "Most do."

Changing the subject as we meandered through the crowds, I quizzed him about his security purchases.

With Jim being the ship's electro-technical officer it came as no surprise that he was into gadgets. He'd taken some time off from the day's shopping to install security cameras in the corridors of the accommodation block and the way up to the bridge. He'd also bought a somewhat less kosher supply of pepper spray and a couple of stunners for the bridge crew, now concealed in compartments under the operations consoles. Not much as far as weapons went but it was better than nothing, and if found the authorities might have less of a fit than if they found us hoarding a stash of guns.

I idly wondered if we could install a concealed home for Horatio too, as it seemed he'd adopted the bridge. "Hope Bosun's buying him some fresh crickets."

"I'm sure they sell some juicy bugs somewhere around here. You've gotten quite fond of the spider," Jim noted.

I winced, "I wouldn't go that far. Hmm, let me see. Spider … big, black, hairy and very fast. No, I'm not sure fondness is the right term." Although, if I searched my heart I wasn't sure I was being wholly honest with myself. "Well at least, he's not something I'm going to pick up and cuddle."

A tingle between shoulder blades had me scanning the crowd, my eyes zeroing in on an impressive man who strode through the crowd with purpose. He might have been clothed in black pants and a black hoodie but you couldn't hide that flaming hair of red gold. "My god, he's shaved his beard."

"Actually, I did that for him last night," Jim confessed. "He thought he'd best be presentable for the coast guard's hearing into the pirate attack."

In that moment I realised Jim was looking at him with the same keen interest as I was. "You like him don't you?"

"Of course. He's my friend."

"No, I mean more than that."

Jim glanced down to study his shoes. "That's my problem."

He was hinting for me to butt out but hell, I was a journalist. We both watched as O'Reilly walked up to his targets, seamen De Silva, Sharma and Lasseter, no doubt trying to gain their trust. Damn my traitorous heart. What made it notice him? "He's bad tempered, authoritarian and arrogant."

"Are you trying to convince me or yourself?" Jim looked at me with a grin. "I've observed that you two work well together as a team."

"That's the job. It doesn't mean anything. It's not as if he's worse than your average newsroom editor. Basically you treat them with a healthy respect. Like a bomb that could go off at any moment."

"Nah," Jim chewed on that, "He's not that bad. I've known him for a few trips now. We often end the day over a quiet drink in my cabin. He's got a wide interest in the nature of things, the state of the world, life in general. Makes for some interesting conversations."

"Sounds like a sales pitch to me. Are you trying to convince me or yourself?" I threw his question right back at him.

"I'm just saying, if you approach him right, he's got no guile. He is what he is. Yes he's volatile but there's an honesty to it. He doesn't leave you guessing what he's thinking."

I gave a store holder some change in exchange for some breadfruit chips and passed some to Jim. "I doubt O'Reilly and I are ever going to enjoy the level of friendship you two have."

"You won't know if you don't try."

"You saw him first," I countered. "I'm not after stealing him from you."

"Hardly. Since I'm never going to have the relationship with him you could." We watched the man under discussion end his conversation with my enemies and head off away from us. If he'd seen us he was being careful not to show it and blow his cover. He was supposed to be my enemy too.

"Fancy a dance?" Jim obviously had decided it was time to get both our minds off of things.

We wandered down to where the local musicians were playing various drums, some of steel, some wood covered with what I guessed were animal skins. A large, beautiful woman belted out a number that sounded a bit African, a bit Caribbean, maybe even a bit Indian, the words perhaps French or the local creole. Who knew? It sounded great. The musicians were proud, confident and happy. The vibe was catchy.

Jim proved he had the groove, his moves liquid, flowing with the beat.

I shed two years of war zone, injuries and an uprooted life. I let go, feeling my way into the music. Until I was the music.

We must have spent a good hour there before we wandered down to the edge of the beach to refresh ourselves with a cold drink. Iced tea made from lemongrass, though I wasn't sure there wasn't a bit of the local rum in it. "Thank you for a marvellous evening Jim."

"It's been my pleasure. I guess we'd better get you back to the ship. What do you have on tomorrow?"

"Survival at sea."

"Ah, going for the dunk then. They might yell at you a bit but it's usually good fun and at least in this climate quite refreshing."

"The 'they' is just Captain Larue. Looks like my friend Deman hired the whole damn school just for me and Adeela. She's off to some hospitality school the day after tomorrow, to learn how to fold napkins and cook some fancy dishes."

"She'll have fun then. We always have a very international crew so being able to cater for all tastes is pretty important. A seaman who doesn't enjoy his food is a grumpy seaman."

Which segued my mind back to my challenge. "Remind me to get the purser to order in some Guinness for O'Reilly then, and whatever are the ingredients of Irish stew. Whatever might keep him in a good mood."

"I think Ireland's cuisine, in recent times at least, has become as international as the ship's. I notice we're back at our earlier discussion."

"Not really. I mean, on my own he'd be too much to handle. I don't like having to tread on eggshells."

"Then don't. Lay down the rules. Openness and brutal honesty."

"Says you, hiding your own interest. Nice idea but everyone has triggers. Some get more volatile about it, others get devious and manipulative."

"And what are your triggers Ry? What wounds from childhood do you carry? What do you do just like your parents did?"

"Gah, you want me to go there?" Who came up with questions like that on a first date. Date? I couldn't think that way about Jim. Any more than I could think about Reilly as anything more than hot. No! I growled at myself, don't think about that either.

But Jim's inquisitive nature wouldn't let up, "In the interests of openness and honesty."

"Well I guess my dad was centre stage. A bit needy. As in needing people's admiration and approval. While mum was an explorer at heart, wanting to do her own thing without being told how. I take after mum a bit so I guess at least some of my triggers are around being told what to do."

"Hence your doubts about Reilly."

And let's just not go there, "What about you Jim?"

"Er, I suppose I started this. Well dad was your ultra macho sort and I think he thought someone had switched babies at the hospital as I surely wasn't his. He tried to get me into little league baseball as a child but I ran and hid for the day. Then there was his horror when I decided to go into electronics rather than the building industry."

"What's wrong with electronics?"

"It just wasn't anything he understood."

I smirked at that, "Which would be your way of making sure he butted out of telling you how to do your job."

I was rewarded with his laugh, "I guess, I hadn't thought of that. Though gadgets always did fascinate me."

"So your dad wouldn't give you approval. What about your mum?"

Jim sighed, "I think she just enabled him. Telling me to go with the flow and just do what my dad asked."

"That must have been maddening. When what you really wanted was support to be yourself."

"I did."

"So your triggers?"

"Easy, people not accepting me. Though I don't blow up. I just go off on my own and do my own thing."

"But Reilly accepts you."

"He does."

"And the job you do is perfect for you as you're your own boss."

"Yeah, there is that. You know you're pretty insightful Ry."

"Just a knack. Been around people a lot. Observed a lot. I've interviewed some pretty interesting people in my time. From guerilla fighters to feminists, from fashion models to hard nosed politicians. They've each taught me something about humanity I guess."

It was Jim's turn to see through me, "You loved your job didn't you?"

My shoulders sagged, "Yeah. Haven't quite worked out how I'll reinvent myself yet."

"Seems to me you already have."

Adeela hadn't returned by the time I got back to the ship so I did a quick workout, on my own, in the gym, then went to play with my new camera gear before turning in for the night.

The alarm woke us bright and early. With enough time for breakfast.

I interrogated my cabin mate as we tucked into a basic feed of toast and cereal. The kitchen really was having a break. "So, spill!"

Adeela blushed, "There's nothing to tell. We had a lovely time walking through the market together. Then we shared a taxi back to the ship."

"And?"

"And," she cleared her throat, "He's meeting me after class today. We're heading out to some fancy restaurant he knows."

"Promising."

She casually flicked a stray hair from her forehead. A tell perhaps. "And you?" Adeela attempted to deflect the conversation. "Jim kept you company?"

"Yeah, and he really is good company. We shopped and danced and wandered. Talked a lot. It was great."

"So?"

"So he's O'Reilly's best friend and I'm not sure he swings my way anyway, if you get my drift."

"Oh!"

Shit. "That's not for…"

Adela looked horrified, "No, I wouldn't gossip."

No she wouldn't, "I know."

Placated, she dug further, "So what did you talk about?"

Other than Reilly, "Hmm, triggers mostly."

"Triggers? I'm not sure I understand your use of that term. As in something you press?"

"As in people have buttons that, yes, can get pressed. Sensitive areas that when touched on cause them to react in ways that have their roots in childhood experiences or later stressful events."

"Wow, that was a deep and meaningful conversation."

"He's an intelligent bloke," and I felt I could trust him. "I enjoy his company."

"So where does O'Reilly fit into all this?" she asked curiously.

I looked at my watch, "Oh, is that the time?"

Adeela laughed at that. "Come on then, let's grab our stuff. Jim giving us a lift again?"

"I hope so," because I'd forgotten to ask the night before. But he was there, waiting, when we came off the ship.

14

Larue was waiting for us too when we got to the school, "Hurry up. We've got a lot of ground to cover today. Got some officials coming in at morning tea. They want to take your statements over that whole pirate thing. Since you'd best be presentable I won't be dunking you until after that, so…" Obviously hassled, he paused to scratch his head and think, "Jackson, give Shirazi a run down on the lifeboat. What it contains, how it works, that sort of thing. That will give me time to set up the conference room for our visitors."

"Er, what if I forget to tell Shirazi something important."

"I'll know," he pointed to one of the security cameras. "I'll have you on an app on my phone. We'll debrief after, on anything you miss. Lifeboat's…"

"On the training vessel on the jetty, yes I saw it."

"Well then, why are you standing here?"

"Sheesh," I muttered to Adeela as we walked towards the jetty. "Anyone would think he was in competition with our favourite Third Officer."

"For grump of the year," Adeela assumed correctly. "I guess they've sprung this official business on him and it's thrown out his schedule."

As we approached the boat we shut up, assuming he had one of his hidden cameras somewhere.

"So, This is a state of the art lifeboat. Fully sealed fibreglass construction with it's own engine. We'll go inside but first let me point out the release mechanism and where the electrical cable plugs in to keep things like batteries charged. That has to be unplugged before the boat is released. The last part of the release procedure happens from inside, within the helm…" I hoped Larue was listening.

I'd just finished giving Adeela the tour of the boat's contents when

Larue's voice came over some loud speaker, somewhere, demanding our presence back at the office.

The captain escorted us to the conference room where the officials were already seated. Larue did the introductions. "Trainee Steward Adeela Shirazi, Deck Cadet Rylee Jackson, meet Mr Daniel Joubert, from the coast guard. Lieutenant Sophie Camille from our police department and Monsieur Vidot from the ministry."

Vidot shook our hands, "There's no need for such formality, please call me Alexi."

"Nice to meet you Alexi."

"Let's grab some refreshments and take a seat," Captain Larue suggested.

I had to admit I was curious as to why we deserved this much attention from people who were obviously high up in their professions. I'd expected at some stage someone might want our statements but this was something more. So I asked. "I'm honoured but curious, why are you bothering with us? We're of no importance."

"I suspect otherwise," Joubert replied. "Certainly we have the statements we require from your senior people but, off the record, your captain led us to believe that there were some supernatural elements that led to your ship's crew defeating the pirates. We'd very much like to hear your take on that."

Oh shit, "Er…"

"We're not here to belittle you," Camille reassured, "only to listen."

"Okay." So I told them. Adeela added her bits at the appropriate spots in the story.

The Lieutenant leaned back in her chair, taking this all in. "So you're saying the ship's owner was there too."

"In the other dimension, yes. He brought a team of people he often works with. I understand he helps out the local division of protectors where he lives."

"Protectors?"

"Protectors are what the local police got rebadged as by some well meaning marketing gurus who wanted to paint them as warm and fuzzy. More like good guys rather than ogres wielding big sticks."

Sophie laughed at that, thankfully, "So they help the protectors. With what exactly?"

"They help with cases that require special intervention, battling magick users who've gone rogue, accessing the akashic plane to find missing people, that sort of thing. Though officially it's Rachel Bashandi who heads up that team, not Deman. Deman funds it. Vladimir Petrov is their liaison with the protectors. Lydia's Rachel's mum and one hell of a good healer."

"Though not of lost limbs," Joubert noted, "Sorry."

"No need for apologies. I'm at peace with my recent limitations, as much as I can be." Mostly. I was determined to put on a brave face either way.

"So what exactly can they do to help, from this other dimension?" Sophie wondered.

"Look, I'm new to all this." I had to admit. "I was thrown into this other world when Lydia healed my injuries. It made a connection between us, such that I can freely talk to her, mind to mind. Seemingly that now extends to the others. During our pirate invasion they were able to keep me informed about what was happening on other parts of the ship. They used telekinesis to pass me small objects like keys or to undo restraints on prisoners. Lydia used considerable will power to help hold the fort on the bridge. And," I hesitated. Did I tell them the rest?

"Go on, please," Sophie urged, avidly.

"Well, Deman and Vladimir had swords in the other dimension. I got the sense that they could use them to fight unpleasant entities that might exist there. Not that there were any with the pirates."

There was a moment's silence around the table and then Monsieur Vidot learned forward, resting his elbows on the table, his chin resting on his steepled hands. "Could you contact one of Rachel's team now for us, mind to mind." He straightened, "Get them to ring this number." He passed me a piece of paper.

It smacked of parlour tricks and I hoped my allies wouldn't be offended but I guessed this lot wanted proof. "Give me a moment." I closed my eyes and reached out. *Lydia, you around?*

I saw her look up from the patch of herbs she was weeding in the late afternoon sun, being afternoon where she was. She smiled back at me as she took out her phone. *Give me the number.*

A moment later Vidot's mobile phone rang, "Alexi Vidot. Hello? Ah. Very pleased to make your acquaintance Madame Greenfell. Sorry, Lydia, of course. And please call me Alexi. Yes, sorry to impose. Perhaps you could raise my cup from the table but be careful, it's still got some tea in it."

And she did.

Stunned silence ensued. Then, "Thank you Lydia. No that will be all for now. We'll likely be in touch with your daughter's agency. Yes, you too. Delightful woman," he muttered to himself as he hung up.

"I believe she's going out with Vladimir's boss so I wouldn't get your hopes up, um, sorry."

"Not at all, your frankness is refreshing Ms Jackson. Well I've seen and heard what I wished to."

The others concurred.

"That being the case," he opened a satchel onto the table and took out some documents, passing them to me and Adeela. "We are pleased to offer you both dual citizenship in the Seychelles. With visas granted to your destination in Australia. Your embassy, Ry, informs me that it would be best to go through the process of replacing your Australian passport when you get back home as it can take a while." He turned to Adeela, "The British Embassy has confirmed your identity Ms Shirazi. The consulate remembers the work of your father. They will expedite matters and make sure that a British passport is waiting for you when you get to Australia. You'll need to arrange to collect it from their embassy in Canberra. In the meantime if you'd present yourself to them in their embassy in our city they'll get you to complete some forms and get the process underway. End of the week would work for them, they said. On behalf of our government may I welcome you to the Seychelles."

Adeela had tears of gratitude in her eyes, "I don't know what to say. I'm deeply honoured."

I was surprised too, though I suspected they saw us as an investment. "I'm in your debt," there I'd put it on the table.

Vidot laughed. "You're truly as intelligent as your captain claims, Ry. Yes, we may well call in our marker at some time. For now enjoy our island, your island, and I wish you both success in your studies."

After that Larue's threat of getting us to evacuate from the training vessel and swimming out to a life raft didn't seem much of an ask.

We dried off from that little odyssey and spent the afternoon learning about operating short range radio, how to survive a sinking vessel, attract attention from potential rescuers and how to fix a leaky life raft. Larue also explained how to find North or South by the stars, depending on which hemisphere we were in. Since it wasn't night time we got to use a state of the art computer simulation for that.

By the end of the day we were once again weary, yet feeling buoyant, given our new found legal status; citizens and seamen.

We gathered our stuff and headed out for the evening. "Becky's over there waiting for you."

Adeela looked puzzled, "Who?"

"Your suitor."

"Oh, Cook," she laughed. "Can I tell him what you shortened his name to."

"Don't you dare." God knows what I'd get in my food. "Go and enjoy your evening out."

"You too. Isn't that Jim's rental over there?"

There was someone in the car. I figured Jim would have his head buried in his computer tablet. "See you back at the ship."

I went and knocked on the passenger door of the rental.

Jim hurriedly undid the locks and let me in. Wise man, not taking risks while he was reading. "I know a nice little bar that serves finger food."

"Sound's the go," I approved.

I settled into the front passenger seat but as I secured my seatbelt I happened to glance in the rear vision mirror. Was that a car, half a block back, pulling out to follow us? Or was I just being paranoid? Jim hadn't seen them yet.

As we headed into town I kept glancing at the rear view mirror.

"Something worrying you Ry?"

"Probably imagining things. And this is really cliched but, there's a black sedan that appears to be following us."

"Hmm," he glanced up at the mirror and frowned. "See what you mean. Let's take a few odd back streets. If they're simply, like us, heading into the city centre they won't follow us."

But they did. "Well damn," Jim muttered.

"Jim, you keep ahead of them as best you can. I'm going to get us help."

"How?"

"Don't suppose you know the number for the police around here."

"No idea."

"I was afraid of that. Okay. I'm asking you to trust me. I'm about to go into a ....." how did I describe this to him without worrying him? "Er, sort of a trance."

He glanced at me doubtfully.

"Look, just trust me, okay?"

"Okay."

"Cool." Now who could I contact? Most of my contacts in Australia would be fast asleep, it being the middle of the night there. Then I remembered Takemoto had heard me when we were dealing with the pirates. *Takemoto, It's Ry. Can you hear me?*

What the…?

Jim Northey and I were heading into Victoria to a bar but we've picked up a tail. Not sure what to do. We've got no weapons to speak of. Can you call the cops?

Can I tell them where you are right now? What's your number plate? Even better what's theirs?

Er. I'll have to pop out of trance mode. Hold on for a sec. I let my focus return to my body and opened my eyes. "How're we doing?"

"Well they're not shooting at us but I think they're trying to force me to speed up. Probably planning to get us on some remote stretch of road and ram us off some cliff or something."

"You've been watching a few too many movies," I nearly laughed, any other time I would have. Trouble was there was a chance he was right. "Need to know the name of the road we're on and I need our number plate to tell the cops."

"Can't see it from here. Look in the glove compartment. There might be something on the paperwork for the rental."

"Ah yeah, here it is," and handily there was a pen too. I jotted down the number plate of the car behind us, make and colour on a used fuel docket. Writing things down always helped me remember them. "Okay, going offline again."

"I'll just keep driving then," Jim commented forlornly.

Takemoto, I'm back.

Took your time. I've got the cops waiting on the phone.

Great, I read out the registration numbers to her and told her the road.

What about a phone number they can call you on?

Er, I've got one with me but not sure if I've got coverage for the Seychelles.

Give it to me anyway.

So I did. The phone rang almost immediately, pulling me back out of my trance. I put the call on hands free so Jim could add his two cents worth to the conversation if necessary.

"It's Lieutenant Camille here. We'd prefer you didn't come through the central business district. Could you turn up the hill onto the Sans Souci road that goes to the National Park.

"Up to Morne Mountain?"

"That's correct. Parks are sending up their pet drone to monitor your situation. We're liaising with their rangers to set up a roadblock"

"You want me to zigzag up those hair pin bends." Jim moaned

"Don't panic Mr Northey. They haven't tried to ram you yet," the Lieutenant reminded him. "Maintain your speed. We hope to have a helicopter in your vicinity shortly. Keep this line open."

"Will do," I hoped there was plenty of juice in the phone's battery. "There's the turn Jim."

"I see it. See if you can operate those controls and get that sunroof open."

I scanned the dash panel, nothing, then looked up and noticed a switch on the roof. I loosened my seat belt enough to reach up and hit the button. I could now hear the approaching drone, though it was keeping a distance. Probably wary of being shot at.

A voice from the backseat distracted me, I looked over my shoulder, "Lydia!' in etheric form. "What are you doing up? It must be the middle of the night where you are."

Hey. I'm over 60. Happy if I get six hours sleep these days. Anyway, your thoughts were loud. Now why don't we go on the offensive and spook them?

"Who are you talking to Ry," Jim, glanced my way, troubled.

"Long story but a friend of mine, Lydia's in the back."

"If you say so." His tone said otherwise.

"Look, I got us help didn't I? Just keep that trust going. God, have you seen the view?"

"What view? All I'm looking at is the road. Tighten up that seatbelt. The road's about to start it's zig zag."

I sat back in my seat but spoke out loud so Jim, and dare I say the police who could be near the phone on the open line, knew what I was about. "So what are you suggesting Lyd?"

Do what I'm doing. Project yourself into their vehicle.

"You're probably more skilled at projection than I am. Why don't you?"

Because, one, they don't know me. Seeing you in the car with them may more than startle them. And, two, I think it's something you're capable of. You should have a go.

"But how do I get them to see me? Jim can't see you."

Only because I didn't want to startle him into driving off the road. Best warn him now and I'll show you.

"Ah, Jim. Lydia's just going to become visible. Don't freak okay."

I sensed Jim rolling his eyes, "Yeah okay." Then he glanced in the rear vision mirror and swore. "Fuck, you weren't kidding. Er nice to meet you Lydia."

"And you too Jim. But it takes effort to do this so I'll just fade back if that's okay. I'll still be here and Ry will still be able to communicate with me."

"Er, thanks," Jim acknowledged, his eyes never leaving the road as he took a particularly tight bend.

"So how did you do that Lyd?"

Same as you did during the pirate attack, just bring the image of your body with you. May I assist?

"That would be great Lyd. Ah, Jim. I'm going offline again. Going to try something."

"You do your thing. I'll just watch the road. Whoever's behind us is a damn good driver. They're gaining. Wouldn't be surprised if they're waiting for an opportune moment to ram us over that hypothetical cliff we spoke about earlier."

I could see the sweat on his brow, the fierce determination in his eyes, "You're doing great Jim. I trust you to keep us safe."

"Hell. No pressure then."

Okay, I spoke now telepathically with Lydia as I slipped back into trance. Letting go of all resistance. Letting go of all worries by trusting Jim. *I'm ready.*

Open your mind's eye, Lydia coaxed. *Let it be empty of everything except the vision of you sitting in the backseat of their car. Envisage that they will see and hear you but not be able to touch your physical body which remains here. You are safe and protected. I won't let any harm come to you Ry.*

I followed her instructions, aware of my awareness, shifting and flying to its intended destination. "Hello boys."

"Fuck." Sharma, who I was now sitting beside, on the backseat, swore. He tried to lash out and hit me but his arm went straight through me, fortunately without generating any weird sensations.

DeSilva turned around in the passenger seat to see what was going on, "How the hell?"

"Now boys, let's be reasonable about this. That's your ship's ETO in that car you're chasing. What harm has he ever done you?"

"If he's allied himself with you that's his problem," Lasseter, the driver, judged.

"That's a bit harsh. And what of me anyway? All I did was phone for help. I didn't know your friends would be ambushed."

"Someone's to blame," Sharma decided, "We haven't been able to get past Cook to get to Shirazi. You're handy."

"So, what? You plan to force us off the road?"

"Hey, you took the mountain road. Don't blame us if we take the opportunity."

"We took this road because we didn't want you skittling any innocent pedestrians." But I could see I was getting nowhere with them so I returned to my body. "They won't see reason," I announced to Jim and Lydia, and to Lieutenant Camille if she was still listening.

"I don't understand," Jim moaned. "I'm just innocently driving a car."

"Not so innocent in their books, you're my friend and that's enough."

"Bastards. What now? Has Lydia got any suggestions? I've got another hairpin coming up so I'm going to need to concentrate."

Actually I do have an idea, Lydia sounded hopeful. *Why don't we flatten their tires?*

"We can do that?"

Sure. It takes a little concentration but no more than you just used to project your image to them. It's like the telekinesis we used to get you keys and free O'Reilly from his restraints during your pirate attack.

"And you used will power to help hold the bridge door while we were trying to get to you. Okay. How do we do this?"

Form your intent, clearly in your mind's eye, but wishing them no harm that might karmically bounce back on you. You just want to stop the the car. Keep the problem and solution clear in your mind. See us rejoicing as we leave them far behind. Visualising that positive consequence is critical to success.

"If someone's about to do something, can you hurry up please," Jim complained. "They're right up my tail end trying to give me the hurry up. I don't want them ramming us, the insurance on this rental might not cover it."

"Let's do this then. Lydia, you take the tyres on the left and I'll take the right. Jim, we're offline."

"Yeah, yeah, I'll just try to keep us from careening over some breathtakingly beautiful, jungle laden cliff."

Somehow I knew things must be getting bad if Jim was waxing lyrical about the landscape. I did as Lydia had instructed, focusing on the air valve of the back tyre. Some part of my mind was aware that Lasseter was now having trouble keeping their car from fishtailing around the road. Now to stop the car dead in its tracks. I focused on the air valve of the front tyre.

"We're losing them," Jim rejoiced. "Hangon, they're abandoning the car and running into the jungle."

I opened my eyes and could hear the sound of an approaching helicopter, "Find somewhere to pullover."

"Are you mad, what if they come back out of the bush and jump us?"

I had a moment's presence of mind to switch off my phone. I could always get the last number back if I needed. "I don't think so. That's the police arriving in that chopper. Now let's get our stories straight. They were close enough for us to see who was in that vehicle. Enough for us to be sure that they were the same people we suspected of attacking me on the ship. We had good reason to believe that they meant us harm, even if we can't tell them about my conversation with them in their car. Hopefully Lieutenant Camille is with them."

The Lieutenant was. She studied the state of the suspects' car then wandered over to us. "You're going to have to tell me how you did that, Ry? Firstly how did you know to look out for a tail. Start there."

"Hm, perhaps this is for your ears only," I nodded, indicating the other cops within easy hearing. We walked a little away, to the edge of the road. Then I told her.

"Etheric warriors, out of body travel and now telekinesis. You truly do amaze me." and for some reason she wasn't doubting me.

"I had help. I couldn't have done it without Lydia's instruction."

"Is she here now?" the Lieutenant wondered.

I looked around but couldn't see her, "No. She's probably gone back to sleep."

She took a moment to pause and consider everything then turned to give instructions to the other cops. "Get a tow truck up here and impound that vehicle until we can contact whoever they rented it off." She eyed Jim, leaning against our car, shaken. "Perhaps you and Jim would like to hole up at my place for a bit. I doubt his nerves are in a good state at the moment. My home isn't far from here. Come have dinner with me and we can talk more."

Well at least we weren't being arrested for having caused havoc and mayhem on their roads. "That's very kind of you Lieutenant."

"I think it's time you started calling me Sophie. After all, I think we're going to have a bit to do with each other."

And just what did she mean by that?

15

Jim was still looking pale when we got to Sophie's house, as directed. "Are you all right?" I asked him as we walked to the door.

"Yeah, just …"

"I know," I gave him a hug.

He snuggled into me, breathing in deeply as if breathing in my aroma.

"Hey, I'm sweating."

"Don't care."

"I think you're taking advantage of our recent scare."

"It's working isn't it?" he pulled back and grinned. Yeah he looked more himself.

"Gah!" Did I now have two complex men in my life? I distracted myself by knocking on Sophie's door.

"Come in," she yelled from the other side.

We pushed the door open and entered into a simple wooden bungalow. Light and spacious. Very open plan. Our hostess was nowhere to be seen, "Like your place," I called out.

"Thanks. I'm in the kitchen. I'll be out in a sec. Make yourselves comfortable."

Jim had already done just that, taking up one end of an elegant, cotton covered sofa. He patted the space next to him.

I rolled my eyes but sat there as invited, turning to him, "Jim, we need to discuss this."

But Sophie took that moment to come into the living area, carrying a large tray of drinks and nibbles. "Nothing much, I'm afraid. I figured you missed out on eating out in our little city. So I heated up a few of my leftovers from last night." She pointed to a tray of savoury looking balls, "Gateaux piment, or what you might call chilli bites, made with yellow peas, chilli and onion, coriander leaves and cumin. Deep fried, so not very healthy I'm afraid. In the bowls are some spiced chickpeas and some saffron rice. I'm not big on the meat you see. Hope you like the beer."

"You're a lifesaver Sophie," Jim declared as Sophie passed him a glass.

"You cooked all this?" I wondered.

Sophie beamed at my obvious amazement. "Things can be a little expensive in the Seychelles so most of the locals have a few skills at turning the local produce into edible morsels. Hope you like bananas. I've got some wrapped in banana leaves and drizzled with honey and vanilla. That's dessert."

"Um, I don't know what to say," was there a ploy in here somewhere? "Thanks for the rescue."

"What rescue? You did all the work. And thanks by the way for letting us know what was going down. I know the road we sent you on can seem a bit hairy."

"A bit," Jim winced.

"At least they didn't ram you. I know that was a hire car," Sophie noted.

We all knew things could have escalated. We'd been lucky. "Did you find them?"

"No, the jungle is pretty thick in those parts. But if I was them I wouldn't want to spend night-time in the jungle. Not that we have any major predators or anything like that. It's the creepy crawlies they want to watch for; the spiders and scorpions get very active at night. Then there's the tree dwelling Boom-slang snake. You don't want to inadvertently walk into one of them. People have been known to die of internal bleeding from their bite."

I laughed nervously, "And they say Australia is full of venomous creatures out to get you. Honestly I think we've been unfairly labelled."

"A stereotype no doubt. On the brighter side we've already gotten some footage from the security camera from where they hired their vehicle. Want to see?"

"Definitely."

"Help yourself to the food. I'll go get my computer tablet."

I spooned some tasty morsels into a bowl and took a sip of the beer. My first beer in two years away from home. Life was good.

Sophie returned and passed me the computer tablet that had a freeze frame of what they'd captured showing on the screen. There was no mistake, "Yep, that's them."

"You know the suspects then?"

"Honestly I only know them by their surnames. I never got around to asking the captain for their first names. Seamen Sharma, Lasseter and DeSilva, from the engineering section of the Merkwood II. They've had a hate session on me after two of their comrades were taken out by thugs when Adeela and I were trying to make an escape from the hell hole we were in. She was on the run from those in power because they feared she might start a human rights or at the very least a women's rights movement. I was trying to get out because I'd just survived a bomb blast, not quite intact, and wanted a way to get home."

"So the men who died, the suspects blame you for their deaths."

"I think they're frustrated because they can't do anything to those who did it so they're taking it out on us instead. Easy scapegoats."

"Or not so easy scapegoats," Sophie mused. "You're still in one piece."

"They beat her brutally one night," Jim pointed out.

"Then, we suspect, they gave the hiding place of the women on board to the pirates." I didn't bother mentioning the graffiti. It seemed too trivial in comparison.

"There's little doubt in my mind that they would have rammed us and pushed us off the road tonight. They were just waiting for the right spot." Jim was sure of that.

"Until all their tyres went mysteriously flat," Sophie liked that bit of the tale. "That was good thinking on your and Lydia's part, Ry."

Jim looked at me, mystified, "You told her?"

"For some reason Sophie believes me and I don't think it's because she's gullible. Why is that exactly?" I asked the woman in question.

Sophie took a sip of her beer then sat in an adjacent armchair and proceeded to tell her tale. "My mother is what is locally termed a bonne femme de bois, a woman of the woods. A kind of shamaness. The locals look to people like my mother to protect them from ghosts, zombies and black magic. She works her trade in charms, spells and potions and she has the sight."

" Zombies!" Jim flinched.

We both ignored his reaction, "And, I'm suspecting, you inherited some of her wisdom," I tactfully broached the subject.

Sophie didn't look keen to admit it, "Possibly. I was raised on my father's logic. He's a maths teacher you see. Then I survived the rigours of my training in the police academy, in France. But still, there are times when I feel things. But you need to understand that this is a deeply Christian country so individuals with my mother's skills are treated with a mix of reverence, fear and superstition. I tread carefully, given my position."

"We won't betray you Sophie."

She took a mouthful of one of the chilli balls and seemed to turn within for a moment. Then her eyes sprang open and she stared directly at me. "No, I don't think you will. Jim, too, I trust. And one other who is coming to my front door even as I speak."

A loud emphatic knock at the door confirmed her statement.

"Come in Mr O'Reilly," she yelled out.

And he did, looking puzzled. "Ya got a security camera out here or somethin'?"

"Kind've," she laughed, as if the question was inconsequential..

But I knew the truth in that moment. Her security camera was her mind. She was undoubtedly a bonne femme de bois like her mother, or at the very least had the potential to be.

"I heard you'd had problems," Reilly got straight to the point.

"We managed," Jim overcame his worries about zombies to speak up and for some reason known only to him decided to place an almost intimate hand on my thigh. I couldn't decipher the look he gave Reilly. An unspoken question, a challenge or a 'why weren't you there?'. I couldn't work out which.

Their eyes met and though I knew they weren't telepathic a world of something passed between them. Jim left his hand where it was. "Jim, what are you up to?" I asked hesitantly.

"Just seeing where we stand."

Sophie coughed. "Reilly, please join us. I'll get another bowl and a beer."

"Thank you." Reilly smiled at our host who turned and escaped to the kitchen leaving us appraising each other.

"So it was Sharma, Lasseter and DeSilva?" Reilly asked, taking the nearest available armchair on the other side of the coffee table, perhaps all the more to stare at us.

"It was," I put my beer down, "Sophie has some security camera footage of them and I spoke to them but unfortunately they just want someone to pay and that person seems to be me. They think Adeela is too hard to get to as they'd have to deal with Cook."

"You spoke with them?"

Acutely aware of Jim's proximity I only just managed to keep my mind on the conversation. I was really more troubled by what I was going to do about these men than I was about reporting what had already happened. I mentally slapped myself, getting my brain back in gear. "I projected an image of myself into their car, enough that, to them, I actually seemed to be there. Bit weird though when DeSilva hit me and his arm passed right through me."

"Effin' 'ell. So that didn't freak 'em out?"

"No," sadly. "So Lydia and I deflated their tires." That still gave me a moment's glee just thinking about it.

"Using some kind've tele-whatsit," Reilly guessed.

"Isn't she amazing?" Jim beamed.

"Hmm, I tend to agree."

What? Had O'Reilly just said that? Um, this was getting embarrassing. Not to say intense. Yeah I was kind of fond of both of them. Possibly fond was too soft a word to describe how I felt. Jim was really easy to like but why the hell Reilly interested me just plain flummoxed me. Keep your mind on topic, I swore to myself. "They're still out there. Sophie's got an APB out on them." There, that should shift the conversation.

"And Sophie's interest? In a car that was merely following another, albeit at moderate speed. Hardly warrant's the police's interest."

"I think it's more that we're of interest to Sophie." I could be wrong but that was my hunch.

"Clever of you Ry. And you're right," Sophie rejoined us, handing Reilly a beer and a bowl. "I'd like to float an idea past the three of you." She took a map from a shelf on the wall and then rolled it out on the floor between us.

"The Indian Ocean," I noted. "What of it?"

"Well if it was a country you'd have to say it was one of the more lawless on the planet. Most of the world's oceans are. Countries only have authority over their territorial waters. There are vast swathes of ocean that are no-man's land. Peopled by pirates, smugglers, illegal fishing trawlers, waste dumpers, human slave traders and so on."

"Hang on a moment," I interrupted, "Are we talking about the past or the present? Slaves? Really?"

"Who do you think crews most of the illegal vessels? Men desperate to escape either the poverty of their countries or who are simply sold to the companies. Indentured to their owners to work in appalling rat infested conditions for little more than minimal food. They work all hours in all conditions. And if they can't, well there would be more than a few skeletons at the bottom of any ocean. The sick and the tired don't last long out there."

"What about Interpol?" Jim wondered.

"A land based organisation. They're hamstrung as much as the countries that border the ocean. If they can gather enough evidence that they can track back to land based criminal organisations then they have a chance but often the money that is made on the oceans far exceeds any fines they throw at them."

"That's terrible, I had no idea it was that bad out there," but my investigative reporter's nose was twitching. Was there a story here that I could sell to my agent?

"The big shipping companies like Merkwood do what they can to police and report what we see," Reilly remarked. "We have schedules to keep though and usually stay within the main shipping lanes. What is it you're after Sophie?" he asked suspiciously.

The lieutenant nodded in my direction. "Ry, you've already shown with your car hopping that you can project yourself anywhere. Plus you have a strong alliance with the owner of the Merkwood line who, along with his friends, have abilities not unlike your own. You said they undertake work for the Protectors in their city."

"I did but I can't speak for them. I'm not their representative."

Sophie's enthusiasm seemed to dim, "I understand, We're not expecting miracles. As a country in the middle of it all, along with Mauritius, we're particularly vulnerable. The Merkwood II often calls at both island nations for supplies and R&R. I'm authorised by my government to ask if you might ally with us, unofficially. We don't want this arrangement on the books."

"I think that is for the captain and the shipping owner to decide," Reilly reminded Sophie. "And you still haven't told us what you want from us?"

"Evidence. And where evidence isn't possible then intel. We don't expect you to stray from your usual cargo run. Just be our eyes and ears. Be our ally in the fight for some law on our ocean."

Gathering intel was pretty much what Deman wanted me to do too. But what did he or the Seychelles government really hope to achieve? "Would it really make that much difference?" I mused, as much to myself as anyone. "No one owns the ocean. The laws to protect it are inadequate. International committees rely on consensus agreement which is rarely possible. Take whaling for instance. It only takes one country to defend what they see as their centuries old right to take what they wish and the whole thing comes unstuck."

"The ocean laws are mush, I agree," Sophie nodded sadly. "But we are not alone in the fight. Many rich philanthropists fund vessels that do policing, of a kind. They've learnt the hard way to stay on the edge of the law but they are out there. You would be one more asset on our side. Be one more set of eyes and ears."

"And you're hoping I could get onto suspicious vessels, through out of the body or projection, to look around at their operations."

"Exactly."

"I'd want rights to report some of this in the international media. When it wouldn't get in the way of getting the crims to justice."

"We could draft an agreement to that effect."

"Ah-hm!" Reilly cleared his throat.

I took his meaning. "We'll think about it. In the meantime I'll broach the idea with Deman and depending on what he says we'll need to involve the ship's officers."

Sophie relaxed back into her chair and took a well earned sip of beer, "Understood, entirely. To possibilities," she raised her glass.

"To possibilities," I agreed.

"And thanks again for the save, Sophie," Jim put in.

"We haven't exactly caught them for you yet."

16

Back onboard, I first checked with Bosun to make sure Horatio had been fed, then I set my alarm to wake me up an hour earlier in the morning. Ugh! I had a thousand ideas spinning in my head but it was no point using the internet at this hour to put in a video call to either Deman or my editor. They would both be sleeping right now. I looked at my watch and figured I had time to take up O'Reilly on his offer of a little sparring practice in the gym. There was no need for him to act as if he was my enemy anymore, since we knew for sure now who my real enemies were.

Jim was in the gym too, working out on the bench press. That was a surprise. I hadn't taken him for the physical type. But then maybe a lot of my assumptions about Jim had been wrong. One of those assumptions had been his lack of interest in my gender. Well that was plainly off key. Maybe I had to get my head out of its fixed stereotypes of what comprised a man, or human of any persuasion, for that matter.

O'Reilly was in the middle of the room, practising his kata on the padded floor mats. He certainly was an enigma. An arrogant pain in the neck one minute, protective, dictatorial and then this, all poise and fluid grace, like a dancer on steroids.

What, if anything, should I do about the two of them? Or was even venturing there fraught? Third Officer O'Reilly was my workplace superior. Jim was my friend. Did I really want to mess with that?

"Stop thinking whatever you're thinking about Ry and get yourself over here," O'Reilly commanded.

I truly hated obeying anyone. There was a reason I'd become an investigative reporter. I was a one woman show. But I was mature enough to know when I could rail against authority and when it was better to shut up. I went and faced him on the mat. "Can you teach me some of that? It looked beautiful."

He choked, "I wasn't aiming for beautiful, I was aiming for deadly. But, very well. We'll have to adapt some of it for you but let's give it a go. First bow to me."

"What?"

He laughed at my shock. "It's tradition to start a kata with a show of respect to your teacher or at a tournament to the judges. If not me then imagine someone ya do respect and that you're honouring them."

"I do respect you O'Reilly but bowing's another thing altogether."

"How about if we bow to each other as a show of mutual respect."

"Yeah," I mused hesitantly, "I can do that." The tradition seemed important to him.

"Now set your feet apart, like this. This is a basic fighting stance. Knees slightly bent. It lowers your centre of gravity and makes you more stable."

"Less talk, more show," I grumbled. I wasn't in the mood for him to play the all knowing teacher. Even if I wanted him to teach me. Yeah, I can be difficult at times. It had been a long day.

He sighed, aggravated, "Very well. Step to the side of me and a little behind. Try to copy my moves. I'll work through it slowly as a whole first and then break it down into chunks."

"Okay."

I mimicked his moves, a bit befuddled at times. Though I didn't have his finesse I could see the reason for most of the moves. I imagined an opponent and his weapons as I flowed through the dance of blocks and kicks. Reilly's yells as he punched out startled me at first but then I figured they were part of the practice too and would equally startle my imaginary opponent.

Wisely I didn't attempt his spectacular leap into the air, gracefully rotating and landing on his feet like a cat. That seemed to be the end as he stood and bowed towards me so I did likewise. "Right, shall we take that a piece at a time."

It was like learning the moves of some fancy ballroom dance. I kept my imaginary opponent in my mind's eye and that helped.

"She's good," Jim, who'd stopped his weights to watch, commented. "She has focus and intent."

"She has potential," O'Reilly grudgingly agreed.

"Hey, I'm here. Talk to me, not around me."

"I think you have some natural skills Ry," Reilly turned that penetrating stare back on me. "Let's hone it shall we?"

We worked out for another half hour but I was beginning to flag. "I need sleep." I put it out there like a plea. "I need to get up at the crack of dawn to talk to Deman and my editor." At least that sounded like a better excuse than the fact I was running out of energy.

"Fair enough. You've done well."

"Here, here," Jim agreed, looking up from wiping down the benches and putting away the weights. You didn't want a mess of weights rolling around if the seas got rough.

I edged towards the shower, "I'll go and clean up. Catch up with you later." Since my enemies were somewhere running around a jungle I saw no reason for the guys to wait around.

But Jim and Reilly were both still waiting for me when I came back out, standing either side of the exit, like royal guards on alert. "Really, there's no need. I don't think there's anyone else onboard who's going to accost me."

Jim grinned, "Depends what the accosting involves. We might have a few ideas."

My eyes narrowed, "What are you two up to?" They'd said very little during our drive back from Sophie's yet somehow I knew they'd come to some kind of understanding. What it was, I hadn't a clue. What it was about, I suspected.

"I think I've given of my time and deserve a thank you." Reilly folded his arms and gave me the glare.

What the? "Thank you. I really appreciate your time. I enjoyed tonight."

"So did I," he stepped forward, really close. He lifted my chin.

I forgot to breathe. Those emerald green eyes transfixed me. Traitorously my body yielded as he lips met mine. Was that the ship that had moved?

He broke away and we just stared at each other.

"Ah, hm," Jim tapped me on the shoulder.

I turned to him, puzzled. My mind no longer functioning after Reilly's kiss. My brain sizzled into a further melt down as Jim French kissed me, his tongue questing for ownership of my mouth. He pulled away but not before he stroked my hair affectionately. "I see a little more of the brunette in you every day. The real you."

"Come on," Reilly interrupted, "We'll walk you back to your cabin. They still haven't caught that trio and there's no saying for sure they won't find their way back on board."

"Damn." Or were they just using that as an excuse to chaperone me. Where was this heading?

I grabbed my stuff and followed them out the door. Reilly locked up the gym, entering the code into the panel outside it. My brain had a moment to start reworking. "I'm honoured, really. But if this is some kind of competition to see who gets the fair maid? You've been friends for too long. I don't want to come between you."

"Then don't" Reilly put it plainly.

"What he means," Jim elaborated, "Is that we won't argue over you. We'll just adore you, each in our own way."

Adore. That was a very strong word. Not too far removed from the L word. God. This was messing with me. My world was changing too fast and somewhere I'd lost control of it. I really did need sleep. I couldn't think clearly and was in danger of making messy, potentially life altering, choices.

We paused outside my cabin door. "I'm not inviting you in. Aside from the fact that Adeela might be back."

"From her hot date with Cook. I doubt it," Jim chuckled. "I think he booked them into a seaside villa for the night."

Well at least my alarm wouldn't wake her up too early in the morning. Like a worried mum I hoped Adeela knew what she was getting herself in for.

O'Reilly bent down and kissed me on the forehead. "No such luck for you. You've another two days of hard study ahead of you. This will have to wait," whatever 'this' was. "In the meantime one of us will drive you to and from your training. No roaming around on your own until they catch that lot. Is that understood?" he asked firmly.

I did my level best not to childishly roll my eyes. "I didn't plan on running amok."

"Just make sure you graduate." From Reilly that was an order, as usual. Though if either of them had the remotest idea of having some ongoing relationship with me I guessed it would be easier if I was a legitimate part of the crew rather than Deck Officer in name only.

"Of that I intend to do my level best."

Jim patted me affectionately. "I'll be waiting for you on the dock in the morning. Sleep well Ry."

"And just how am I going to do that with a bunch of unruly hormones raging through me?"

"You'll work it out," Reilly decided, matter-of-factly.

"Think of us," Jim suggested.

Then I did roll my eyes, groaned and went inside.

17

Though the nimble fingers of my remaining hand had dealt with my needs the night before I'd still been plagued by hot and steamy dreams involving Jim and Reilly in various positions that only my overly active imagination could have come up with. Sheesh. As the alarm wailed in my ear I woke restless and edgy. I swiped the alarm on my phone to off and threw myself out of bed before my body got other ideas, like drifting back into fantasy land.

I pulled out my laptop, checked I was connected to our satellite internet, and made my first call. "Rylee Jackson to speak with Deman Merkwood, if he's available."

"He is not," his stiff shirted admin, a Mr Whiting, informed me. "He's in transit to a meeting. Can I take a message?"

Hmm, he couldn't really call me back, I'd be in training. "No, that's fine. Just tell him I called and I'll try and call him again later."

"Very good Ms Jackson," and he hung up.

"Hmph," though I couldn't fault the efficiency of Deman's admin, he still rubbed as a little too, um, robot-like. A bit of banter would have been polite, it wasn't as if Whiting didn't know me.

I tried my agent next "George, How's it going?"

"Rylee, where the hell have you been? You don't call. You don't write," he joked. I'd called him two days ago.

"Got one hell of an idea to run past you?"

"I'm still waiting for some video footage of whales, albatross, pirates, anything?

"I'm keeping an eye out for the wildlife and as for the pirates, how many times do I have to apologise for not videoing any of that for you. I was in the middle of a crisis."

"You often are. It's where you go."

"Well how about this?" and I told him about Sophie's proposal.

"Brilliant. Do it!"

"Whoa up George. Still a lot of people to involve if the idea's to get off the ground. And I need to get my basic sea cred if I'm to work at sea in an official capacity rather than as a passenger they're humouring."

"Well get to it then. Shouldn't you be getting ready for your day's training. Slacker," he joked. Yeah my agent often teased.

"I've got time for some breakfast. I'll call you when I know more."

"Just tell me you're doing okay," his tone more serious and concerned.

"I'm doing okay."

Jim was on the dock, with the same hired car we'd fled in the day before. Perhaps the hire company didn't know about our run up the mountain. The less they knew the better.

Jim stepped out and walked around to open the passenger door for me, "Allow me."

"Um, Jim, thank you. Really. But you don't have to do that."

He actually pouted, "I thought if I acted the suave gentleman I could win your heart."

"I like you already."

"I was hoping for more than like."

"Just be yourself. Like when we sat on the beach the other day. There was a comfortable companionship in that."

He nodded in agreement, "There was, wasn't there?"

"And you know why that is Jim?"

"Er…"

"I don't have to compete with you."

"Oh," his expression brightened.

"Can I ask one question Jim, which I hope won't offend but I need to know?"

"Am I using you to get close to Reilly?'

I swallowed hard, yeah that had been the question, "Er, yeah."

"Ry, I fell for you from the moment you and your overly bleached hair came through my door. There was something irrepressible about you. It was clear even then, that Reilly was stricken with you."

"Hah! He hated my guts."

"Nah. He might have been trying to tell himself that but there was clearly a gleam in his eyes. I sorrowed, in that moment, for I knew I couldn't have you. I couldn't take you from him."

"He didn't have me. I'm my own person. I make my own decisions."

"Clearly, and as you've yet to make one on that matter, all options are on the table."

Hell, no pressure then. "You'd better get me to the training school on time before this car turns into a pumpkin or me some slave girl."

"Hmm," Jim's honey brown eyes sparkled with mirth. "That might have possibilities."

"Jim!" I growled in exasperation.

Larue worked me through more maritime theory that morning. Types of anchorages. Cloud formations and what they could tell you about incoming weather. Even where to be in the event of a tsunami, as far out in the ocean as you could get over the deepest water.

By the time I came up for air the clock had gone well past twelve and my stomach was rumbling.

"Grab yourself a sandwich Jackson and have half an hour off for a stroll. It'll clear your brain for this afternoon."

I'd have liked nothing better but, "Actually, I made a promise not to go roaming until the police catch some individuals who tried to run me and a friend off the road yesterday."

"I'd heard gossip about that but didn't know whether to believe it. Okay, well go and sit out on the pier at least. There's a security camera out there, covering our training vessel. We'll keep an eye on you."

"Appreciate it captain," I gave him a respectful salute of

acknowledgement.

A light sea breeze had gotten up. Enough to ruffle my hair. The breeze whispered over my bare shoulders, tales of sailors past and promises of future adventures.

My spirit seemed to float with the breeze, lighter than it had been in a long time.

As I ate my sandwiches I was suddenly aware of Lydia's presence beside me. Fortunately she hadn't projected a solid form or her sudden appearance might have freaked out whoever checked on the security feed. "Hello Lyd."

"Beautiful day you have here."

"Paradise, I guess, or close to it." I wouldn't spoil it by mentioning the prices in town, the venomous creatures or the stifling afternoon heat that occasionally slammed into you like a wave.

Lyd's lips twitched at the corners. "Yes, well, I guess every Eden has its serpents. And how are you doing?"

"Confused." There was no hiding my thoughts from Lyd so I didn't bother. Both men came readily to my mind.

"You and either of them wouldn't work, but together. Yes I think there might be balance there."

"But what if we can't juggle it? If it unravels, what then?"

"All relationships have two things in common, risk and work. You take the risks or you live a life of solitude. You do the work because everyone is different, has different needs that have to be met to keep them feeling valued. With balance the risks and the workload even out. Honesty and openness do the rest."

"How did you get to be so wise?" I wondered, out of admiration.

"Running an orphanage you often end up working with many trauma damaged souls. Kids ripped from all they've ever known, who have to learn to trust a new set of adults and hope that they'll love them even a fraction of what they had before. And all those kids under one roof. Different egos. Different issues and interests, all vying with each other to survive. Not much different to everyday life really."

"No I suppose not," I tried visualising Riley and Jim as two kids. What would be their needs? Jim would want companionship, comforts and the beautiful things in life. Riley would want to be 'the man', to protect, to control, to strategize.

"Learn about them," Lydia suggested. "Why they are the way they are."

"I already know a bit about Jim. He wants the acceptance his father never gave him. The right to follow his own path. To be authentically Jim."

"And you bared a bit of yourself to him in the process," Lydia guessed.

"I always thought that when I met the right man, or in this case men, I'd just know. I'd be swept away on a tide of emotion, so entranced by them I'd have no doubt about what to do next."

Lydia laughed, though a tad nervously, "Those types of beginnings often lead to ruin. At the very least you find out too late who your partner really is, sometimes even after they've walked you down the aisle. There's a whole section of the population who try to win a woman just as you said, sweeping them away on a tide of praise, chocolates and flowers, only to later reveal themselves as controlling egomaniacal monsters. Having won you they require you to worship them and serve them, subverting your own needs and alienating you from your friends."

My eyes narrowed, "Speaking from experience?"

"A long time ago. I learned my lesson the hard way. The therapy afterwards launched me on a new life. I've kept an active interest in relationship dynamics."

"And you have a new love life."

Lydia's face blossomed in joy, "Yes, he's a wonderful addition to my life. I'm still keeping him at a slight distance but…"

"You think he's a keeper," I caught her thought and finished her sentence for her. A potentially bad habit that maybe I shouldn't get in the habit of with telepaths.

She chuckled, "Yes. He is a keeper. And I might have not dared to go there again but after years of solitude and fleeting affairs I think I deserve to take the risk. I'm trusting myself because I know this time I have the caution, the wisdom to ask questions and to look beneath the surface."

She'd given me a lot to think about but I didn't get a chance to do that. Larue had a busy afternoon planned for me. Some hideous challenge called celestial navigation. Thankfully not all of it as the whole was a huge subject. Enough to give me an overview and that truly was enough.

I finished the day with an exam covering what I'd learned during the day and some basic applied mathematics for good measure. I scraped it in within the time allowed, handed it to Larue and nearly ran for the door.

He blocked my escape. "Think of it this way Jackson. You'll have an appreciation now for what your officers know."

"There's that."

"No more theory. For now."

Phew. Though the 'for now' sounded ominous.

"We'll take the training vessel out tomorrow morning. I'm putting together a skeleton crew. We'll head out at dawn since we have to get you back in time for your final exam and then we'll have your graduation.

Dawn? Fuck. "I'll be here."

As I made my escape I looked on the road, trying to spot the hire car. Nothing. But there was a rumble in the distance. The aggressive bark of a large engined motorcycle. I stared as the garishly yellow and slate grey monster of a bike pulled up in front of me. "What is that thing?" I asked it's rider as he got off it.

"An Aprilia Caponard. 1200cc. Rally model." He passed me the jacket and crash hat he'd had strapped to the pillion seat.

"I'll boil," I muttered as Reilly helped me into the kevlar reinforced jacket and strapped the hat to my head. With some questioning of my wisdom I used my etheric arm for balance, swung a leg up and over the seat and settled behind his back, wrapping my one and a bit arms around him as best as I could. "Where are you taking me?"

"You didn't get a very pleasant experience of the mountains last night. I thought we'd go up to the Mission Lodge Lookout, to watch the sunset."

Sounded good to me. Though no further conversation was possible, I couldn't hear myself over the engine. I relaxed into the rhythm of the ride as we fluidly travelled the windy road as if it was made for the bike.

We reached some old ruins and Reilly pulled over, "Hop off."

"Someone lived here?"

"I think, if travel guides are to be believed, it was built by some missionary society as a place for children who were dumped on the island after the abolition of slavery."

"Poor souls."

"Indeed."

But the sombre history did nothing to detract from the view. A view that revealed the full extent of the western side of the island. "There really is a lot of unspoiled beauty here." And I had dual citizenship of this remarkable place. How lucky was that?

While I took in the panorama Reilly emptied one of his side panniers of a tarp, food and drinks. Like a knight of old he lay the tarp on the damp ground for both of us to sit on. Then he passed me some finger food and a light cider which was imported and therefore must have been hideously expensive. "Is that your bike? It doesn't look like something you could rent."

Reilly affectionately gazed at the mechanical beast. "Wilcher lets me keep it on the ship. It doesn't take up much space. What with the inquest and all I didn't have time to get it out before now." He slipped out of his jacket.

Good idea. I did the same. As I wondered if there were any mozzies up here to chew on me, Reilly passed over some spray. "No nasty chemicals as far as I can tell."

"Thanks," I covered my arms, my ankles and the back of my neck liberally. "What's the food," I wondered as I shifted my mind from the mozzies that might chomp on us.

"I stopped at a local Indian restaurant. I've noticed ya 'ave a preference for vegetarian so I got us some veggie samosas and some cauliflower and potato bhajias, sort of fried veggie fritters."

"Yum," I picked out one of the fritters to try. The cider went perfect with the heat of the food. "Reilly, can I ask you some questions?"

One eyebrow lifted, "Is this an interrogation?"

"No, more like looking under the bonnet when you're thinking of buying a new car."

Reilly got my drift, "And what would ya be wantin' to know about this car?"

I went with the analogy. For some reason it seemed safest. At least less rude. "Well, like how it was made and what it's quirks and foibles might be."

"Hmm, I think when they made this car they didn't have much of a budget. Ya might say the chief designer and the chief engineer argued a lot, even comin' to blows. In the end the car was better off out of the factory, out on the open road where it could reach its full potential."

"At sea?" I quizzed, wondering how that had come about.

"Eventually. If we're talkin' about this car's foibles ya might say it went against the grain. Bugger the regulations and the standards. It was impounded once and that was not something to its credit. After it got out it looked for new horizons. That's when the ocean beckoned."

Hmm, "So forgetting the car analogy, what annoys the shit out of you?"

"Ouch, ya really do want all the dirt. Ya're askin' me to reveal my underbelly."

"Can you blame me? Okay let me guess some of it. You have a short fuse and you don't like disrespect. I've figured that much out working for you."

He shifted as if uncomfortable, "Yeah, well ya'd be right on both those things. Add to that I don't like to see anyone bein' physically abused. Even unwarranted verbal abuse pisses me."

Because of his parents, I guessed. "You're a protector. I admire that about you."

"Yet ya're a hard one to protect, aren't ya Ry?" His fiery green eyes blazed for a moment.

"I like my independence. The right to make my own choices." He'd better understand that from the start.

"And why would that be, since we're diggin' deep here?"

Shit, fair's fair. "That would have a lot to do with having an egocentric apprentice megalomaniac of a father and a mother who railed against his attempts to control her."

"An apprentice megalomaniac?"

"Well, he didn't quite make it to the top of his field. Though he's still working on that, as far as I know. I keep out of his path as much as I can. Mum finally divorced him, took him for quite a bit actually. She's living life her way now and though she has the occasional friend with benefits I think she plans on staying single."

"Makes sense, given her experience. And you Ry? What do ya hate? Apart from buddin' megalomaniacs tryin' to control ya."

"Being ignored. I think it's why I enjoyed being a journalist, being in front of the camera. It filled a hole left by my childhood."

"No hidden desire to control either me or Jim?" he asked but I could tell it was more of a tease.

"God no. I feel strongly about people having the right to be who they are."

"Even being short fused."

I grinned, "Even that. At least it's honest. See it from my perspective. My father was, is, devious and calculating. Often with a hidden agenda. Whereas you're, well not transparent but," I looked for the right word. "If you want to express your opinion you leave very little doubt about what it is. I might not like it at the time but at least I don't have to look for any hidden meanings." I ate another fritter, washed down with some of the cider Reilly had brought along.

We sat and finished eating in companionable silence, passing each other juicy morsels with a grunt and a nod.

"Ya used past tense when speakin' of your career Ry. Why is that?"

I shrugged my left shoulder, as if the stump said everything. "People would want to look away from that."

"People or you?" he asked incisively.

Bugger. Was he right? Was I prejudiced against myself? Was I limiting my options because of how I, myself, saw people with disabilities? "Maybe a bit of both."

Reilly smiled, seemingly pleased with the honesty of my answer, "Audiences can be educated."

"Even if they can, there's the television companies who buy what I produce. Bottom line, they're not going to take risks, not when they're already battling to keep their budgets afloat due to all the online competition for audience."

"So make yer own online channel. The tools to do that are out there aren't there?"

"Hard to make money from but yes, it can be done. But what's my content? It has to be of interest."

Reilly thought for a moment, "If it was me, I'd look to the sea. Pirates, environmental garbage, battles for territorial rights, the wildlife. Got to be somethin' there. And fits seamlessly with what Sophie wants us to help with."

I took another sip of cider. I'd already had a few tentative thoughts along those lines. Even a nascent blog that was starting to get a bit of a following. "Combine a life at sea with my journalism."

"Why not? I know Jim just went shoppin' for ya for a heap of new camera gear. Ya must have already been mullin' over the possibilities. Stop fart-assin' around. Commit."

"Easy enough for you to say," I scowled, "I still need to graduate tomorrow if I'm to be even halfway legitimately employed."

"Which is why I'm not makin' any moves on ya tonight."

I didn't know whether to be relieved or disappointed. I wasn't really ready to step off that cliff yet. Or was I?. "And there I was hoping you were wining and dining me with designs on my body."

"Postpone that thought until tomorrow night. For now I just want ya well fed, rested and admittedly protected. That and Larue called me while ya were doin' yer test this afternoon. He told me you were strugglin' on some of the celestial navigation basics."

Damn, "I thought I'd done okay."

"Ya will," he went back over to his bike and then pulled out a heavily padded instrument which he brought over and handed to me.

"A sextant?

"Mine, so don't drop it."

I wouldn't dare. "I have to admit it's a mystifying contraption."

"It's just a curved ruler for measurin' the difference in reflection between two objects. Hence the mirrors. There's a telescope for lookin' through and shades you can put in front of the sight so ya don't burn yer eyes out lookin' at bright objects. Why do ya think so many pirates of old had a patch over an eye?"

"Actually I'd never wondered."

"And ya call yourself an investigative journalist. Where's yer curiosity? Come and stand here. Hold it like this." Reilly came behind me, damn near an embrace, as he explained its use. He was bringing the theory to life, his enthusiasm for his subject contagious. It was like my mind was syncing with his and suddenly there it was, the understanding washed over me like a tidal wave, leaving only clarity in its wake. "I think I've got it."

"What about there, give me the angle and position?" He tested me.

As the sun set and dark descended on us the stars burst forth out in all their glory. Reilly pointed out Orion, rising in the East. It would travel across the sky and descend into the West in the early hours of the morning. Since the Seychelles was just south of the equator it wasn't possible to see the North star Polaris. Instead Reilly directed my attention to a grouping of stars called the Southern Cross and explained how to tell them from other cross shaped constellations. But my focus was distracted by a sound I caught on the wind, "Did you hear that Reilly?"

"I did." He frowned and turned his head from side to side, trying to get a sense of the direction.

"It's coming from the jungle down there," I pointed.

"We can't go in there. Anythin' could be crawlin' around in there now it's dark."

I knew that wasn't fear speaking but wisdom and caution. "Perhaps, there is a way. Hold me. Let me relax against you."

"With pleasure," obviously pleased by the prospect.

I slipped my awareness out of my body, like a hand leaving a well loved glove. It was becoming easier to do this. Still it was difficult to see.

Only because you are limiting yourself by your preconception that it's dark, Lydia murmured through my mind.

Were you spying on me Lyd?

Hardly. Your mind entered the akashic. We're all connected here. Of one mind. To your left I think, she suggested.

I left the implications of her statements to mull over later. Instead I steered my mind's eye left. *There. A body. Good grief. Is that?*

The one you call Sharma.

Gah! He's crawling with insects.

Then ask them to leave.

I can do that?

In the akashic they are as much apart of you as anything else.

So I didn't need to be polite about it. *Depart*, I ordered. They ignored me.

Maybe Horatio then, Lyd suggested.

You want me to connect up with the akashic version of Horatio? Can I even do that?

I have no idea. Why don't you investigate the possibility.

A man was lying on the thick jungle floor, likely dying, and I was contemplating making some mystical connection with a spider.

To help him. He's being eaten alive.

I cringed. She was right. I let my mind's eye drift to the ship's bridge. The ship wasn't going anywhere but the bridge was still manned, Seaman Merryweather on duty. I found Horatio peering out from behind a console. Would he sense me? I drifted my awareness down to his level. Staring into his mesmerising multifaceted eyes. He looked straight back at me and we had a moment. More than a moment. Hell, I suddenly realised why Horatio had been roaming the ship. He felt an urgent need to find a mate. As dangerous as that prospect could be for him he felt a biological imperative to pass his packet of sperm over to a receptive female of his kind. *I can't make any promises but I'll ask around and see if anyone on the island has a female of your kind as a pet.*

I didn't get words back in my head but I did get some kind of non-verbal sense that we both understood each other. And then the unbelievable happened. He did his own version of an out of the body experience. A shadow of a very large black spider separating from his physical body and travelling with me, back to the man in the jungle. *Lyd*, I whispered, *watch over Horatio's physical body while we do this.*

Of course.

If I'd wondered if the jungle life would sense Horatio I was left with no doubt that they did. Insects frantically fleeing in all directions. The huge etheric spider hovered over the man and nothing was coming near.

I'll be back, I communicated with the spider. *I'm going to get some help.*

I allowed myself to once again feel Reilly's warm arms around me. "Call for an ambulance Reilly. And call Sophie. Tell her we've found Sharma."

But Sophie was already ringing on Reilly's phone, even before I finished my sentence. Coincidence? I didn't think so as I suspected the woman really was as much of a bonne femme de bois as her mother. Reily put the call through to speaker phone.

"I've got a couple of paramedics on the way and two emergency workers with slash hooks," she announced.

"Tell them to hurry. He's in a bad way. I've got something watching out for him but I don't know how long it will stick around."

Sophie chuckled, "I know what you've done Ry. Hang on. I'm just about there."

Once again cop cars and officials crowded the mountain. As the medics disembarked from the ambulance I edged away from Reilly, "I need to show them where he is."

"Remind me again why we're helping him?"

"Because," did I try to tell Reilly that everything was one whole, all connected. Hell, yes. He was going to have to take me on as I was, or at least as what I was becoming. "Because he's as much me and you as the jungle here, the earth, the sky, everything that lives and breathes and everything that doesn't. He doesn't know that, which is why he's been part of their attack on me but their ignorance doesn't make reality less so."

Reilly frowned, "He's me? You?"

"Not the outer shell, but at the core, yes. I'll explain later. I have to guide them in."

"Past the snakes and other bities."

'Horatio will show me a safe path."

"Horatio!"

But I didn't have time to explain, "This way," I indicated the direction to rescuers and plunged headlong into the forest, plugged into Horatio's acute sense of vibration and smell. Sophie, beside me, passed me a torch, "Even so, this will help."

We found him in short order and stepped out of the way as the team lifted the injured man onto a stretcher. "Snakebit," one paramedic hissed. "He'll be lucky to survive the night."

But I knew Lydia would channel some healing energy into the man once Horatio returned to his body and she was released from her duties there. I thanked the spider and he left. Though I'd felt his passing hope that I would be true to my word and see if there was a female black Brazilian tarantula being kept as a pet on the island. I mentioned it to Sophie while we walked back to the ruins, following the medics.

Reilly met us at the edge of the forest. "You know it's very hard to be protective if I can't do anything to help."

"But you did help. You watched over me while I left my body."

"It's hardly the same thing."

"Actually," Sophie interrupted, "it's critical. You did well tonight but you both know very little yet, of what exists in the otherworld."

And wasn't that food for thought? "What lurks there?"

"The Akashic is a record of every action, thought and belief that has been imprinted on it. Including the individual and collective fears of all sentient beings."

Yikes, "So what are you saying Sophie, that bogeymen exist?"

"Exactly. And just like in your day to day world you are most likely to draw to you what you resonate with, what you fear, or what you believe to be true. Fears take form within it, to reflect what you expect. So if you believe in demons then your fears will manifest as such."

"I wasn't actually afraid of going into the Akashic before you brought this up," I accused, a shiver running down my spine.

"Ignorance isn't bliss, Ry. Lydia's been watching your back but there are things you need to know about. Everyone at this level of consciousness has fears. You need to be aware of what those fears are. Be careful what you take into the otherworld. Your state of mind should be calm, positive and resonating with the highest good."

"Or… duh duh duh da!"

Reilly gritted his teeth. "So she needs to be prepared but how can I protect her?"

"Two things. Your love for her. That is your greatest weapon. A weapon of light. The second is the higher vibrational beings that you can call on to help you. They hold free will as sacrosanct so they won't come to your aid unless you ask."

"Angels?" Reilly didn't sound convinced.

"If that's the form you're most comfortable with. Actually they are high frequency formless beings of light. What names you give them are for your convenience, not theirs."

"All well and good," he muttered, "but I'd like somethin' physical I could use too."

Sophie took a deep breath and closed her ebony eyes, seemingly going deep within, then she opened them again to stare at him. "I have what you need. Come to me tomorrow afternoon while Ry's doing her final exams."

18

A new day dawned, one filled with both anticipation and trepidation. I'd be navigating a real vessel this morning. I was surprised to find both Reilly and Jim waiting for me. Jim, as was his way, opened the passenger door of the car for me while Reilly rolled his eyes, "She's not helpless."

"Pull your head in, Reilly," I impolitely chided. "Let Jim be Jim. You be you. And I'll be me. No-one's asking you to open car doors for me but if Jim wants to that's alright by me. If you both truly want a relationship with me then it's going to have to be one where we accept, or at least tolerate, each other's uniqueness. We don't have to be public about it but between us there has to be absolute openness and honesty."

"Here here," Jim agreed, now in the driver's seat.

"I take your point," Reilly reluctantly agreed from the back seat.

"Why are you both here anyway?" I wondered.

"Larue needed to find you a crew. Didn't he tell you?" Reilly smirked.

No he hadn't. Damn. "Wait a minute? My crew?"

"You'll be the captain today. Larue your chief officer and I'll be your engineer and communications officer."

"And Jim?"

"Anything you want me to be," he hazarded an affectionate glance in my direction. "Though most likely general lackey and steward. I'm doing your lunch today. Hopefully you won't need an ETO for this trip but if you do I'll be there."

Bloody hell!

Larue was outside the college waiting for us, "Captain Jackson, your ship awaits."

I gulped. And there I'd hoped the boys had been joking. "Honestly, isn't this a big ask?"

Larue chuckled, evilly, I thought, "Not if you keep the red channel markers on your left as we head out and remember the order to raise the anchor before you try and motor out."

Ugh! I needed to get my brain in gear. Think like a captain. That's what I needed to do. "Okay, first order is that we have a crew meeting. Make sure everyone knows what they're doing and where we're going. Then I'll plot the route."

"Excellent," Larue patted me on the back. Whether it was real approval or he was being patronising I wasn't sure but I took it as the former. I always preferred the glass half full approach.

Thankfully we got underway with no problems. More, I suspected, due to the competence of my crew than me but at least Larue wasn't frowning at me. We tied up at a jetty on the nearby island that had been our destination and after Larue got out the picnic table and fold out chairs Jim set the table with our somewhat early lunch. A modest feast of sandwiches and a platter of tropical fruit. With the pizzaz, fitting a maitre-d, Jim opened a bottle of chilled white wine, imported from my own country. "An Eddystone Point Riesling, enjoy."

Not a cheap wine I was guessing. "Nice," it had a refreshing taste, almost a hint of citrus.

"I'm bringing the Guinness next time," Reilly muttered, but he seemed to enjoy the wine.

"To possibilities," I offered the toast and everyone, including Larue, clinked their glasses together.

"Speaking of which," Larue announced, "After we get back and Ry's done her exam we have some officials coming in for her graduation."

"What?" I squeaked. Er, "Why?"

Everyone else ignored me. Reilly considered it. "I have a meeting with Sophie but I'll be there. What time?"

"Fifteen hundred hours," of course Larue gave the time in 24 hour clock. "The lieutenant is coming too so that shouldn't be a problem. Time enough for Ry to ace her test," his stern focus on me punctuated the fact that he wouldn't accept anything else. "Then she can get cleaned up."

"I'll bring her a freshly pressed uniform," Jim decided.

That pleased Larue. "Excellent. Well finish up. The day's getting on. When you're ready let's pack this up and head back. Not forgetting that the return trip is still part of Ry's practical assessment. I don't want to see any slacking on procedure."

I couldn't help myself, "Aye Aye, Sir." I said somewhat flippantly.

Larue just laughed. After a week of my company he'd grown accustomed to my cheek. He chided me nonetheless. "You'll make a fine captain oneday Ry but remember, respect."

"Sorry Sir," and I was, but we grinned at each other anyway.

Back at the training school, the exam proved to be no easy multiple choice or 'tick and flick'. Larue obviously took the course standards seriously and I was glad he did because I knew, as a member of the crew of the Merkwood II, that our lives depended on each other knowing our jobs. I sailed easily through the stormy waters of shipboard safety only to nearly founder on the celestial navigation. But I thought about what Reilly had shown me the night before and that helped me visually picture a fair bit in my head. For a journalist it had always bemused me that I learned best through pictures and doing. Words just weren't enough. Wisely Larue had guessed this and adapted his teaching style to my way of learning. Not something that would have been easy to do for a large class but given I was getting one-on-one, thanks to Deman's generosity, it had been possible to work through the course in a different way. I'd never make an engineer. Never design a boat from the ground up. But as I called up the pictures in my head and mentally used the sextant in my mind enough, I hoped, came to me.

With a sigh of relief I put down my pen and looked up at Larue who was sitting at a nearby desk, "Finished."

"Excellent. Well hand it over and go and freshen up. Northey's out in the foyer with your clean clothes."

I didn't grit my teeth as I handed over the papers but I felt like I could have. I was rigid with hope and expectations. My future hung at this moment. But standing there worrying about it wasn't going to affect the outcome now.

I went to the foyer where Jim greeted me with a hug and understanding in his eyes. "The best will be Ry, you'll see. Here," he handed me a plastic bag with my clothes and a few toiletries he'd thrown together. What looked to be high end shampoo and, oh heaven, lemongrass scented soap. How had he known?

He ignored my stunned expression. "I'll do your hair when you come out," he informed me.

Hell, I didn't want to contemplate a life without the luxury of Jim in it. Could I have the week over and study harder? Had what I'd done been enough?

Blessedly the welcome water of the shower flowed over my back taking at least some of my angst with it. I pretended I was a drop of that water, a tiny part of a huge river, flowing to the sea. A sea that accepted me in its embrace. As mother. As home. Wherever that thought had come from it calmed me, knowing that all I had to do was flow where the river was taking me. I reached out to the guides that Lydia had told me about. Those who watched out for me. "I trust. I give thanks." And as Jim had said, "The best will be". It wasn't for me to know which outcome was going to be that 'best'. I'd done all I could. I just had to step out the way now and not block that outcome, whatever it might be.

I dried off and quickly dressed, noting that Jim had even shined my work shoes. I decided against makeup. I wasn't going in front of a camera and my face, au naturale, had its own strengths. If I was going to a gala I'd still 'put on a face' as my mother used to say but for this, I'd just be myself. I opened the door to Jim, "I'm ready for the hair," not that I couldn't have brushed it myself. It turned out having one's hair brushed by someone you cared about was a deeply pleasurable experience. "You'd better stop now Jim or I'll smell of arousal."

"Well now. I'll have to store that one in the memory banks. Let me just take a little bit more of that bottle blond away. I think you've got enough new growth that I can recut it now, in such a way that the blond bits will just look like highlights." He went into his happy space and snipped away. "There now."

I peered into the mirror and was pleased. "Neat!" Then I sighed. "Well let's go and see if this was all worth it. Whether Larue's marked my papers yet."

Larue was busy talking with Reilly and Sophie when we came out of the bathroom. They all looked in our direction. Was I embarrassed? Nah. Well maybe a bit.

"I like what Jim's done with your hair," Sophie commented.

"What?" Reilly asked. "She doesn't look any different."

Sophie rolled her eyes in my direction and smiled. "The others will be here shortly. We're waiting on a contingent who are clearing the airport. They took longer than normal to get through customs and quarantine. You know what it's like these days. Someone sneezes somewhere in the world and they all get jumpy."

After a string of pandemics had rattled the world it wasn't any wonder. Though I was glad they hadn't put the ship's crew through the wringer when we'd disembarked in Victoria. Maybe there was some new threat out there. I hoped it didn't get in the way of our eventual return to Australia.

We didn't have long to wait for the others, who turned out, surprisingly, to be a lot of people I already knew. Our own captain and chief officer. Adeela, naturally, as she was graduating too. Cook, well, I guess he had an interest there. There were a few Seychelles officials I'd already met and, lo and behold, Deman and Rachel. "What are you doing here?"

"Why, coming to your graduation of course." Deman wrapped me in a warm hug. "Vladamir sends his apologies. He's tied up on protector work."

"And Lydia has a couple of new children she's settling into the orphanage," Rachel added. "She says you'll understand that she's still with you."

"Yes, I know," Lydia had never been far when I needed her, since we'd met in the otherworld. I knew I only had to think of her and we could touch each other's mind.

Indeed, came her whisper. *And congratulations.*

I don't know yet, I pointed out to Lyd.

No, of course not. Lyd smirked in my mind. *Though you could know a lot if you wanted to. All in time. I shouldn't push.*

"This is a lot of fuss. I'm not that important" I complained to no-one in particular. "I don't even know if I've passed."

Larue let me out of my misery. "Of course you passed. What teacher would I be if I couldn't train a bright and able student."

I blushed at the praise. And liked the fact he'd notice I was able, even if, to use my term, unidextrous.

"And me?" Adeela asked, her brow furrowed with worry.

Larue groaned, "Both of you need more faith in yourselves. I have your results from the hospitality school Ms Shirazi. You have nothing to worry about. Now before you both completely upstage my little ceremony let me get up on the podium. Ladies and gentlemen. If you could take your seats. Ry and Addela to the front row."

Duly organised Captain Larue took the stage. Captain Jefferson Wilcher and Deman Merkwood stood a little off to his side.

"Thank you all for coming today." Larue commenced his short speech. "As you know the maritime school usually takes a short break at this time of the year but I was persuaded by the two men beside me that it would be in the college's interests to run a customised course for two people they thought worth the effort.

Adeela Shirazi was uprooted from life in her own country, just before joining the crew of the Merkwood II. She has shown herself to be an efficient and amiable steward. She spent the first part of her week with us here before finishing her current studies at the local hospitality school where she impressed the teachers with her aptitude. Ms Shirazi. Would you come to the stage and accept your certificate?"

Everyone clapped enthusiastically, especially Cook.

Larue shook Adeela's hand and handed her the framed certificate. "Your results have been officially recorded and it is the hospitality school's hope you will return to them should you consider training as a ship's cook."

"Thank you Sir," her eyes glistening with moisture, she returned to the audience. I gave her a quick hug. Cook beamed at her and reached over the back of her chair to give her an, almost, professional pat.

Larue waited while we settled then scanned his notes before looking up and speaking. "Ladies and gentlemen, I'm ashamed to say that when Rylee Jackson first came through the college doors I did wonder. How could she do what was required of the course? She soon set me straight."

A few in the crowd, including Reilly, gave knowing laughs.

"Ry, as she prefers to be called, had recently come to one of those junctures, a point of no return, that many of us face in our lives. Her life changed in a moment. Yet rather than wallow in pity she has remade herself. I am proud to have met Ry. She has inspired me with her resilience and tenacity, even when faced with the terrors of celestial navigation. It is with great honour that I call Rylee Jackson to the stage to accept her certificate."

Shit. I felt the stares of the crowd on me as I walked up to Larue and shook his hand, "I just did my best, that's all."

"And your best included some of the highest scores I've seen on both your test and your practical. I'd better see you back here to continue your Bachelor of Science in Nautical Science Rylee or I'll track you down."

"Continue my what?" I thought I'd just been meeting the basic requirements to be a fully fledged member of the crew.

Laure grinned, "We thought we might scare you off if we told you what we were throwing you into. This week was our chance to assess your aptitude. Deman sourced your university records from when you did your BA in Journalism. With that and references from Wilcher and Pertwie I was able to sign you off for a fair bit of advanced credit. It seemed particularly silly to make you do the unit on English and Communication Skills. You've already completed a lot of the first semester but if you continue the course will take you into areas you're perhaps not familiar with such as maritime law, some physics and basic boat architecture. There's a bit of marine engineering towards the end of the course. Ship operating procedures I expect you'll romp in."

I paled.

"You'll be fine," he chided, "You've a better mind for it than you think and I'm sure that Captain Wilcher will pair you with people who can give you plenty of experience to draw upon. Practical work first for you I think, then the theory can just fill in the gaps. Don't sweat it Jackson, it'll all come to you in its own time. It's like eating an elephant. You just bite off one small chunk at a time."

Not that the mostly vegetarian in me fancied eating an elephant but I got his point. "Well that all depends on my employer," I glanced at Deman. As scary as what they were proposing was, it did give me a path to a future, "but I'd like the chance." Though, physics?

"Excellent."

Deman shook my hand, "You know you've got a job in my company if you want it. Not because I'm doing a friend a favour but because you're that good and I only employ the best."

"I really appreciate that Deman. I'm still considering what my future might be. Much depended on today."

"Well, you're over that hurdle now. We'll talk more about it later."

Wilcher held out his hand, "Hurry up, if we don't get off this stage there'll be no refreshments left for us."

I shook his hand, "Of course sir. Thank you for coming, sir."

"You've proven yourself to be a valuable member of my crew, Jackson. I'm sorry if I saw you as cargo when you first stepped on board."

"Apology accepted," I nodded to the rapidly disappearing nibbles, "shall we?"

As we walked off the stage he quietly talked in my ear, "Think about what Larue said about further training. I agree with him. You have the potential to work up through the merchant navy ranks, if it's a life you want. You'd need to continue your training and log at least 18 months at sea to become a fully fledged Deck Officer. It's not an easy life but it has its merits. Have a think, once you get back home, then get back to me with your decision."

After I'd been congratulated by everyone who'd come and the celebration started to die down Adeela made her apologies. "We've still got the weekend to ourselves on the island. I know I haven't been around much. I feel like I've deserted you."

I waved my finger at her, "None of that. Go lap him up girl."

She glanced at Cook, glanced back at me, and grinned, "Thanks Ry. See you back on board then, when we set sail on Monday."

"Stay safe. DeSiliva and Lasseter are still out there."

"I'll play it safe. I think Bek's got some island hideaway picked out for the weekend. Snorkeling, bird watching, hiking. That sort of thing."

I snorted, "Yeah, I've no doubts about what 'that sort of thing' might include. Watch your heart too Adeela. It's early days yet."

"You too," she glanced knowingly in the direction of Reilly and Jim. "Both of them?"

I shrugged my shoulders. "Who knows, like I said. It's early days. See you onboard Steward Shirazi."

"And you Deck Officer Jackson," She gave me a mock salute.

As Adeela left with Cook, Sophie meandered over to me, idly twirling the stem of her half full wine glass, "Can I have a word?" She nodded to an area a bit away from the others.

"You've found Lasseter and DeSilva?"

She pursed her lips, "We have a lead we're following but nothing yet. No, I approached someone about your spider's little issue."

I snickered, "His desperate need to drop his load. By the way, he's not my spider."

"Horatio might disagree. I think he's taken quite a liking to you."

I shivered, "Actually, I'm mildly arachnophobic." More than mildly.

"But you're okay with Horatio. You worked together yesterday. You get on."

"I guess. I sort of relate to him. Not just the whole missing limb thing but, oh, I don't know. He seems out of place yet he's making the best of the world he's got."

"Do you think he could be captured? He's kind've free range at present isn't he?"

"I think if there's the chance of delivering his parcel of sperm to a female he'll let himself be captured. I'll speak with him."

"You speak spider?"

"Well, not words. Sort of a non-verbal communication. I haven't worked out the how or the why of it. It just works."

"The owner of the female is keen to speak to Horatio's owner to set up a meeting of the two."

"Does the female have a name?" I wondered.

"Delilah, I believe."

Reilly sidled up to us, "What are you two ladies deep in discussion about?"

"Sex," we'll he'd asked. "We're pimping Horatio out. I guess in human terms you could say he has a full sack and is feeling a primal need to get rid of his load."

Reilly choked. When he recovered he pulled out his phone. "It's O'Reilly, put me through to the Bosun. Hi Singh, enjoyin' my shore leave. Speakin' of which, I have two ladies here discussin' yer spider's sex life. He has? Well that makes it easier. Look I'll hand you over to Lieutenant Camille," he passed over his phone to Sophie. "Devender Singh," he explained to Sophie.

Sophie took down Devender's contact details, promising to get back to him shortly, then hung up and handed the phone back to Reilly, "Apparently Horatio returned to Devender's cabin this morning and is back in his usual enclosure. He doesn't know why the spider came back but it should make setting up the, um, meet-up, easier."

I had a rough idea why. Horatio must have taken me at my word, "Hopefully Delilah doesn't chomp on him."

Sophie grimaced, "Ouch. I'll keep my fingers crossed for him."

"Maybe your mum could do a protection spell for him."

"For a spider," Sophie laughed, "I think she'll get a chuckle out of that. I'll speak with her."

Reilly nudged me, "Now that we've sorted out Horatio's life I have plans of my own. Time we left, Ry."

"Er," it appeared life was still rushing headlong towards me, "I'll just go and grab my certificate."

"Quit stalling Ry. Wilcher already took your certificate and Adeela's, he'll have them dropped off at your cabin. We told him you're spending the weekend snorkelling and hiking."

Sophie's eyes twinkled with mirth, "Have a good weekend Ry. I'll ring you if there's any news on your assailants."

Jim was already waiting in the car, a different one from what he'd had before. This one was a lipstick red open top convertible. An Audi TT, if you please.

"Where're we going?"

"We're heading to the North West of the island, a secluded cove. We've booked a rental there." Jim explained, from the driver's seat. "Hired you some fishing gear, Reilly. The guy at the shop remembered you. He knew your favourite surf rod. And he gave us a generous discount."

Reilly settled into the backseat while I took the front. "Cooking gear?"

"I checked with the rental," Jim replied. "Everything we need's there. I stopped at a mart this afternoon and did some shopping for us. Most of it's in that cooler beside you."

"Aren't we going back to the boat?" I wondered in mild panic. I needed, well, stuff.

Jim smiled in the rear vision mirror "All taken care of Ry. I packed for you."

"Er," I wondered what he'd packed, "ok."

Jim opened up the throttle and I felt the wind ruffle the top of my hair. I hoped these two appreciated the wind blown look because that was going to be me when we stopped. Ah well, it was worth it to lean back in the seat and enjoy the sky overhead, the jungle smells and the sounds of birds in the tree-tops. It was like flowing through nature. I felt my life flowing like that too, towards some unknowable outcome. Such was uncertainty. I'd long ago realised fears weren't bad. They were just designed to keep you safe. But you didn't give them full rein over you or you missed out on the full potential of all that life had to offer. So I leaned back in my seat and embraced the ride and my equally high speed trip into uncertainty. In the unknown lay everything.

The 'bungalow' was indeed tucked away among the trees, a couple of minute's walk to the beach. Fly screens covered windows that contained no glass but they did have shutters to keep out the odd passing storm. A broad, raised veranda graced the front and the back.

Jim opened the fly screen door for me, "Your room's this way."

"I get a room of my own?" Well, that was a relief.

"We thought you might want breaks away from us. And of course your own bed to sleep in if you don't want to, you know…" he waggled his eyebrows at me.

I relaxed somewhat. Not so pressured then. I stowed my 'stuff' in my room, a generous suitcase of clothes and toiletries Jim had pinched from my cabin on the ship. Then I went to help him bring in the groceries.

Reilly did his he-man thing and carried in the amply laden cooler, "Where'd ya want this?"

Jim showed him.

"I'm going to head out and see what tha fishin's like," Reilly announced.

"Good," Jim decided, "Catch us a couple of decent sized ones and I'll cook them up for dinner. I'm going to start on making salads."

"Do you have to? Reilly groaned.

"If I want my friend to live a long and healthy life, yes I do," Jim gave him the look.

It was the first time I'd seen anyone challenge Reilly's choices. I did my best not to gasp.

"Hmph," Reilly replied and took his surf rod in the direction of the ocean.

"Really," Jim muttered, "that man would live on nothing but Guinness, bread and potatoes if he had his way."

But I had to disagree, "I don't think Reilly would ever be that stupid, though it might be what he prefers. He's just letting his inner child show."

"Is that so? So what does that make me?" Jim wondered.

I found a cold soda water in the cooler and opened it, chugging down a welcome mouthful, "The adult," most definitely. "You're the wisest of us, I suspect."

Jim groaned, "Now I'm Yoda." But there was a laugh underneath the grumble.

"Can I help you with the salads? I'm not much of a kitchen hand," I waved my one and only, "but I can give it a go."

"You can put those things in the fridge for me but then, maybe, go give our inner child some company. I think he's feeling lost and uncertain."

"Uncertain?"

"About, well you know, the dynamics of our situation and how it's going to work. He is a worrier you know."

I rolled my eyes, "Yeah, I worked that one out." And here I'd thought I was the nervous one. I emptied the cooler into the fridge then strolled down to the beach.

He made an impressive silhouette against the setting sun. The man and his surf rod. The hunter gatherer out to provide for his family. And, by the look of the fish already on the cleaning board at his feet a good fisherman. He hadn't scaled it yet so I looked through his kit and found what I needed.

Reilly looked down at me, surprised, but said nothing and went back to watching his rod. He'd had a tug on the line and now was letting out some line, trying to lull the fish into a false sense of security so it would take a deep bite rather than a nibble. Yeah, I'd fished with my cousins a time or two so I knew the game. If the fish was too sneaky or too suspicious it would just take little nibbles of the bait until it cleaned it all off the hook. I watched the master in action, out of the corner of my eye, as I cleaned the fish.

There! The line gave a sharp pull and Reilly gave an equally sharp pull back. Keeping the tension on the line he reeled it in. It seemed we'd have enough fish for tonight. Not that I was big on the whole carnivore thing but hell, Reilly had caught it.

While he detached the fish from the hook I set about finding the bait Jim had bought for him. I handed him a handful of wriggly somethings and he stared at me, stunned.

"What?" I wondered.

He shook himself, "Nothing, just ya're the first woman to ever do that for me."

"What, pass you bait? It doesn't need brain power to work out that that's what you'd need next."

"It's not just that you anticipated my need. It's that you would touch somethin' most would see as disgustin'."

I shrugged my shoulders. Yeah they were icky but … "I want to eat too," even if my preferred idea of seafood would be some edible seaweed I could use as a sushi wrapper of soup flavouring.

He just shook his head and went back to fishing, intent on the line. He caught one more and cleaned it while I bagged up the others, "That's enough I think for now. I'm a firm believer in only taking what you need. Despite what some illegal fishing trawler operators think, there is a limit to the number of fish in the ocean. I love fishing, it's kind of like a meditation for me. I have to watch the rod so I don't tend to think about the innumerable daily things that clutter my mind. But I do feel a little guilty for taking the catch."

"I think it's like in that movie, Avatar, Reilly. We acknowledge we're part of an interconnected system and that us, being sentient beings, have a responsibility to care for that system. We're alive, we consume. We can't get away from the fact that eating a fish is eating a living being but we can do it respectfully, humanely and with gratitude." Or be vegetarian, but I kept that to myself as that was not my decision to make for him. Like he said, the act of fishing gave him peace. I wouldn't take that away from him. Though I might see what else would give him peace.

"Well, I'm grateful for the company. Thanks for coming down. Even if you'd just sat there and done nothing it wouldn have been great."

I was mindful of what Jim had said. "There's no need for you to be on your own, Reilly, unless you want to be."

"Sometimes. But today, no." He picked up the surf rods while I picked up the bag of fish and we headed back towards the bungalow.

"I guess I have to apologise."

"What tha hell for?"

"Well, I had a lot of thoughts going through my head about how the hell we were going to make things work, you know, you, me and Jim. It never even occurred to me that I wasn't the only one who might have stuff going through my head. It was selfish of me."

"Ah, thanks. Actually Jim and I have been worryin' about whether we're pushin' ya into something you were neither ready for or inclined to."

"Well I guess it comes down to whether we're talking about two simultaneous relationships or a poly group. Personally I think the latter would work better."

"You do?" Reilly sounded surprised.

"Well think about it this way. You and Jim have an established friendship and I come along. If I start going out with each of you separately, or as might be the case, hopping between your beds, each of you is always going to wonder about the relationship I'm having with the other. That's not going to be good for the survival of your friendship with Jim."

"Well," Reilly seemed a little fazed by the frankness of our discussion, "I guess I've had that worry too but Ry, I'm not, well, you know…"

"Into men sexually, I think Jim and I would both be surprised if you were. It's not who you are. But let me ask this. Would seeing your friend naked bother you?"

"No, not at all. He's more like a brother to me. We shared a sauna once in Finland and that didn't bother me."

Promising, "So how would you feel seeing him, um," don't beat around the bush Ry, "fucking me?"

His eyes widened, "To be honest I don't know. Possibly turned on. Possibly jealous. Not sure."

"Well at some stage this weekend we're going to have to find out."

"Is that on the cards, yet? Shouldn't we get to know each other more first?"

It was the wisest option but, "And when we're back on board the Merkwood II?"

Reilly shook his head, "The captain wouldn't like it. It could cause jealousies among the other crew who are essentially celebate between shore leave. And then there's yer reputation. If word got out, others might try for ya, willin' or not. It's a problem many women in the merchant navy face, even when they're clearly not involved with anyone. Some men will always hope, and if frustrated enough take their chances. Ya need to keep your cabin door locked and bolted at all times."

"Already do, but as you've just said. We're going to have to keep things off the radar once we're back onboard. So we only really have this weekend. At least until we get to Australia. I'm not a slut Reilly," I felt obliged to point out, "but we can't waste this time."

"I would never think that of ya. Ya've just caught me off guard is all."

Jim was waiting on the verandah for us, "What are you two in deep discussion about."

Reilly laughed nervously, "Beyond yer wildest dreams Jim. Let's eat. Then we'll talk."

19

"So what do you think of your new country?" Jim asked as he passed the potato salad. It was a safe topic of discussion.

"It's more than I ever hoped for," I had to admit. "Travelling around the world as I've done, doing documentaries, I've never put down roots. I have a converted garage at the back of my mum's place for those times I do grace Australia's shores. It'll be nice to have somewhere else as a base, especially if Deman's willing to have me working with you guys on the Indian Ocean run."

"Hmm," Reilly mused, though not sharing whatever was going through his head.

"Share," I encouraged, or was that demanded, "let's not have secrets between us."

"Well I hesitate to say because nothing is certain with us at the moment."

"When is life certain?" I wondered.

"Okay, point taken. I've been thinking of investing in property here. Like you say, it's convenient. Our current run across the Indian Ocean often takes us past here, Mauritius and sometimes Madagascar. Property here is very expensive though."

"Not as expensive as Australia," I pointed out.

"Yeah well," Reilly rolled his eyes, "nothing's as dear as that. But there are a lot of extra charges for foreigners buying here."

"Which there should be. You don't want people coming in and buying up the place on spec to the extent that the locals can't afford housing."

"Like what's happened in Australia," Reilly could see where my pet gripe was coming from.

"Anyway," it occurred to me, "I could do the buying. I'm a fully fledged dual citizen afterall."

"Ya 'ave that kind of money?" Reilly wondered, sounding like he didn't believe me.

"I've a bit stashed that I could use as a deposit and it's not as if I'm paying my mother much rent for the converted garage space. As I say, Deman's virtually guaranteed me a job. Barring some misogynist bank manager I should be good for a loan for the rest." Though it might not be my gender they took objection to. I thought of my solitary arm-ness. "We could get a property, put it with a property manager who could rent it out and maintain it when we're not here. Make a bit of money renting it to high end tourists."

"Ya'd want a high end property then," Reilly countered, playing devil's advocate, "that's going to cost."

Jim, who'd been sitting back listening to our banter finally saw fit to interrupt, "What about a simple hideaway. There are artists, writers and honeymooners that would love that. This place is up for grabs, and being as it's a little out the way, the price is not objectionable." He left the table and came back with a sales brochure. We stared at him.

"You were already on this page," I noted.

"Came up in discussion when I was renting it for the weekend. I'd been thinking of the investment and convenience potential."

Reilly tapped the table, like a judge calling for order in the court, "Might I remind you both that we're getting ahead of ourselves."

I disagreed, "Not really, this is a separate issue. It's a sound financial investment. We get a building engineer to check the place out, tomorrow maybe. If we still have any doubts about the wisdom of what we're proposing we put the idea past Deman's accounting and legal gurus. I'm sure they could advise us and if we proceeded they could draw up some agreement that protected each of us. We could even be our own company."

Reilly groaned, things were getting away from him, "Go and freshen up, Ry. Clear that busy head of yours."

"Not yet. We haven't discussed the other elephant in the room and Jim needs a hand with the dishes."

"Leave the dishes."

"Uh, uh," Jim shook his head, "this is the tropics. Leave food scraps around and you're asking for an invasion of ants, cockroaches and god only knows what else. We'll need to put the fish carcases into a bag and freeze them until we're leaving."

Reilly looked suddenly horrified by Jim's vision of an insect armageddon, "You're right. Okay, let's clean this mess while we discuss the elephant. Do you know what she's suggesting?"

"I can imagine," Jim, waggled his eyebrows suggestively. "Why should women be any different to men? How many men do you know fantasise about having two women at the same time? It makes sense women might have fantasies the other way around."

"Fantasy is one thing," he turned his attention back to me, "do you realise the mechanics involved?"

I coughed, oh well, I guess I had to be as open and honest as I was requiring these two to be. "You might not like what I'm about to tell you but, here goes. I once got a call from George, my agent, about whether I'd do a doco on a private, members only club. Apparently an adults only channel thought it would make great late night viewing and George thought we might be able to sell it to one or more of the more open minded tv stations as well."

"You did a doco on a sex club," Reilly looked aghast as he scraped the fish remains into a plastic bag and tied a knot to stop the contents escaping.

Jim just grinned, "Only you. Do tell."

"Well I took the job but there was one condition the manager of the club and the members who were on its board demanded. They would only allow me to document activities I was willing to participate in myself. So…"

Reilly sat back down, tea towel in hand, as if to steady himself,

"What did you agree to?"

"Oh well," how to make light of this. Say it as quickly as possible I suppose. "I was assigned to Mistress Emelia who took on responsibility for my actions in the club. In return I submitted to her guidance while in the club. As Jared, my cameraman wouldn't agree to such an arrangement, it fell to me, otherwise we'd never have gotten to do the doco."

"And if Jared filmed anything he shouldn't?" Jim asked, intrigued.

"I would be punished. Actually I ended up being punished anyway. I don't make a very good sub."

Reilly rolled his eyes, "Why am I not surprised. So what did you learn from doing this documentary?"

"Well it's more what I learnt from the experience. Don't worry, you won't find any embarrassing footage of me on the dark web. And when I was on camera, doing interviews or pieces to camera, I was wearing a black wig and loads of goth makeup. I even used a pseudonym."

"Wise," Reilly agreed, "but ya're still not sayin' much. Let's try it this way. What did ya enjoy?"

"Oh well," I blushed, "most of it really. It was all a game and the members were very considerate given as I was only there as what they classed as a 'tourist'. I found I liked having my hair tugged. Hmm, the sensations of ropes and fabrics on the skin, it was a rather sensual experience. Not much into the hard core whipping but lightly done, it was like a massage on the back, did wonders for the circulation."

"And," Jim nudged. He knew there would be more.

"Well, I tried various, what they called scenes. All worked out in detail and negotiated beforehand but that didn't take the fun out of it. I didn't like the headmaster caning my ass. Although it was fun dressing up as a schoolgirl. I refused the doctor-patient scenario, so not my thing. The very idea turned me right off. But the captured wench of two lusty pirates. Now that was fun."

Reilly shook his head in amazement, but he seemed as avidly

interested in the tale now as Jim, "And these pirates. They 'did' ya at the same time?"

I squirmed, the memory making me hot, "They did." But I was afraid now, "Do you think less of me now?"

"Never Ry, though astonished, yes. Ya truly go where angels fear to tread."

"Oh I had a cast iron legal agreement drawn up before I went in there. Plus Jared had my back and I had a safe word. I made sure I wouldn't experience anything I didn't want to and the club was equally careful. Their reputation was on the line too. They didn't want any bad PR."

"Jared, yer cameraman" Reilly prompted, "he died in the explosion that injured ya."

I looked away, swallowing the moment, "Yes."

Jim, who had just let the water out of the sink dried his hands, walked over and wrapped me in a comforting hug, "Were you close?"

"No, not in that way. Not really." Who was I kidding? "It was more of a convenience. You go to some of those strange and dangerous places, you keep your risks to a minimum. We were more like work partners with benefits. We certainly weren't exclusive. Though sometimes we'd pose as a married couple if we thought I'd be safer that way."

Reilly came over to join the group hug, "I'm glad he was there for ya. Ya used condoms?" he asked casually but I understood the implied meaning.

"Yes we did. I'm clean, if that's what you're wondering. I'm on the pill too. Wellard was kind enough to replenish my supply when I came on board."

"I haven't been with a woman since Seattle last year," Reilly announced to no-one in particular. "I had a full medical before this trip."

"I can't say that I've been that restrained," Jim admitted. "Though I take precautions. And I need to say something before we go further. I don't think I can ignore some of my needs."

I understood where he was coming from, or at least I was guessing, "You're bisexual. I don't have a problem with that, as long as it's casual. If you ever wanted to bring someone into our circle it would have to be by our mutual agreement though."

"Absolutely," Reilly concurred.

"I can live with that," Jim agreed. "Shall we?"

I laughed at the insanity of it all, "There's nothing impromptu about this is there?" Shouldn't there be?

"We're not planning a one night stand. Ry. Any woman who passes me fish bait is a keeper."

"She did what?" Jim asked, astounded.

"Sheesh," I didn't know what all the fuss was, "you'd think I'd passed you a box of chocolates and a glass of bubbly."

Reilly laughed, "Go freshen up Ry, we'll be in in a moment."

The moment continued past my shower. They were obviously in deep discussion which made me wonder whether I should go out there and join in.

In the end I decided to give them space. My only real decision seemed to be whether to dress in some of the brand new lingerie that Jim had packed for me, and obviously bought for me, or go naked.

Being hopeful I thought I might expedite things by going for the latter option.

I snuggled under the bed clothes. Not that there was much snuggling needed in the tropical night air. A simple sheet sufficed.

The door scraped against the wooden floor. Jim came in, "I hope you're not asleep in that comfy bed Ry."

"I'm hardly going to sleep when my heart is hammering in anticipation."

"Then I'd best not keep the lady waiting," though there was no speed in the way he leisurely stripped his clothes. First the buttons of his shirt, he slowly undid them from the top down, revealing a perfect chest with just the slightest wisp of hair. He undid the buckle of his belt and slid the belt out of its loops with a flourish, throwing it on the bed with a look that met my eyes. Oh shit, everything in me clenched for I knew then that while Jim would never abuse me he might very well give me a little bite to my pleasure.

He slid his trousers suggestively down his legs, until they pooled at his feet and he stepped out of them with a grace that only he had.

My breath hitched as he came towards the bed, his eyes on me until he pulled the drawer of the bedside table open. "I didn't tell Reilly, because I didn't want to get his hopes up, but I stashed a few things in here earlier, just in case." He pulled out a large bottle of lube and a small iridescent purple butt plug still in its packaging. "Damn," he swore, as he struggled with the impenetrable shrink wrap.

I laughed and in that moment delight replaced all the nerves I'd been feeling. "Don't you hate that stuff. Do you want me to go and get a knife?"

"Don't move, I'll be back," he hurried out and returned with a pair of kitchen snips. He still mauled the packaging, hard to do otherwise, but he finally managed to extract the hard won plug."

Anticipating where this was going I rolled onto my stomach and prepared myself for the invasion, which didn't come. Instead came surprise as his hand slapped my ass, "Wha?"

"Reilly may not be experienced in kink but I am. I'd enjoy finding your kinks. What's your safe word?"

"Pink, I can't stand the colour unless it's bright and in your face. Pastels are not my thing."

"So noted. Pink it is. So are you using it yet."

"That little paddle on my ass, hardly. You just caught me off guard."

"Excellent." His hand landed on my ass again and felt warmth radiate from where he'd made contact. "Harder," I groaned.

"How hard? I'm trusting you to tell me Ry. I don't want to spook or hurt you. Only to give you what you'll enjoy."

"You can use the belt strap, just not too hard." I suggested cautiously. I was feeling my way with Jim as much as he was with me.

The sudden whack of the leather stole my breath?

"Too much?"

"No, good, really good."

"Three more then. Count them?"

"One," oh yes, he had that just the right amount. He was a master at this. Another depth to Jim I hadn't expected.

"Two," my thoughts stopped. All I could feel was my ass.

"Rylee?" Jim inquired.

"Drifting," I purred.

"Oh really," he chuckled. "I didn't intend for you to go into subspace yet. One more."

"Three," I purred, hardly aware of anything as his fingered lubed me and he gently inserted the plug.

"Be a good girl and keep it there. Now roll over."

When I did I noticed Reilly, standing in the corner of the room. He'd clothed himself as a pirate, a makeshift wooden sword at his side. His white shirt, loose and billowy, teasing with a hint of flesh. But if he was a pirate he was a shocked one. Shock, horror and desire fought for command of his face. I worried, "Still don't think poorly of me Reilly?"

"No, no. Just it looked like abuse but you were enjoying yourself."

And I knew how he felt about abuse. One of his triggers. "Actually," my mind now sobering, "Jim and I were dancing. That fine edge where a little pain morphs into pleasure. Too much, without my consent would be abuse. Too little and, well it wouldn't be boring but it might not do it for me."

"He was making you submit." He commented, clearly confused.

"Absolutely not. He was topping, not mastering me. It's entirely different."

"Let me ask you this," Jim questioned his friend, "How did it make you feel to watch?"

"I, … I wanted to be the one causing her to bliss out."

Even resting, rolled on my back I high fived the open palm Jim offered me.

"What?" Reilly wondered.

"Odds are that you're a top not a dom. Which kind of suits our dynamics."

"What's a top?" Reilly's intelligent, inquiring brain was kicking in.

"Simply put, a pleasure giver. While the so-called bottom, in this case, was Ry?"

"I thought we were goin' to have sex? You know, pirates plundering the fair maiden."

"That too, but that only takes a couple of minutes. This extends the experience."

Reilly was silent a moment, worrying us with his reaction, but then…"I want to learn."

Jim coughed, clearing his throat. Then he smiled. "The best way to learn is to experience being on the receiving end first."

Reilly backed away from the bed, "You're not spanking me and you're not coming near my rear end, with anything, Jim."

Jim flushed with anger. "I don't force my way on anyone. I won't deny I love you Reilly. Suck it up. But since I love you I have no intention of doing anything to you that you don't want, let alone might hate me for."

"Guys!" It was time to step in. "Before this heads towards disaster can I make a suggestion, Reilly?"

"What?" he asked suspiciously.

"Let us lick you."

"Where would you lick me?"

"Not your bum or your cock. No oral sex. This is what's called a negotiation Reilly. You set the limits."

"I'm okay with those limits."

"Okay, then what's your safe word? What word do you choose to mean stop? A word we won't confuse with a contrary no that really meant 'more please'."

"I'll use yours, pink wasn't it?"

"Then come here. I'm sort of holding in this plug at the moment so getting up out of this bed might defeat my efforts." I didn't like Reilly's lack of trust but right now wasn't the time to question that. I approached the nearest piece of flesh on him, and licked.

He rewarded me with a groan.

"More?"

"Please."

I inched up towards his right nipple and tentatively flicked it with my tongue.

"God, ya teasin' me. Harder."

I gently scraped the flesh with my teeth then covered the tip with my mouth and sucked, hard. His back arched as he moaned in pleasure.

"What's your safe word, Reilly," I paused to ask.

"Pink, why?" he asked suspiciously.

"Nothing you haven't agreed to but if you don't like anything, use your damned safe word," did that sound a little terse? I gave the nod to Jim. We were about to find out just how much Reilly would tolerate. As I continued my ministrations to his nipples Jim moved to lick Reilly's leg, hard and firm. Reilly firmed too. His mind might not trust us but his body did.

"Geezuz Ry. Suck my cock." Reilly moaned.

"It's not normal to renegotiate your boundaries half way through a scene. You might say we coerced you later," I was half teasing him, but I meant it too.

"Please suck my damn cock."

My eyes met Jim's. He shrugged then moved out of my way as I meandered my licks down Reilly's body, slowly towards that desired spot.

Reilly growled.

"Jim, I'm ready." I knew he'd get my meaning.

As my mouth finally descended down the length of Reilly's cock I felt the tug as Jim removed the plug. I kept my mind focused on my job at hand as he fingered cool lubricant into my tight ass. I let the wetness of my mouth do the same to Reilly's cock.

I heard a condom packet being opened. Anticipation clenched my solar plexus. It was a while since I'd done this. I was putting a lot of trust in Jim.

I fought hard not to lose my concentration as I felt Jim nudge my opening, working his way in. Hell, I'd never stopped to ask how big Jim was. I'd never seen him naked and fully aroused.

Reilly's had a long and satisfying length to it that I sucked like an icy pole. Jim had the breadth.

"Push back when you're ready," Jim murmured in my ear.

I did, tensing at a moment's discomfort and then it eased. And I was his. I sighed at the pure connection of it and went back to my task at hand, mastering Reilly's cock. I made like a pole dancer, my tongue twirling around it, then milking it. He felt close. "No coming yet," I ordered.

"What?" Reilly groaned in a mess of pleasure.

"Discipline is your trade. Be disciplined now. You don't come until I do and I don't come until Jim does." I'd drawn the line in the sand. Now I went back to tormenting him.

Jim held my ass firm with both hands and found a rhythm of his own. It was all I could do to hold off my own need to come. "Jim?"

"More, I want more of you," He fucked me harder.

I felt my eyes rolling back in my head as I yielded to his reins. I was… I don't know what I was. My brain ceased to function.

Jim came a fraction of a second before he yelled out a victory cry. Reilly cried out too, near drowning me in cum as my insides went into a meltdown that rolled through me, wave after wave.

We all collapsed into a puddle of languid limbs, a cool breeze fluttering the curtains. I drifted for a while. When I woke up next it was dark and Jim was noticeable by his absence, where he'd been at my back. I quietly crept out of bed, throwing on enough of yesterday's clothes to decently wander outside where I found Jim sitting on the steps of the porch. He was looking in the direction of the moon but I don't think he noticed it or the gecko that was peering at us from the branch of a nearby shrub.

I sat down next to Jim and put an understanding arm around him.

He sighed as he leaned into me. "He doesn't trust me. I thought he knew me."

I knew the deep pain behind those words. "Give him this weekend Jim. All his life he's tried to be the man, the protector, the authority figure."

"I know," He mumbled, but he didn't sound in the least appeased.

"And you need our complete acceptance of who you are." I shone a light on the issue.

"You accept me." He noted.

"Hardly an issue for me, but yes. I put myself out there acknowledging my inner kink so I know it's an important thing for me too."

"So what do we do?"

"Words won't do it. We have to show him, probably a number of times, that we respect his boundaries."

"And if it doesn't work?"

"We go back to plan A. You and I have an open, committed relationship. How we fit other people around that core is up to us."

"If Reilly won't trust me I don't think I could bear …" he left it unsaid but I knew that if I had Reilly and Jim didn't at least have his trust then it would drive a wedge between us.

"I know. Hey," I gave him a friendly nudge. "It's a beautiful night. We're not sleeping. Let's go for a drive. Chuck us the keys." The Audi looked a fun car. Might take our minds off of things.

He had them in his trouser pocket and held them out to me but his look was mournful, "Ry,"

He was trying to tell me something with his eyes. I didn't understand. I grabbed the keys with my one hand and that's when I realised. I sagged back onto the steps beside Jim, "Well that's a bummer."

It was his turn to put a companionable arm around me, "I'll adapt a car for you. You'll see. Have to be an automatic. Voice activated for shifting the gears between park, drive, reverse and neutral. Voice activation for the handbrake too."

"You can do that," Hope welled up.

"A bit of programming. A few control arms. No pun intended. I'd have to find someone with the machining skills to make some of the bits."

"We'll ya'd need a bleedin' an engineer for that. Could be ya know someone who trained as one before he went the officer path. What the hell are you two doing out here in the middle of the night?"

"Looking at the full moon," I fibbed.

"Liar," he spat. "You preach openness and honesty so I expect the same from you. Both of ya."

He had a point. "We were discussing you, actually." There, that was said.

"I know I was an ass. I reacted before I thought. Hell you both know I'm an asshole at times. Maybe I need some unconditional acceptance too."

Hell, "How long were you listening back there?" I wondered.

"A while," He sat down purposefully, next to Jim and getting the man's eye, he placed a hand on Jim's thigh. "You're my best friend. I didn't mean to hurt you with my show of distrust. I don't actually distrust you. It was a reaction. Probably one I learned off my father who's a homophobe of the first degree as well as a misogynist. Actually I think he hates most people except for himself."

"It's a touchy area for me," Jim explained. "Growing up I was called, at best, effeminate. The kids at school were worse."

"I can imagine," I murmured to myself.

"The thing is," he continued. "I've never identified as particularly gay, hetero or even bisexual. I'm just, well, me."

"Where'd you grow up?" I wondered, trying to visualise a context for the tale he was telling.

"The backblocks of Colorado. Cattle country. Immense landscapes of mountains, plains and snow. I loved the wide open spaces. But once I graduated I moved to Seattle. Partially the attraction was the chance of a job at one of the big tech companies. The other was the scene. It allowed me to explore so much but still I couldn't find an identity as such. I drifted until I scored my first contract on board a vessel heading west. At sea no-one cared about what my background was, only that I could do the job and not let down the team. Since my work was specialised I found a certain amount of autonomy, and a kind of power. I found a place to hide from my family and a place to call home."

"And you found me," Reilly pointed out, "We've become fast friends. I don't want to lose that because of a moment's stupidity on my part. Don't I deserve more than one chance."

Jim sighed deeply, "I want to give you that. It's just that I know that sex strips away all layers of pretense. At some level you must feel a little uncertain of, how should I say this…"

"Macho challenged." I tried to joke but watched them both carefully, with an eagle eye.

Reilly tensed, "If that's true then that was buried in my subconscious long ago by an upbringing I'd rather forget."

"Forgetting it won't help," I guessed. "You need to shine a light on it, Reilly. I'm no therapist but I don't think you can change it unless you first accept it's there and the reasons why it's there."

"The reasons?" Reilly winced, "at some level I've taken on my father's attitudes."

"Not consciously. Your subconscious did," Jim mused, "probably because it thought it would protect you in some way from your father."

"Protect me?"

"Can you imagine what your childhood would have been like if you'd been like me?" Jim posed the question.

"Shit. I'd be dead. No ifs or buts. He was and still is that kind of man."

"Exactly."

"So how do I go about convincing my subconscious that it's perfectly fine to give you the trust that you know I want to?"

"Baby steps," I figured. "We wear it down by showing you time and time again that we won't ever breach any boundaries you impose on me and Jim.

Reilly relaxed a little. I think he was hearing what I was hearing. That Jim was willing to take the risk. But Reilly wasn't one to leave things to chance. "Middle of the night brainstorming aside, I probably need to see a professional. I've carried this shit around with me long enough. My issues weren't a bother to anyone else except me until it was no longer only me I worried about."

I choked back a laugh. Even Jim snickered a little.

"What?" Reilly demanded, none too happy with either of us.

I braved the answer, "Well I'm not sure your issues haven't coloured your working relationship with those who serve in the lower ranks."

Reilly frowned at that, "Is that journalist speak for I'm a pain in the butt at times?"

I bit my bottom lip and grinned, "I couldn't possibly answer that. Look, seriously Reilly, despite or even maybe because of your rough edges, I don't know the why of it, but I'm attracted to you. I can't help what my heart feels," let alone my hormones. "I have no wish to change you. I just want your trust in both me and Jim. If we're to have a long term relationship that lasts through the ups and downs everyone faces then we'll need that. Trust and love."

Both men stared at me.

"You said the L word," Jim whispered.

Well duh, "I don't go around having these kind of in depth discussions with just anyone."

"Damn it," Reilly swore, rubbing his brow. "She's right."

Uh oh. I knew I'd been the one to mention the L word but my energy levels were beginning to flag. It was the middle of the night after all. And I didn't like the look of the bug that was trying to alight on my arm, "Anyone on for going back to bed?"

Fortunately both Jim and Reilly dove at the opportunity to end the discussion, for now. I swatted the bug before it could do me or anyone else harm then we meandered back inside and collapsed in a heap on the bed.

20

I woke, alone, to the smell of freshly cooked toast. I threw on some clothes from those that Jim had packed for me, then followed my nose into the kitchen. Reilly was buttering toast and Jim was setting plates on the table. "Looks good," I commented, finding a cup and pouring myself a cup of tea that smelled faintly of vanilla. "Any jam?"

Jim passed me a jar. "Raspberry. I hope that's okay."

"Raspberry's good."

Reilly put a plate of chopped up papaya, mini sized bananas, passion fruit and pineapple on the table and passed me a plate.

"Thanks. I feel like I'm getting the royal treatment here."

Jim laughed, "Nah, you get to wash up."

"Hmph," but it seemed fair. "So what's the agenda for today?"

"Sex, bungolow inspection, sex, buy bungolow, sex, fishing, more sex." Reilly summed up the plan. "Somewhere in the middle of that we'll eat, drink and be merry."

"Ok...ay", various parts of me mulled on that, expecting a certain amount of wear. Would I be able to stand up by the end of the day?

Jim sat down next to me and patted me affectionately, "By sex he means everything from cuddles, romps in the local rock pool, massage, whipped cream to, well, whatever works. Expect to be pampered, not used, Ry."

I leaned into him and nuzzled, "Thanks." Whipped cream? "I did wonder how I was going to meet both your needs."

"Your needs come first," Reilly sat down heavily in his chair. "You're the glue in this relationship after all."

"I disagree, I see Jim as the catalyst. Without him we might spit and snarl at each other."

"Me, snarl?" But Reilly smiled. "You might be right."

Jim looked between us both, "You're forgetting, Reilly is our protector and our authority. God help anyone who gives us any grief."

We all laughed at that.

I did the dishes after breakfast. Jim dried. Reilly put away. After that team effort Jim went to ring the property's owner and Reilly went looking on the internet for a local building inspector who might be available on the weekend. It occurred to me Deman might still be on the island, so, not wanting to deal with his admin, I found a comfy chair and let myself drift. Like an eagle soaring the skies I narrowed in on Deman's location. He was sitting out on a cafe deck with Rachel, seemingly having a bit of well earned rest and recreation, enjoying the best that the capital of Victoria had to offer. He sensed me and looked up, instantly alert. "Ry, what's up?" He was careful to be looking at Rachel when he spoke so that no-one thought he was speaking to thin air.

"Nothing dangerous. More that I need your business nouse."

I laid out to him what all the details Jim, Reilly and I had hashed out the night before. "What do you reckon?"

He leaned back in his plush dark green leather executive chair, steepling his fingers under his chin. "Give me a moment to think."

I gave him that.

He leaned back forward and looked at me intently. "You think this relationship of yours will work?"

I shrugged, "As much as any. There's been mention of the 'L' word and while there was a bit of shock no one really flinched. Aside from the romantic stuff, which is still yet to evolve, I trust them Deman. They're my friends. And you know how I value my friends," him being one of them.

"I'm not going to tell you to be careful with your heart Ry. Hell knows that whatever Rachel, Vladimir and I have is complex enough. I'll have Whiting contact our legal people. I'm sure they could draw you up an arrangement that would protect all parties and fax it through. But I have something I'd like to put to you.

Reilly was staring at me intently when I came out of my trance. "You're supposed to tell me when you're going to do that so I can stand watch."

Oops, I guessed saying he'd been busy wouldn't cut it. "I'm really sorry, I guess I need to get used to the fact you've got my back."

"I always had your back, I just didn't want to admit it."

Jim passed me a glass of water, "I'm guessing you went to talk to Deman."

"You could have just phoned him," Reilly griped.

"I could have but then I'd have to have dealt with his annoyingly overprotective admin. Honestly, you don't want to have to deal with Mr Whiting. Rude, doesn't quite cover it."

Reilly's green eyes sizzled, "You need me to ream someone out, I'm your man."

Jim choked.

I bit my lip, "I appreciate it. Anyway, he has a proposal for us to consider. He's been talking to the government here about using his ships as part of their monitoring of the oceans. With, of course, us doing what Sophia discussed. Part Surveillance, part documenting. Media coverage if I can get it. Given all that, Deman wants a base here. Somewhere he can make secure, house a few vehicles and whatever might be needed in passing. Plus there's the fact Rachel has kind've fallen in love with the place."

"So what? He wants an office in Victoria?"

"No, he wants something hidden out of the way. Here. If we're agreeable his company will buy and manage the property. He'll also front any taxes and costs. In return we'll pay a peppercorn rent of one dollar each a year."

Jim looked disappointed. "I don't want to rent it. I want to own it. My heart's become kind of set on it."

"Well," how did I throw this out quickly and duck?" "Deman would make a gift of it to us if two or more of us ever married. In the meantime he wants to beef up the security around here and build a garage. He and Rachel, even Vladimir, might stay here from time to time, when we didn't need the place. Since he knows the schedule his own ships run, he'd know when we weren't here. In the meantime we wouldn't have any loans to worry about or any assets to split if we parted ways."

Reilly thumped down in the nearest cosy armchair. "You can't mention marriage and splitting in the same sentence."

"I thought I split that paragraph up well enough."

Jim sat down too. It looked like the three of us were having another heart to heart. "I can see the advantages with Deman's company buying it, especially since we're short on time. Purchases like this can take up a lot of time wading through the bureaucracy. Plus we wouldn't have all the problems that come with managing a part-time rental."

"Let alone the taxes and maintenance costs," I added.

"It's a generous offer," Reilly seemed to have recovered from the use of the 'M' word. "What's he want in return?"

Ah, there was my, correct that, our Reilly. Looking out for our interests. "He wants us. He wants me to commit to working for his company, permanently, rather than seeking work with his company on a sailing by sailing basis. He wants the three of us to commit to working together as a team, ostensibly doing what our shipboard roles require but with the added stuff on top. He's offering a generous remuneration package but we'd be expected to go above and beyond to earn it."

"And will you, commit?" Jim left that word hanging in the air. A word that could mean many things to the three of us.

Damn it! We had to make a decision on this if we were to grab a chance at this property. "Hell, Yes. What about you two?"

"Do we have to do a three musketeers thingy?" Reilly groaned.

Jim rolled his eyes towards the ceiling, "Just a yes or no will suffice. Yes, from me. It's a no brainer."

"Yes then, you two aren't ditching me, from any of this."

Well, phew. "Deman said if we agreed we should go ahead with contacting the real estate and getting an inspection. Then we send the final contract through to him. He's staying at the Hilton Resort for now. Leaving on Monday after the Merkwood II departs. If we're quick about things we can start the ball rolling and then he'll deal with the rest."

Reilly handed me his phone, "Let him know. We'll get things underway. We only have this weekend."

"I don't need your phone Reilly. I think I can project a simple yes without leaving my body. Give me a moment," I brought an image of Deman to my mind, found him finishing his coffee with Rachel and sent a *Yes*.

Understood, came the quick reply.

"He got the message."

"I'll go and ring that inspector I found online?" Reilly went to do just that.

"Real estate agent said he had a prior commitment, he can't get here for an hour," Jim explained to me.

Reilly returned, "Inspector's organised. He's only a few minutes away. Said to ring him once the real estate agent get's here. He thought it might help with the negotiations if he points out any flaws as he sees them."

Smart. "I guess now we wait." I mused.

"Nah, there's no fun in that," Jim decided

"I hope you're not suggesting we go for a romp in the bedroom," by the looks of them both the thought had crossed their minds. "I don't want to be halfway to an orgasm and we get an interruption."

"Voice of reason," Jim decided. "How about we get Reilly to take us through some of those Karate kata moves. They looked complex but beautiful."

"It's only complex because if you're following the instructor you have to keep changing your perspective as you move around," Reilly found his element. "Okay, outside. And despite Ry's dive in approach I'll slow it down and we'll take it step by step."

21

We spent a good hour out in the yard, learning the various blocks, punches and steps and putting it together. Left, right, center … yeah it had a flow."

A car pulled up in 'our' drive and a petite man I didn't recognise got out. He looked mildly official in his clean white shirt and business slacks.

"Hi."

"Bozoo madame, I am John Vidot. Your boss, Mr Merkwood, is interested in purchasing these premises?"

"Bozoo Mr Vidot," Reilly took charge, "I'm Reilly O'Reilly, this is Jim Northey and this is Rylee Jackson.."

"Reilly and Rylee, amusing"

Reilly wasn't amused, "I have a building engineer on standby. I'll just give him a call and tell him you're here." He disappeared back into the house to make the call.

I stepped forward to shake the man's hand, "Bozoo, I gather is Seychelles creole. I must learn more of it."

John, who'd seemed a little intimidated by Reilly, brightened. "You're interested in our culture and customs?"

"For sure. I recently became a citizen but I know very little of your ways."

"My sister, Veronique, would be honoured to teach you, madame. She doesn't charge much."

"Next time our ship stops on the island I'll be sure to look her up if you'll leave me her number. And please call me Ry."

"Plezir"

"Jim," Jim offered his hand, "and don't take Reilly the wrong way. He just wants to make sure that everything's right with the purchase."

"Plezir, Jim. I understand entirely. The property has not had much use for a while, what with the tourism downturn. The property's owner was so happy when you arranged the rental for the weekend. I assume everything is in order."

"It's a lovely place." I agreed.

Reilly returned, "Paul Payet is on his way. Can we offer you a drink Mr Vidot?" Reilly had finally remembered to be cordial.

"Please call me John as it seems I'm on first name terms with your friends already. Something cold perhaps?" John asked hopefully.

"Come into the kitchen," I led the way, "I'm sure we'll find something to your liking."

The engineer, Paul, soon joined us, a stocky man with a no-nonsense manner. He and Reilly seemed to mesh and disappeared with torches, a tape measure and writing paper, muttering about verandah poles, bathroom plumbing and the standard of the electrical wiring."

Jim frowned, "I could have told them the wiring is fine. A little dated, but it's safe."

I gave Jim an affectionate, consoling nudge, "I think sometimes our Reilly gets caught up in the moment of being in charge and forgets about the skills and competencies of others."

Jim laughed at that, "A bit. 'Our' Reilly?"

I shrugged, "Just saying. We'll kick him up the bum for it later."

The real estate fella, John, looked between us, confused. "You sound like a married couple."

I instantly clamped my hands over my ears and started muttering "Nah, Nah, Nah"

Jim snickered. "Well you see John," he explained, rolling his eyes at my antics, "We're having enough trouble with the 'L' word. We're a long way off the 'M'."

John shook his head, "They're just words. I can see what's between you and it's made of strong stuff."

After an awful lot of negotiation we sent John on his way with his promise to send a contract through to Deman, ASAP, and a copy to us. Then we cornered Reilly, "Did you perhaps forget something?" I posed the question.

Jim had his arms folded.

You could tell Reilly knew something was up but he looked confused, "No, I don't think so?"

"So you remembered to consult your friend and electrical engineer on what he thought of the bungalow's wiring before you went charging off with the building inspector?" I put my solitary hand on my right hip and gave him the raised eyebrows look.

Reilly winced, "Shit. I didn't mean. I completely forgot."

"Yeah, you forgot to consult," I readily agreed

Reilly looked at Jim and knew he was in the shit. "I really am sorry."

I thought I knew a way to fix this but I didn't think he'd like it. Though it might just go a little more of the way towards giving our relationship a strong basis to build on. "Words are easy, Reilly. We value your ability to take charge, strategize and protect but there are going to be times we'll want you to loosen that precious control of yours and treat us as the assets we are. What we need is a demonstration that you're willing to hand those reins over to us. It comes back to that trust issue we discussed last night but it's more than that. We need equal value in this relationship," I explained it as nicely as I could.

"You have it."

"No, we don't" Jim countered.

Reilly sighed, rubbing his face with his hand, "How do I make this right?"

That's what I loved about Reilly. When faced with a problem he faced it head on rather than deny it. "Let us tie you up and have our wicked way with you." Before he could protest I added, "With Jim respecting the boundaries you negotiated earlier. And you have your safe word."

Reilly looked between us but his focus was on Jim who he'd clearly insulted. "And this would mend this between us?"

Jim nodded, "You can see it as therapy or funishment, whichever you wish, but do this and the slate's cleared."

He stood very still while he thought, then Reilly came to his decision, "Okay."

Reilly watched intently while Jim rummaged through his box of goodies, "Why did you pack rope?"

"Hope."

"And what's this?" Reilly reached over to check out the plastic apparatus.

Jim smacked his hand away. That got him a glare from Reilly, "It's a strapon, okay?"

Reilly looked to me, knowing I'd be the only one capable of wearing such a thing, "Did you know about this?"

"Hell no but I'm thinking this is a real treasure trove." I felt like a kid in a toy shop. "I hope you have a bigger butt plug or two in there, that last one was kind of loose."

Jim didn't know what to make of either of us, "Patience. First let's deal with our resident control freak."

"I'm not a control freak," Reilly stood his ground.

"Well you're about to prove it, aren't you," I pointed out.

I took a strand of rope and let it run through my hand, a juggling act to be sure but it didn't seem to have any scrags or loose bits, "Nice."

"I'd hope so, given what I paid for it." Jim took the strand off me and felt the weight of it. "Good choice Ry, this will do nicely."

"Shall we set up in the bedroom?" I wondered. It was the most private place we had after all.

"Yes, but let's lock the front and back doors. We don't want anyone walking in on us. Might as well turn our phones off."

"No we won't," Reilly countered. "What if Sophie rings with news of our suspects?"

"Hmm," I found my phone and made a call. "It's Rylee Jackson. Hi, yes, could you put me through to Lieutenant Sophie Camille. Hi Soph, just letting you know we're switching off our phones for an hour or so. Cool." I hung up.

"She said she has her ways."

"What exactly does that mean?" Reilly demanded.

"It means she can yell in my head if she has to. Look, go find one of those wooden chairs in the kitchen and bring it into the bedroom. And go lock the doors while you're at it."

"Why?" he asked suspiciously.

I turned and glared at him, "Are you forgetting about something again Reilly, like trust?"

Reilly swore and stomped off to the kitchen, as ordered.

"You sure about this Ry?" Jim whispered to me. "He could hate us for it. He's not exactly used to playing this way."

"Jim," I could see his courage was flagging and I needed some way to give it back to him, "we only have this weekend. We need to strip away our respective layers and see what's at our core. It's a danger, yes…"

"But we have to find out some time," Jim finished my sentence.

I patted him reassuringly, "One way or another we'll try and keep your friendship intact but you have to admit, the moment you put a hand on my thigh at Sophie's you changed everything."

"I did, didn't I? Okay, no regrets, here goes. He's coming back."

"Strip," Jim commanded Reilly.

I think both Reilly and I were taken aback by the sudden depth of Jim's voice. I recognised it as someone in dominant mode but I doubted Reilly would know the reason for the change."

"Take a seat," with noticeably practised hands Jim tied Reilly's behind his back

"What now?" ever seeking information, Reilly wanted to know.

"For now you sit and watch." Jim turned his back on him and instead turned his attention on me. "I know you're not submissive Ry but would you be up for playing it?"

"You want me to bottom for you?" Yeah, why not, I could act.

"Yes."

Naked I took my place on the floor. Taking a simple kneeling position I placed my right hand on my thigh, palm up. I turned my gaze to the floor and waited. It looked like we were about to play out a scene, for Reilly's benefit no doubt.

Jim walked slowly around me. I felt rather than saw. I heard the footfall of his steps. His breath changing as he appraised me. The stroke of his hand, his praise. I waited.

I saw his feet, felt the heat of his body at my front as he came full circle. His hand firmly gripped my short hair and tugged my head back. I avoided his gaze.

"You may look at me sub."

I used that permission to seek out his eyes and found them, hot with desire.

With just his index finger he caressed my lips. Gently that finger nudged my lips apart and invaded.

"Suck."

My tongue danced around his finger like it was made of gold, a precious honour to be savoured. I mourned when he removed it.

His wet finger traced a line down my chest, where first he found one nipple, then the next. "Keep quiet for me."

Which was almost impossible as he tweaked each rosy nub with increasing pressure, to the point of nearly pain, but something else. It was like he knew exactly how much I could take. I knew he watched me intently. Yeah I was no submissive but I felt a strange urge not to disappoint.

"Give me your hand sub," he raised me up and guided me towards the bed.

He angled me so as to give Reilly a view, though I doubted he could see it all. He'd said not a word but my focus wasn't on him at the moment.

"Make yourself wet for me."

He hadn't given me permission to speak and I wasn't sure of how much protocol we were adhering to. I wanted to tell him I was soaked already. But I guess there can always be more.

My fingers used the plentiful moisture to coat my fingers then I found my nub and gently caressed a single finger tip over it.

Jim didn't tell me not to, but he obviously had other ideas, "I want to see you fingers sliding into that cunt of yours. Yeah, like that." It was a command, with the slight touch of a purr about it.

"Jim, you can't leave me like this," Reilly protested.

"Can't I just? Are you safe wording out Reilly?"

"No, but…this is hell."

"I've taken your control, Reilly. You have no choice now but to watch while I fuck my willing sub."

"Ry, make him see reason."

Jim answered for me. "She won't say anything. She knows I haven't given her permission to speak and that I'd have to punish her if she did. Mind you, perhaps I'll make her your whipping boy. Ry, will you take Reilly's punishment for complaining. You may answer this."

Oh boy, I remembered ass spanking. The warm glow of the skin afterwards. "Gladly, master."

"Excellent, roll over then. It will be five because Reilly protested and five because he appealed to you to override my command. I will do the counting."

"One,"

A firm but restrained hand slapped my butt cheek. He wasn't out to hurt me. This was for show as much as for tweaking my pain-pleasure boundary.

"Two,"

His hand warmed my other butt cheek. It was all I could do not to squirm as I anticipated each of what followed.

I felt myself drifting. I felt Jim rolling me over. He gently caressed my face, "You go into subspace so beautifully. But I'm not finished yet. Come back to me."

My eyes fluttered open and stared languidly into his. "I'm here."

"Do you want this? For me to fuck you? I wasn't sure if you were saving there for Reilly. You may answer me."

"If Reilly's okay, I am. I want you, Master." I playfully used his title.

"Well," Jim addressed Reilly. "I don't want you hating me if I take what you feel is yours."

Reilly's eyes softened, "No Jim. I won't hate you. And don't let the master in you go just yet. It's a side of you I've never seen before."

"Very well," Jim's voice deepened again into that commanding almost baritone again. Taking charge he rearranged me on the bed to give Reilly a side view, I supposed. "Put your legs up on my shoulders, sub."

And I knew why. I clenched in anticipation. This was going to be deep. Just an edge of fear caught me, "Permission to speak master."

"Go ahead."

"I, no forget it, I trust you."

"Of that I am glad and deeply honoured, precious. Have no fear, I'll take this steady. Any discomfort, give me another colour other than your safe word."

"White." It was quicker to say than pale pink if I started getting uncomfortable.

His broad cock nudged at my entrance and I had to relax to let him in. It helped that I was so wet already, which had no doubt been planning and preparation on Jim's part. "Easy, precious. Take a few breaths. Deep one in, and let it out.

And as I let it out he slid right in, "Oh my effing…amazing."

Jim laughed, "With such praise I can only let you off that breach of protocol. Now take what I can give. Take all of me."

I felt stretched. I felt connected in places I didn't think it was possible to feel. "Please," I murmured, forgetting myself.

"I cannot deny you," Jim purred. He set up a slow and steady pace at first. Both being gentle with me while I got accustomed to him and at the same time tormenting me. Holding that desired release like a distant star in the sky. But it was there.

I think the pace was tormenting Reilly too, as I heard a groan of frustration. But he too held his peace, having learned that I might 'suffer' for his infractions.

Jim found his rhythm.

I watched the man in wonder and awe as he found his zone. He was in the flow. A master of his domain. And I was that domain. I yielded and he took. A volcano boiled within me. Some vast magma chamber rumbled to life. I was trying to hold off coming, for Jim's benefit but fissures were forming in my resistance. The hot lava of need was beginning to consum³e. I cried out as I thrust up to meet his thrust and we erupted together. Gentleman that he was he eased my legs from his shoulders then he smothered me in kisses, nuzzling me and caressing me. "My wonder, my joy."

Sometime later I drifted back up to the surface of my consciousness.

"Hey, you two, wakey wakey. Someone untie me."

Jim groaned and near fell out of the bed, legless but struggling to right himself. He fumbled over to Reilly and undid his ropes, "Well done man," then with that faint praise he staggered back to bed and collapsed,nearly on top of me. I grunted and pushed and managed to regain a smidge of Ry-space.

Surprisingly Reilly clambered up onto the bed, behind Jim, draped an arm over him and we all drifted back off into a half doze.

Arwen Jayne

22

Ry, wake up Ry, came Sophie's urgent voice in my head. *Switch your damn phone back on you. You've had your hour. You didn't say you were going comatose.*

I groaned and got up, retrieved my phone, switching it back on. It rang immediately, "Sophie? What's up?", I put the call on speaker phone so the guys could hear.

"Lasseter was spotted on a security camera about half an hour ago, heading your way. It could be a coincidence he's going in that direction but if not. What did you do? I've been mentally yelling at you for the last half hour. I was starting to think he'd found you already and you were all unconscious. Any longer and I was going to send out some uniforms to check on you."

"Sorry, Sophie, in hindsight Reilly might have been right. We should have kept at least one phone on."

Reilly rolled his eyes and raised his hands to heaven.

Jim interrupted, "I hear a car pulling up in the drive."

"I'll stay on the line," Sophie decided. "Keep your phone with you so I can hear what's going on."

Reilly ducked low below the window and peered out the very corner. "He doesn't look armed but everyone stay down low. I'll go see what he wants."

"No!," I said quickly. "It's safer for me to project myself. He can't harm me in my etheric form."

Reilly nodded, "Come here then. I'll hold you while you go out of your body."

I quickly tranced out. It was getting easier every time I did it. Like shedding a piece of much loved clothing. Which reminded me I wasn't clothed in reality. I mentally dressed myself in a cool cotton top and light weight shorts and thongs. That would do. "Lasseter. What's your business here?"

"Ry, I'm glad you're here. I heard that Jim had booked this place. I hoped to find someone here who would know where you were."

"Why?" I asked suspiciously. It was on the tip of my tongue to ask if he and his friends hadn't done enough but I'd try civility first.

"To apologise. Sharma, also, sends his thanks for saving him. You didn't have to do that but you did. We were wrong. Very wrong. I understand if you hold a grudge."

One name was noticeable from his apology. "And deSilva?"

Lasseter sighed. "He won't see reason. We argued at the hospital, after Sharma regained consciousness. He's adamant that nothing will make up for the loss of his friends except your and Adeela's deaths. He's a ball of raging fury. I'm sorry, but I can't see him seeing reason anytime soon. Look, they're shipping Sharma home on Deman's private jet when it leaves on Monday. He and I talked. We want to make amends, so, I'm offering to protect you."

Hmm, this was all so sudden, "Keep that thought. I'll be back out in a second." I walked my etheric self back through our front door to give the appearance that I was really there. Not that Lasseter hadn't seen me project myself before but I didn't need to remind him that I had my own defences. I reclothed myself in my physical body and stared into Reilly's concerned eyes, "Did you hear any of that?"

"He wants to apologise? I'll give him damned apology," Reilly growled.

"Reilly, brutalising him will only renew his enmity. I need allies not enemies."

"Is that journalist speak for you don't want me to tear strips of him?"

"In a word, yes. I know what he did is a trigger for you and I respect that. I'm asking you to refrain from acting on that rage. He's offering to help in protecting me and Adeela. My only problem with that is do I trust his word?"

"Can I say something," Sophie asked over the speaker phone.

"Go ahead," I hoped Reilly would listen to her reason if not mine.

"Firstly, while I understand how you feel, Reilly," she targeted her words carefully, "as a cop, I can't condone any sort of vigilante justice. It would be a black mark against you and we're hoping to work with you. We know you have a record but that's long in the past. We're prepared to turn a blind eye to that. Don't muddy things up now. Secondly, I have officers who should be there shortly. If he will voluntarily submit to questioning and a lie detector test I think we should take that opportunity."

I turned to the other man in the room, "What do you think Jim?"

"I'm with Reilly, in that I'd skin him if I could. They stalked you Ry, beat you up and nearly forced our car off the road. That's intimidation, assault and attempted murder," he said, I expected for Sophie's benefit, reminding her of the extent of our grievances against this man. "But the reality is venting our anger on Lasseter would make us as bad as them. Sophie's option is the only viable one, and the only legal one. If we want this sea surveillance alliance we need to play by their rules. We let them take him in, question him and see if he's telling the truth. The rest is up to the captain. He's already expressed his desire to summarily dismiss any of the individuals who did the graffiti on your cabin door, let alone the latter stuff. His future is not ours to decide."

"Shit," Reilly swore, "I just hate that we're powerless in this but you're right."

"Not powerless," Sophie put in, "Merely that you've delegated that power to those of your allies best able to deal with this man. I know you'll do the right thing," or at least she was convinced of it now. "Go talk to him. I'm hanging up. I've got an interview room to book."

I hurriedly dressed in some real, rather than etheric clothes, as I was still naked. Then I followed Jim and Reilly out the door. Though I wasn't sure what I'd do to restrain them if Lasseter got them offside.

Lasseter was leaning against his car. He looked up and straightened to attention, "Sir," acknowledging Reilly.

Reilly glared at him, "You took part in beating up a woman and fellow crew member." Yeah that was Reilly, direct and to the point."

Jim didn't look any less imposing, "And if that wasn't enough you were in the passenger seat when deSilva was trying to force us off the road."

Lasseter's shoulders' sagged in defeat. "I have nothing to offer in my defence. I allowed myself to be carried along on the strength of deSilva's hatred of Jackson and Shirazi. Rushil Sharma, and I both realise now we were wrong. Rushil, owes his life to Ry and he knows it. He's ashamed. So am I."

"Ashamed enough to give a statement to the police and submit to a lie detector test?"

"You don't trust me. I wouldn't expect you to. I wouldn't in your shoes. If handing myself in to the police goes some of the way towards proving my intent then yes."

His assent was timely as a police car came down the drive.

Thomas Lasseter frowned, "You'd already called them."

"Lieutenant Camille did. You were spotted on a security camera, heading this way." So, it wasn't us, we didn't do it. But I hoped we wouldn't lose his trust so quickly.

Lasseter seemed to accept that. "I guess it really is a very small island. Hard to escape attention."

Two burly Seychellois men approached him, each would have made one and a half of him. "Thomas Lasseter?" one asked.

Lasseter sighed, "That would be me." Less certain of himself he directed his attention to Reilly, "I meant what I said Sir. I wish to make amends by helping to protect Jackson and Shirazi. Even the cook can't watch Shirazi's back all the time."

"You're assuming that deSilva will find his way back on board, past my security."

"Your security is excellent sir," Lasseter trod carefully, "but deSilva knows more about the hidey holes on that boat than most. I think he and at least Felly had a smuggling operation on the go. I don't know what but it's a gut feeling."

Reilly's curiosity was duly peaked. "Go speak to the cops, Lasseter. I'll talk to the captain. Ultimately the decision whether you sail with us on Monday is up to the police and him."

"I understand Sir," Lasseter allowed the cops to cuff him and take him away.

"I need a swim after all that," Jim went back inside to find towels and bathing gear.

"Count me in. We got any sunscreen for afterwards?" A swim sounded good. It might help to dissolve some of my mixed emotions. I was uncomfortable with my own lingering dislike of Lasseter. I didn't like holding a grudge. No point really as a grudge only poisoned the holder of the grudge. I tried mentally putting myself in Lasseter's shoes but it was a tough call. Had there been times in my life where I'd hurt others because I'd been picked up and carried along by the opinions of others? Certainly never physically but had there been times when I'd passed on an opinion about someone, for instance, because I'd been convinced by another that it was true? As a journalist I was conscious of the need to fact check before I jumped the gun with any story.

"Stop it," Reilly nudged me, none too gently, in the direction of the beach, his surf rod in hand. "For whatever reason I can feel your emotional turmoil from here. Let me take a guess. You've got the guilts up because you think you should think better of Lasseter than you do. Ry, you can't neatly slot any of us into black and white categories. That includes you and Lasseter. You're right not to want to hate, and I admire that about you, but you don't have to like shitheads either. Some behaviour is just that, shit. Ask yourself this. Would you beat, harass and try to kill someone just because Jim or I told you we hated them?"

"No, hell, I'd hope I wouldn't. I'd want to know why you hated them.

I'd want to be convinced that they'd really done something utterly dreadful and even then I'd hesitate. I know I'm not lily white, afterall I kicked that pirate we downed."

"Because you had first hand knowledge that he'd wanted to kill you. You had more reason than deSilva's cronies to want revenge but you didn't maim or kill him."

"Perhaps, but I did give vent to a viciousness that must exist within me."

"And you restrained me from doing worse. Like I said, you can't put us into neat categories of good and bad. We're all just doing the best we can with what's given to us. No doubt we justify much in our minds but at the end of the day it comes down to intent. The intent to consider others or only yourself. You have nothing to worry about."

Perhaps, but I felt his own doubts and uncertainties. Our relationship was affecting him, making him more conscious of how his own behaviour affected others. "I'm not trying to slot you into some category either, Reilly. I accept you as you are."

"Then do me the courtesy of accepting yourself, grudges and all," he glared at me.

23

The day disappeared on us. Between swimming and snorkelling, a late lunch and going over the contract the real estate agent John dropped off mid afternoon time flew. We knew we'd have to pack up in the morning as we were expected back at the boat by 2pm. A sad longing settled on us for what was rapidly disappearing, our unimpeded time together. Passionately we grasped onto the last vestiges of our time in paradise. Jim cooked up the last of the fish and after we cleared the dishes we retreated to the deck to watch the tropical sunset as it painted its orange and tangerine glow behind a silhouette of palms.

I sipped from my cold clear glass of soda water and leaned against Reilly's hard wiry body, relishing the strength and protection that lay there. Jim sat down on my other side. His hand on my thigh. A favourite place it seemed.

I cleared my throat, it was time to put my problem out there, "I know you guys don't get this problem but I'm, well, a little on the sore side."

Jim winked at Reilly, "We know, we have a contingency plan. Hope you're still feeling hungry."

"Er, not really,"

"Couldn't tempt you with some kirsch soaked cherries, ripe mango and pawpaw, served with a liberal dose of freshly whipped cream and a sprinkling of dark belgian chocolate."

Oh, my, god. I salivated at the thought. "I suppose. If I really, really tried. I could force myself," I snickered.

Reilly offered me his hand, "Come with me."

And we were going to the bathroom, why? "What are you up to? Making sure I wash my hands before eating?" Really?

"Trust." Reilly pronounced that one word with finality. He stripped off his own clothes, sneaking a peak to see if I was watching. Hell yeah.

Then he set about stripping me.

Once we were both standing naked in the bathroom he proceeded to get the shower running, adjusting the temperature. "How hot do you like it?"

"In the tropics, not so much."

He adjusted it a bit then stepped into the pristine white porcelain and glass shower bay and beckoned me to enter.

"You sure there's room enough in here for both of us?"

He picked up the bar of lemongrass scented soap I'd left there earlier, "You'll just have to stay close, won't you. Turn around."

"I can wash myself."

"And where would the fun be in that?" To prove a point or to aggravate me he made circles around my boobs with the soap.

I should have known better than to argue with Reilly when he was on a mission. There wasn't one inch of me he missed, and yeah, there too. "Am I washing you?"

"I'll have a quick shower once we're finished with you," He took the handheld nozzle from its holder and proceeded to rinse me off. "Hmm, good enough. Damned shower bay's too small to do more. We're putting a bathroom reno on the priority list once the sale's through." He stepped out ahead of me, grabbed one of the luxurious bath towels and wrapped me in it. "That should have given Jim enough time to set up."

"For what?"

He dared to smirk. "Finish drying off while I have a quick rinse. No leaving the bathroom. And no peeking." It was a distinct command, not a request.

I was getting curious now.

All was revealed a few moments later when Reilly did the gentlemanly thing and opened the bathroom door for me.

I walked into the bedroom and stared. "We're not eating in the kitchen then," I had my duh moment, realising I was part of the menu, or was that the plate?

Jim had taken my time in the shower to cover the bed with a plastic tarp. And he'd conveniently arranged bowls of fruit and cream on the bedside tables. "You've prepared the key ingredient, Steward O'Reilly."

Reilly took the temporary demotion in good humour, "I have Chef Northey. Where would you like her?"

"Here, I think, she'll be the centre piece."

"Good call," Reilly led me to the bed and nudged me to lie down on the plastic.

I wondered if centrepieces of food displays were meant to speak. I could ask, I suppose. "Permission to speak."

"Granted," the good natured chef, in his check gingham apron, decided. Where'd he find the apron I wondered. Pleasingly it was all he wore. I got to appreciate the scenery. The view got even better when Reilly dropped the towel from his waist and positioned himself on the side of the bed, in reach of the bowls of fruit and cream on am his side of the bed.

"Any chance of a cherry and some chocolate?" My two favourites.

Jim picked a cherry from one of his bowls, "stay perfectly still, my little platter." He placed the cherry to my lips.

I took a bite and discovered he had depipped it. The dual tastes of cherry and kirsch melded in my mouth. I memorised the taste, the moment, the pleasure of that one cherry.

"A chocolate chaser, I think," Reilly fed me a piece of the richest, most decadent Belgian chocolate I'd ever tasted. Or was it the setting that added to the appeal? I didn't care. I took that square of chocolate into my mouth and let it melt there, sliding eventually down my throat. My mind followed it, seeking its essence. But my focus was pulled away by the sensation of Jim and Reilly circling cream around my boobs, piping it in neat swirls. And everywhere it touched the cold of it thrilled me.

With the artists earnestly at work I decided to just give over to the experience. Surreal didn't cover it. I felt the trickle of mango juice dribble down my belly as Jim squeezed a particularly ripe specimen, crushing it in his hands with a look of sheer fun and enjoyment on his face.

Reilly licked at the orange coloured syrup, saving it from running under me and making a sticky mess. "Need more cream on this side I think."

Jim reached over me, careful not to spoil his handiwork. He piped more cream in swirls where Reilly indicated. "A dusting of chocolate would be good. I've grated some." He passed Reilly a small bowl of the stuff then he took up his own.

I doubted I'd ever end up on display in the national gallery, heaven forbid, but my artisans took their work seriously. Finally finishing their creation with strategically placed morsels of fruit. I tried to breathe lightly so as to not spoil their work.

Finally Jim pronounced it finished and passed Reilly a serviette, more symbolically than anything as it would take a whole roll of serviettes to clean up this little mess.

Reilly filled a glass with wine and passed one to Jim, "A good dessert deserves a fine wine I think." They clinked their glasses together.

"Hey!" I complained.

Reilly chuckled, filling a third glass from wherever he'd hidden it. Reverently he supported my head and brought the glass to my lips, "Couldn't have our centre piece drying out could we?"

"I feel like one of those Tibetan sand paintings they spend hours making, only to destroy."

"Ah, yes, the impermanence of things, but the fun is in the destruction too," with that Reilly engulfed my tit in his mouth and sucked.

Jim ran a cherry through the chocolate dusted cream and held it to my lips, before he dived onto my icing sugar coated clitoris, and sucked.

I arched and moaned. Cream and fruit slid everywhere. Chaos ensued as we sated ourselves on our over the top dessert. God, I could really do with one of them inside me right now and had to remind myself sternly that it was I who'd said I was sore. The more would have to wait until the morning.

Somewhere towards the end of culinary mayhem, Reilly scooped me up and took me back to the shower. By the time we came out again Jim had removed the plastic tarp from the bed and was just wiping down a few stray bits that had escaped.

Reilly laid me on the bed then stood back, as if remembering their artwork, or was he, gulp, just admiring me. "Go to sleep Ry. You've earned it."

I didn't need telling twice.

I woke in the early hours of the morning, to the feel of Reilly's length gently filling me while Jim held my short hair in his firm grasp, "Tell me this is okay," Reilly pleaded.

As if it ever wouldn't, "More, please. Take me," and he rode us both to heaven.

We didn't have a lot of time. I'd known all along this time together would be a precious gift. We made a good team, cleaning the bungalow from top to bottom and putting everything alright.

Jim packed our few things and met me outside as Reilly locked the door on our little haven. Just as John, the real estate agent, drove down the driveway.

"Looks like I only just caught you. I thought you'd be longer."

"We have a little matter of some sightseeing to attend to. I'm supposed to have been seeing your beautiful island and I have little to report," I explained. I needed the half truth of that to cover our real activity.

"Your island too now, Ry." John pointed out.

I kept forgetting I was a dual citizen now. The memory of it pleased me, "So it is."

"Any must see tourist spots you could recommend, John?" Reilly asked. "We only have a few hours before we have to be back at work."

"Hmm, well there's the rum distillery tour, various museums, a short ferry trip to Curieuse Island to see the giant tortoise farm, but honestly I think there's plenty of old French architecture to look at in the towns and plenty of beautiful beaches still to see. Why don't you just drive along the coastline for a bit and see what you see."

"I'm always up for a scenic drive," Jim admitted.

Unless he was being chased by thugs, but I kept that thought to myself, he didn't need to be reminded. I vividly remembered how stressed he'd been by the whole experience. Come to think, I had been too. "Has Deman signed the contract on the bungalow?" I asked hopefully.

"He has, If you like you can leave the keys with me now. Deman's signed on with us to manage the property. He has told me to take my instructions from you on anything you need."

I remembered our need for a double shower bay but there was plenty of time to plan that once the contract was finalised. I'd research a few designs in the meantime and put them to the guys, "Thank you. We'll be in touch."

Reilly handed him the keys, "Until next time."

John wished us safe travels and left. We took one final longing look at our new, almost, home, then piled into the rented Audi and drove off to see what sights we'd find.

24

2pm came too soon. Back aboard the Merkwood II Captain Wilcher called us, Adeela and Cook into his office. "I've asked you here to discuss the matter of Seaman Thomas Lasseter. Lieutenant Camille is holding him at present until we determine what charges are to be laid."

"Sir, if I may speak?"

The captain laughed, astonished, "And since when did you ask for permission, Jackson?"

I couldn't help it, I blushed, looking down to try to hide the heat in my face.

"Well that wasn't the reaction I expected. I don't think I want to know what lies behind that. Speak your piece Jackson."

Thankfully the heat had cleared from my face, "Sir, none of us entirely trust him and I, more than most, have reason to think poorly of him but, if he truly wishes to help I say we use him. He may have further information on deSilva's smuggling operations or at least be able to give us some insights into how he managed to operate without detection."

"Camille hoped you might see it that way. Though I'm hesitant to reinstate a crewman involved in so many" he sighed, looking for the appropriate words, "misdemeanours. Even if it was under the influence of his peers."

"He did seem remorseful," Jim offered. "I agree he has to pay for what he and his pals did but I know that if he goes to jail he could grow cold at heart and deteriorate as an individual. If we were firm but not vengeful, maybe he could grow past this. Lasseter's best friend's in hospital and though, by some miracle, Rushil Sharma may keep his leg there are still worries about his mental capacity as there was a lot of brain haemorrhaging before Ry found him."

The miracle that he referred to had been Lydia, "You asked after him?"

"After Lasseter turned up at our bungalow, yes. Call it a healthy mix of curiosity and suspicion. I wanted to check on the story."

"Well done, " Reilly praised his friend. "It was good thinking to find out Rushil's situation." And no doubt he was kicking himself for not having done likewise. "Captain, Northey's right. Prison is a harsh place for any man, or woman, come to that. It's a training ground and recruitment facility for organised crime."

Wilcher nodded, "I'm aware of your unique insights into prison life, Officer O'Reilly."

Reilly winced.

"And," Wilcher continued, "that you turned your life around. You'd like me to give this man a chance?"

"Truthfully sir, I hate his guts. I'd like him to rot in hell for beating on Ry and nearly driving her and Jim off the road, but yes, I think it's worth the chance. Especially if he feels indebted to us. We could use that. With an abundance of caution."

"And you, Chef WakwaDlabazane? I value your thoughts."

"Just keep him away from Adeela, sorry, Shirazi, sir."

"Steward Shirazi?"

"I don't think I'd feel comfortable around the man sir but if he's not assigned to the kitchen I," she looked at Cook, "I think my back's covered, sir."

"Indeed," Wilcher leaned back in his dark green leather captain's chair, "I like an abundance of caution. Okay, we'll bust him down to ratings level. If he proves himself I may reinstate him but for now I'll make it clear to him his future's hanging by a thread, which it is. But..." He paused for emphasis. "Before I dismiss you and you head off on your respective duties I will say this. None of you are fooling me. I don't know what the lot of you did while you were on the island and I don't want to know. Though clearly, in one case it involved a shared bungalow, since three of you were there when Lasseter found you. The ship's owner has informed me that it's now his base of operations on the island.

I don't need to remind you that the two ladies present need their reputations intact if they are to avoid being seen as available, how shall I put it? Commodities. Neither do I want to see any lustful looks across the room, casual brushes against each other as you walk past or dare I say any impromptu activities in broom closets or other available hidey holes. I expect and demand absolute professionalism from all my crew. Is that clear?"

"Absolutely sir," Reilly readily agreed.

The rest of us pitched in, bolstering that agreement.

Wilcher rubbed his face with his hand, "Just, I didn't know, be officious occasionally, O'Reilly, you're good at that."

Reilly sputtered.

"You too Cook. No-one's going to believe any modern woman is going to fall for the rants and yells of a manic cook."

Cook snickered, quietly.

"And me, sir?" Jim wondered.

"Just be yourself Northey. You usually are. Dismissed."

God, Reilly was going to be unbearable. I sent a look of support to Adeela. Yeah, we had each other.

"And Northey," Wilcher called out after us, as an afterthought.

"Yes sir?"

"Install a hidden camera in the vicinity of Lasseter's cabin. I want to know who visits him. If he earns it we'll give him his privacy back later."

"On it sir."

25

Preparing for the boat's departure kept us all busy, into overtime. We left at full tide, just as it was about to turn. It was the middle of the night but cargo ships don't run nine-to-five. It was three in the morning when I finally crawled into my bunk after a busy evening running messages, keeping coffee up to the officers on deck and taking readings. Yeah, cadet deck officers were Jacks or Jills of all trades but I sensed a shift in the crew's acceptance of me now I had my basic ticket.

I'd had to overhaul my opinion of hierarchies. Apparently not all were about an elite and powerful ruling class loading it over their underlings. I couldn't speak for other ships but on the Merkwood II respect and status came with your proven ability to do the job. The more you knew, the more you could do and the more you could contribute to the well being of the crew, the safety of the vessel and to making sure the precious cargo arrived safely to its destination, the further up the rung you climbed. Rank was an obvious symbol of that ability but the opinion of the ship's community was measured in a more invisible way. By graduating I'd obviously climbed one of those invisible rungs. Too tired to philosophise more than that I sank into a deep sleep, serenaded by Adeela's gentle snores from the bunk above.

The alarm woke me at seven. Barely four hours sleep. I needed to throw myself in the shower, grab breakfast on the run and get to the morning deck meeting.

Chief Officer Pertwie, Seaman Merryman and I were taking the next shift from the captain and O'Reilly.

Reilly's eyes were like two impenetrable green diamonds, his face carefully expressionless. But I felt him in my heart. *I feel you.*

Reilly frowned.

Shit had he heard me? But I had no chance to wonder about it as the captain was calling us to attention. "We need to get back on schedule. We'll sail on past Mauritius this time and head for home. Pertwie, I've plotted a rough course for us, to take us to Fremantle. If you could cross-check that and make any needed adjustments."

"Yes sir."

"Merryman. A whole heap of containers fell off a ship on our route last week, I don't want us bumping into them, keep your eyes peeled."

"Sir," Merryman acknowledged.

"Jackson, you're taking readings but I also want you checking the international cyclone, hurricane, typhoon tracker. And get us the long range forecast for Mauritius, Madagascar and Perth. Build us a picture of what's going on out there. In this season there's likely to be a storm or two lurking. I don't want to have to report to Deman that any of our containers have added to those already bobbing around out there."

"Sir." I used Merryman's simple acknowledgment. truthfully, I wasn't sure whether to answer his question yes or no. Certainly we didn't want containers falling into the sea but yes I'd do what was asked.

"Excellent. Come on O'Reilly, let's go see if Cook's got any breakfast left for us.

See you in the gym at 3? Rather optimistically I sent the thought to Reilly.

My hope was bolstered when he gave a subtle nod of his head as he left the room, without making eye contact with me.

After lunch Bosun caught me in the corridor, "Horatio's escaped again. I was just coming to tell the captain."

"I think the captain's still on his rest break. He did the 4 to 8 am shift with Reilly."

"Ah, no matter then. I'll catch him later."

But I was curious to know, "How'd things go between Horatio and Delilah?"

Bosun smirked. "We managed to get him out before she turned nasty about it. The owner's promised me that if and when, you know…"

"When Horatio's time comes," I offered.

"Yeah, that. Unfortunately the males are not as long lived as the females. But, Delilah's owner promised I could have one of the female offspring if I wish."

"Maybe you should get one anyway and keep her separate from Horatio. He seems happier on the bridge. I wouldn't be surprised if we find he's back up there."

"But he needs to be contained before we land at Perth."

"So he needs an enclosure up there. Look I can't speak spider per se but Horatio and I are able to communicate. It's non-verbal but we understand each other."

For some reason Singh didn't doubt me, "That's excellent. So do you think you can have a word with him about not being out and about when we land? I don't want quarantine fumigating him."

Strangely, given my arachnophobia, neither did I, "I'll …have a chat with him."

Something prickled up my spine. I looked around, scanning the area.

"What is it?" Bosun asked.

"I don't know. Just a feeling I guess."

Singh frowned, "I'll walk you to your cabin."

Yeah, that might be wise, "Appreciate it. I'm probably still a bit paranoid after all my previous hassles."

"I don't blame you one bit. Pays to listen to your gut." He saw me to my door, "Go and get some rest. Oh, and if you see Horatio when you're up on deck tonight, I'll have the fridge restocked."

More hapless crickets. "I'll look after him. How'd he get out of his enclosure anyway."

Bosun looked guilty, "I may, perhaps, have let him run around my cabin. He must have gotten out through a vent."

Enterprising spider.

Once in my cabin I threw myself in the shower to freshen up, then crashed on the bed, face down. A couple of hours, yeah that would do. I groaned when I realised I'd better set the alarm so I got up in time to meet Reilly if he'd truly gotten my message. Should I try to get through to Jim too. Why not? *Jim?*

Huh?

Gym. 3 o'clock. I kept the message simple.

I am so not hearing you in my head. I'm delusional.

Not my problem. And I slept.

My nap ended with my alarm screaming in my ear, warning me I had ten minutes to get to the gym. Since I hadn't undressed to lay down on the bed for a nap I didn't have much to do except rake my fingers through my short hair and give it a shake. But racing out the door wasn't an option since my spine chill. I sent my awareness down the passage ways that led from my cabin to the gym. Nothing. Okay then.

Safely outside the gym I entered the code and walked in, finding Jim already there, on the weights. "You got my message then."

"Yeah, but how?"

"I don't know. I seem to be getting better at a few things, the more I use them. First up I could only hear Lydia, then I found out Takemoto could hear me. On the island, Sophie."

My explanation was interrupted when Reilly slammed the door open. "Why the hell were you sending your feelers down the corridor? Something you should have told me about?" Not waiting he swung the heavy door shut and bolted it from the inside.

Er, I wondered about other people wanting to get in.

"I block booked it," Reilly muttered. "Now, priorities first, then explanations." He swung me into his embrace and ravished me with a kiss. I responded in kind.

"Bugger," Jim swore, "why didn't I think of that?"

"Because the two of you were two busy talking. You," he poked me not too affectionately in the chest, "let your awareness down. You should have felt me approaching."

Shit, "You're right." I'd just assumed I'd be safe once I got to the gym but what if someone not so pleasant had been lying in wait for me? "I sensed something earlier when I was going to my cabin. I should have been more careful."

"And," he waited for me to come to the realisation on my own.

Oh, "I should have let you know."

"Exactly. We all know I'm the overbearin', over protective bastard in this relationship but I can't protect if I don't know. Even without what we seem to have, I'm responsible for ship security."

"It was only a prickle up my spine," I felt a little defensive.

"And with your apparent abilities that's a big deal."

"Okay, point taken."

"Good, now since when can you transmit thoughts into my head?"

"I wasn't sure I could. It was just such a pain pretending we were nothing more than fellow crew. I wanted that connection and my mind took charge of that and did the rest."

"She got into my head too," Jim admitted.

"Excellent," Reilly was really pleased. "I can have this whole secret life going on in my head and no-one need ever know."

"Could get tricky if you start picking up my every thought."

"Then we'll each practice blocking." It seemed logical to Reilly.

"I'm not sure that's the way to go," Jim thought about it. "Like Ry says. It's her longing for connection with us that forged this. Why don't we see how far we can take that."

Reilly thoughtfully rubbed his chin, "If we're going to be working as a team it could come in very handy."

"If we take this as far as Jim's suggestion, there'd be absolutely nothing we could hide from each other."

"Exactly," Jim gave a thumbs up, "Nothing to hide and therefore no reasons for confusion or distrust."

"Hmm," Reilly looked suddenly thoughtful, "You're going to find out all about my time in prison and why I ended up there."

"So," Jim said it for me, "do you think that will change what we think of you?"

"Maybe."

I was no therapist but I thought I had an answer to this particular worry, "Do you identify with your time there? Do you see yourself as an ex-con and nothing more? Does that time currently shape anything about you?"

"Probably explains a bit why I'm a cynical bastard."

"Don't forget protective," I offered.

"And with a good head for security risks," Jim commented.

"Okay, some good came out of it and no I don't identify as an ex-con. My identity is my job."

I happened to think he was more than his job but I'd argue that one later.

"I can hear you," Reilly reminded me.

"Shit. And I suppose you'll get to see some of my memories of war torn countries and actrocities I've seen, reporting around the globe."

"I can provide a lighter side," Jim offered, "though some of my, how shall we say, extracurricular activities may shock you."

"Figured that much already," Reilly snickered. "Okay, enough of this. We won't try to block each other for now. We'll see where that leads. Let's do some kata."

Damn, and there I'd been hoping for something more … intimate.

Reilly's mouth twitched, "That would be after, in the showers, we don't want to leave the gym smelling of sex and hormones. Jim, you doing weights or you joining in?"

Jim thought about that for a moment then put his weights back down. "I know we tried it out back on the island. I'll give it a go but I have to warn you I have difficulties when it comes to reversing moves in my mind, like if you're facing me your left being on my right, that sort of thing."

"Common enough problem, let Ry work it out from watching me and you sync with what she does."

Jim nodded, "Yep, I can do that."

So we worked through a warm up, some basic blocks and punches, then a cool down but I noted Reilly kept it short. He was on shift at 4pm after all. With twenty minutes to spare he nudged us towards the showers. "I'm not going to assume."

I knew he meant me. "Yes," was all that needed to be said.

"Jim?" Reilly asked casually but it was clear negotiations were taking place. Even while he was undressing.

Jim's eyes twinkled with amusement. "Actually, I'm taking Ry on a date after this. A working date" He shifted his focus to me, "I haven't asked yet but I thought it might be a good time to try out your new camera gear Ry." He made swift work of ditching his clothes too.

"Brilliant, love to." I hadn't had any time to look at my new purchases.

Reilly moved in for the kill, so to speak, invading my personal space.

I took a step back but found Jim blocking my retreat, his muscle toned chest against my back. I took a deep breath, gathering my courage, and looked into Reilly's eager green eyes. "You'd best hurry then."

It was times like this that I appreciated the velcro closures on my shirts and the expediency of elasticized waistbands. In a flash Reilly had me out of my shirt and my pants pooled at my feet. I stepped out of them and kicked them to the side. My eyes intent on him like a rabbit watching a fox, knowing that at any moment it was going to be caught and eaten.

Reilly scooped me up, carrying me to the shower bay, which fortunately was large enough for all of us.

He knelt in the shower bay, the warm water cascading over his back, as he found my clitoris with the tip of his tongue.

Jim wrapped his arms around me, holding me against him. I sensed he knew it just did it for me. "No coming yet sweetheart," he mildly ordered, even as fire and need roared through my core.

"Please," I tried not to wail. Even in the locked gym I didn't want anyone in the outer corridor to hear us.

Reilly rose from the floor, like some god of ancient times past, rivulets of water streaming down his chest. "Keep holding her Jim. Let her lean back on you. Yeah, like that." He guided his penis into my core and there it was, connection.

I sighed in pleasure at that completeness, "Fuck me, Reilly."

"Never," he growled. "What we have is too special for that. This is what I will do to you. I will love you."

I knew he meant those hard won words, they weren't words he bestowed easily. I yielded to his onslaught, revelling in his energy, drinking in his need. "Then love me hard and quick."

Reilly grunted as he thrust up into me.

I felt Jim's heart beat against my back and knew he rode that need to. "When I tell you," he whispered in my air, "Then you may come." As intently as me he watched Reilly and judged the moment, even felt it. "Now!"

Reilly's head fell back as he swallowed his cry of triumph.

I sagged against Jim, pleasurably intent.

Reilly swore, "I've got to get dressed and go."

"Go," Jim ordered. "I'll finish up here."

Reilly nodded, "Thanks," and grabbed a towel to dry off while Jim washed my relaxed and contented body. As he grabbed his clothes he turned back with one last plea. "Just remember I can pick up her thoughts and feelings now. Try not to distract me too much while I'm working. Please."

Jim chuckled, "After midnight then."

Reilly moaned, "Great, I'll be trying to sleep then."

"Sweet dreams Reilly," my naughty side murmured.

He grunted and left.

I felt sorry for Jim, "You missed out."

"Sweetheart, I'm hoping to have a lifetime to enjoy you. Turn around." He dried my back. "Bonding isn't just about sex. Though I suspect it's Reilly's fall back to show you he cares."

"He kind've said the "L" word," I remembered.

"And let's savour that miracle while we go play with your toys. By the way."

"Yes?"

"I love you too."

My heart expanded to embrace my two guys, *And I love you*, I sent telepathically so that both might hear.

Already up on the bridge, Reilly listened to the captain's concerns about the low that was forming in the southern part of the ocean. "I'll get Merryweather to find out the latest on that," he assured the captain.

"Do that. Even with Ry's voice dictation system I still have a mountain of stuff to clear. Damn performance reviews. I need an automated way that would read them all and somehow get the salient points into my head. I'll be in my office."

"If I read some while I'm here and made some notes on the side," Reilly offered.

The captain brightened. "That would help. But you'll need to think as if you're me. You're normally too critical."

Critical? "I'll do my best to be supportive, sir."

"Excellent, I'll go and get a few to dump on you."

Hell, what had he gotten himself into. But then Ry's thought hit him. More precisely he would say it enveloped him.

"Are you alright, sir," Merryweather asked, sounding quite concerned.

"What?"

"You smiled, sir."

"Oh really Merryweather. You'd think I'd never smiled before."

"I haven't seen you do so, sir."

Bollocks, was he such a grumpy sod?

Yeah, but you're our grumpy sod and there's nothing I'd change about you, Ry's comments whispered through his head.

Hmm, he liked that degree of acceptance but the fact remained that the captain thought him overly critical and Merryweather had never seen him smile. Like Ry he didn't really want to change himself but maybe he needed to be more aware of his reactions to others.

Just don't judge yourself, Ry urged as she and Jim went to her cabin for the camera gear. *It's alright to be who you are. But perhaps something to think about, how you judge others might reflect how you judge yourself. You have high standards and that befits your role but it doesn't hurt to give yourself, and maybe others, a little slack sometimes.*

Shut up Ry, he chuckled. *Go take your pickies.*

Merryweather heard the laugh and shook his head. No he couldn't possibly have heard O'Reilly laugh. It couldn't have happened. "Sir. That low is forming into a tropical storm. Only a category 2 so far. They haven't named it yet."

"Good work, Merryweather. Make a note for the next shift to keep an eye on it."

Smiles, laughter and now praise, Merryweather didn't know what to make of the change in his boss. "Right away, sir. Coffee?"

"No, that's fine, I'll get one in a minute."

"It's no trouble, sir."

Hell, was the man testing him or something, "I said no. You're a valued member of the crew, not my lackey, Merryweather."

"Yes, sir." He went to make the required notes, but there was a spring in his step. Maybe working the next four hours with the Third Officer wasn't going to be the pain it usually was.

26

It was a pleasant late afternoon on the deck of the forecastle, the very front of the ship. Since the sea was calm it was, for a change, a nice place to be. Even a little chop on the ocean would have the bow of the ship thumping up and down in the waves. But it was smooth sailing today. The calm before the storm, I thought ominously.

"Can I pass you anything?" Jim asked.

"I'll need the camera next. I'll just set up the tripod."

Jim passed the camera over and I screwed it to the mount. "Let's see what this beauty can do."

"How about zooming in on that?"

I peered into the distance. I should have brought binoculars with me. I looked through the lens of the camera instead. "Dolphins!" I exclaimed. And they were having a good play, as dolphins did, leaping into the air for no apparent reason. Merely for the joy of it.

"Do you want me to set up the microphone so you can do a commentary?"

"Nah, not at the moment. I don't know enough about them to sound eloquent. I'll edit together the best of the footage and voice it over once I've done some research."

"And then up on the blog?" Jim assumed.

"That's the idea. Start building up my following. Get my name out there."

"Your name's already out there as a highly respected war correspondent."

"Yes but not as a wildlife photographer. Though possibly you could say I have enough cred to pass myself off as a documentary maker. I haven't got a lot of experience behind the camera. That was always Jared's job." a moment's sadness washed through me at his memory.

"Make the pictures tell the story," Jim suggested, effectively distracting me. "I think you'd call it storyboarding. Though here you'll just have to flesh it out in your mind."

A story, I mused. I could do that. The dolphins were showing me a life of freedom and unconstrained playfulness. Set the scene. Capture the vastness of the ocean that was their playground. Zoom in on them. Two dolphins in synchronised choreography. But were there any little differences in their character? Was one always a nose in front? There, was that a scar on the other's nose? Had it waged a war with some deep sea creature? Yet he, or she, had recovered from that trauma. Wow, look at that backflip?

Up on the bridge Merryweather noticed a shadow of movement on one of the ship's security cameras. "Sir," he alerted O'Reilly.

Reilly looked up from the pile of paperwork the captain had gleefully dumped on him, "What is it Merryweather?"

"I saw something move up on deck. Something or someone. A shadow moved between the rows of containers."

Reilly frowned to himself, now alert. "The chipping and painting crews should have knocked off for the day."

"Yes sir, they have."

Reilly wandered over to the communication console and called up the Bosun, "Singh, have you got any crew members still up on deck?"

"No, sir. Problem?"

"Don't know. Keep looking for that spider of yours. I'll let you know if I need you."

He called Lasseter's cabin next, "Lasseter, this is the bridge, are you in your cabin?"

Lasseter answered promptly, "I am. Reading a book. Captain hasn't decided yet if he wants me assigned to any duties."

"Well I'm assigning you. You want to find out who's lurking up on deck, midship, starboard side?"

"On it sir. And thanks for trusting me."

Reilly grunted in the affirmative, "Stay in communication and stay alert."

His next priority was to locate Jim and Ry, *Where are you?*

Up front. Filming some wildlife, Ry's answer clearly reverberated through his mind. Their telepathic connection was getting stronger and clearer.

There's an unknown person, we think, somewhere among the containers. I'm not going to tell you to pack it up for the day.

I feel your unease. We've got what we wanted for a test anyway. Taking this back to the cabin to play with and then having a meal in the mess before my shift. Jim heard you too, we're packing up now.

Jim could hear him too? But he was relieved that they were heading out of harm's way.

"You alright sir?" Merryweather, asked, concerned by his boss's sudden blank look.

"Sorry Merryweather, just thinking."

Merryweather added the apology and explanation to the list of strange behaviour the Third Officer had shown during the shift.

Reilly followed up with Lasseter, "Anything?"

"Requesting radio silence sir, I'll call you back," Lasseter whispered. And then came the gunshot.

"Lasseter, Lasseter. Reply. Are you okay?"

Silence was the only reply.

Reilly hit the intercom for shipwide, "Security team, report to the bridge. All other personnel clear the main deck. Man down. Suspect armed."

The captain appeared out of nowhere. "What's happened?"

Reilly briefed him quickly while they waited for the others.

"Take your team to the armoury. I'll take over from you on the bridge."

Hmm, is this worthy of filming? I thought to myself.

Damn it Ry! Reilly swore. *You leave the deck now.*

You don't tell me what to do. I've been to places on earth most consider hell.

Reilly sighed to himself. Intimidation was never going to work with Ry and he didn't want a relationship that wasn't based on mutual respect. *You're right. It's not for me to tell you what to do. But I will ask. Please. I need my mind clear to go after this armed man. I'll keep you apprised of the situation.*

Ry mentally sighed too, *Yeah, okay, I get you. We're, reluctantly, heading up to my cabin now. Just bring yourself back in one piece.*

Plan on it, fortunately Reilly was getting the hang of keeping one ear on his brain and one on the outside. He hoped he hadn't looked as out of it this time. Though the captain was looking at him curiously. "Just thinking strategy sir,"

"Hmm," the captain turned away and went to check with Merryweather on what still needed doing for the shift.

Soon Reilly's hand picked security team entered the bridge; Boson, Cook, Takemoto, seaman Patel and Wellard with his medical kit.

"Whose wounded?" Wellard asked.

"Lasseter. Gun shot. Let's get going to the armoury. I'll fill you all in on the way."

You know I could go out of my body and check the area, Ry offered, *I wouldn't be putting myself at risk.*

Have you got any of those protective stones on you Sophie gave you before we left?

They had been a parting gift that Sophie hoped would be backup protection for me when someone wasn't physically with me. *I have them in my cabin.*

Good, all the more reason for you to be there. Do it. But make sure Jim holds you. Let me know as soon as you can.

Once his team loaded up on weapons from the armoury and got to the bottom of the ship's superstructure, aka the tower that housed the bridge, signal tower, accommodation block, mess and living area, he held his hand up for them to wait. "Security cameras?" he asked, his communicator was switched through to the bridge but Jim heard the thought and understood what he was really asking.

Between the third and fourth rows of containers back, starboard side. Lasseter's lying there. No sign of anyone else. Ry's doing a fly over but there's no sign of the suspect so far. I'll yell if that changes.

"Nothing I can see from the cameras, sir" Merryweather answered Reilly's cover question.

"Understood," Reilly turned his attention back to his team. "Okay, Takemoto, you, Cook and Patel take the port side. Boson, Wellard, you're with me. Looks like the suspect has gone to ground but stay alert. He's armed and dangerous."

It was freeing to move through the ship in this way. I'd had no idea how much I'd enjoy spirit flight. I might have lost an arm but through Lydia's mentoring and Sophie's encouragement I had gained so much more. So DeSiliva was nowhere obvious, above deck. What was below? I could really do with a certain someone's spidery senses so I reached out to Horatio and found him still making his way up to the bridge. A long way for a small being but he was a bloody big and fast spider. I had no doubt's he'd be reaching the bridge by the time I got up there for my next shift. *A tasty treat waiting for you when you get there*, I promised.

I got a sense of salivating spider in response, he was hungry.

Any thoughts on where DeSilva would be hiding? Like dark, hidden, out of the way places on the ship. I sent him a mental image of DeSilva.

His suggestion was one I should have thought of, duh! *Takemoto, can you hear me.*

Disturbingly loud and clear, what's up Ry?

Horatio thinks we should check the void space where we hid when the pirates came on board. Would DeSilva know about that?

Undoubtedly, as I suspect he was the one who told the pirates about our location. Now how do I tell O'Reilly that a spider made a suggestion?

I sensed Reilly listening in, *He can hear me, he already knows. I'll go and take a look and give you a thumbs up or down.*

Okay, I'll steer my team that way. I'll tell them it's just a thought I had. Sorry to take credit.

Forgiven, not that I really minded.

It was odd moving through thick steel as if it wasn't there but I was learning to trust my astral body. And I remembered Lydia's comment that darkness, like everything else, was how the brain chose to perceive it and that in reality physics didn't apply in this dimension. So the dark of the hold cleared like a curtain lifting from my mind. And there he was. Since I wasn't projecting an image of myself he didn't see me though he did look around uncomfortably. He couldn't be comfortable. He had no bed to speak of. A few muesli bar wrappers were scattered around. A small, apparently waterproof pack, was positioned on the floor, perhaps as a makeshift pillow. Settling from his unease he went back to reloading the chamber of his gun though I had no idea what type it was. Such was my limited knowledge of such things.

Zoom your mind in on it Ry, show me a mental picture, came Reilly's clear and demanding request.

I moved around the gun from different angles, strangely feeling like I was now like a remote camera.

And a very useful one, Reilly murmured approval. *That's good. Hmm, Glock 37, ten rounds, 45 calibre. Nasty. Explains the state Lasseter's in.*

Worry washed through me, *Will he live?*

Wellard's with him. After we get this bastard you might go lend a hand with your special kind of magic.

I didn't really think of it as magic. More like an ability humans had long forgotten. *Okay. But how are you going to get him? You barge in here he's got the advantage.*

Could you spook him? Jim, who was obviously listening into the mental stream, suggested.

You mean haunt him. Hmm, then he'd know we know where he is. Hang on I have an idea. I woke myself, if you consider being in the physical world waking. I was less and less sure that one state was more valid than the other. "Jim, do you know where the shaft is that goes up to the bridge. Can I get in there?"

"It's a bit of a squeeze but maybe. Follow me."

Knowing where the enemy was we didn't have to hesitate leaving the cabin.

Jim found an inspection port. "There's a ladder of sorts in there but how are you going to climb it?"

"Been there, done that." When Reilly and I had gone to rescue the captain from the pirates. "Trust me."

I wiggled into the cramped space, barely escaping cutting myself on the metal surrounding the inspection opening. Jim passed me a torch. Then, using my astral hand in tandem with my physical arm I willed myself up the ladder. *Wait up Horatio.* I sent a mental image that I was coming up after him. *Need a favor.*

Wherever Horatio was he was soon there. Hell that damned spider moved fast. I suppressed my inner arachnophobia, telling myself not to put Horatio in that mental category that included scary spiders, even if he was large, black and hairy. *Hi friend. Got a job for you if you're interested.* I gave him a mental image of what I wanted done. *I'll stay with your body. I've got astral protective stones on me.* I was counting on them to keep him safe even if I didn't know how Lydia went about it.

Lydia brushed my mind. *Call to the angel of spiders.*

Spiders have angelic protectors?

Don't limit angels to those in the religious literature. Any life form can have beings of its kind in the higher dimensions. They act both as a blueprint for all that evolves of their kind and their protector.

Does he, she, it have a name?

I have no idea. Names are only important to us. Just call on the over-protector of spiders and see what answers.

Horatio came to rest on my good shoulder as I sent out my request. He seemed to know what I was about.

I felt something akin to cobweb silk touch my skin.

Look upon me two-leg, if you're brave.

I suddenly wasn't looking at the wall of the ventilation shaft but instead out, into some kind of primordial forest. Two enormous multifaceted spider eyes stared back at me. Gulp. My eyes adjusted to the gloom and I could make out the body and legs of a dark shining being. A being of light but spider shaped none-the-less. As I studied her, I thought of her as a her, I was stunned by her sparkling beauty. Not unlike the magical quality of a black opal, shimmering with colours that marked danger. Flashes of red, tangerine and gold. Her markings declared to all of creation that here was a being not to be messed with.

For someone who's scared of spiders you haven't died screaming. I'm impressed.

She was impressed? Little did she know the depth of my fear. Or maybe she did. *I'm in awe. I think your beauty distracted me from my fear.* For a moment.

You mean that. You please me human. What is it you want of me?

Well, I was wondering if you could guard my friend here as he travels through the akashic to scare my foe?

Ah, the one in the hold, she'd picked it from my mind. *I think Horatio can stay where he is. Since you have pleased me I will do this small thing for you.*

Thank you.

Don't thank me yet human for I have marked you as my own. I could do with an ally among your kind. You'll do. Though you need work. Later. With that unsettling proclamation made, she disappeared.

Um, *Aranya's on the way.* I decided to name her anyway. *Get ready.* I warned Reilly and Takemoto who were still on my wavelength.

Not being in the astral I couldn't see what was happening but I could feel it. A stream of deep, dark, penetrating fear, like an arrow it pierced through the hull of the ship. Straight to DeSilva's location.

Reilly's amusement rumbled through my mind. *Cook's tripped him up. DeSilva's down like a stone. Ouch, that had to hurt. Takemoto just threw herself on him and kneed him in the balls. Is she pissed or what? Serves him right for trying to turn her into some Somali pirate bride. Though I don't think that would have gone down too well for whoever took her on. Hmm, I'd better intervene before she goes in for the kill.*

I mightn't be able to see but Reilly's running commentary gave me a clear picture. I felt his concern at things getting out of hand and then his relief as DeSilva was secured.

Ats us nai, Reilly muttered to himself in some kind of Belfast slang.

Whatever he meant he seemed well satisfied.

Literally, that's us now. Mission completed, Reilly translated for my bemused mind.

Oh. Can I come out now?

Yeah, send your spider friend on his way. See you at shift changeover. Then later.

Ooh, *yeah, later.* Though I still might have a word or two with him about trying to dictate to me. Like Aranya had said, later.

Horatio seemed to know he wasn't needed. He elegantly jumped off my shoulder and onto the shaft wall, back on his way to the bridge. I suppose I could have taken him but the captain might have objected. This way it was nothing to do with me. But I'd be the one waiting with a morsel for him when he arrived there. I sent a thank you to Aranya as it seemed the right thing to do then I made my way back out of the shaft.

Jim had found some rags to dull the sharp edges of the inspection hatch. He deftly pulled me out. "Where to now?"

"What's the time?"

He pulled out his pocket computer and checked, "You've still got an hour and a half before your shift."

"Excellent. To the infirmary then."

"Are you really going to heal Lasseter?" Jim looked somewhat puzzled.

"Yeah," though I still remembered the kicks and punches he and his friends had given me. "He held up his end of the bargain and paid the price. I might not like him as a person but I'll do what I can."

When we reached the infirmary door it was locked from the inside. Jim banged on the door for me.

Wellard stuck his nose out, "Oh, Jackson, Northey. What can I do for you?"

"We've come to see Lasseter," I explained quickly.

Wellard looked as puzzled as Jim, "Er, okay. I didn't think he was a friend of yours."

"He's not. But do you remember how well I heal?"

Instantly Wellard was alert with curiosity, "I do indeed. I've sedated him so he won't remember you being here."

"I don't need his gratitude. And I'm not promising I can actually do anything but I'd like to try."

"Please," Wellard ushered us towards the treatment room where the man lay.

Going by the heavily bandaged shoulder it didn't take much brain power to work out that was where he'd been shot. "Damn lucky he didn't get the bullet through his heart."

"Damned lucky, " Wellard agreed. "But it may have nicked a lung. I have to tell you that if that lung collapses it's out of my league and we're a long way from nowhere."

"An emergency helicopter from Mauritius?" I wondered

"Too far," Jim put in. "Those copters can only carry so much fuel."

Wellard found me a stool and put it beside Lasseter's gurney. Jim took up a place, leaning against the back wall, watching.

I closed my eyes and settled myself, finding my core.

You can do this Ry, Lydia whispered through my mind, *but first we need to get past the fact you dislike the man.*

You're not asking me to forgive him are you? Because that wasn't going to happen. Hell no.

Not his actions. It was reprehensible what he and his friends did. And I don't expect you to like the kind of man he is in this life.

Then what?

Doing's sometimes better than explaining. Let me guide you.

Ok, but I was still a little suspicious she was wanting me to forgive him.

Trust me, Lydia reprimanded, annoyed.

Funnily enough the fact that Lydia could get annoyed made her someone easier to connect with. I let out a deep sigh and did just that. Lydia had had my back all through my recent life.

Sorry

Lydia tsked. *There is nothing to forgive. Neither my annoyance nor your lack of trust. They're largely irrelevant as you're about to perceive. Now, I want you to remember a time when you felt a great amount of love and bring that feeling to your mind. Sense it. Feel it. Let it encompass you now.*

My mind went, naturally enough, to sex, to the connection Jim, Reilly and I had felt back in our bungalow escape back on the Seychelles.

Now we're going to use that feeling as a tool. And like all tools it doesn't judge. It just does what it does. Think of some aspect of yourself you dislike. Put that feeling on it.

I thought of that grasping side of myself that often wanted to chase after the next big story, irrespective of the consequences. Hell, hadn't that been what led me to a war zone where Jarad had died.

Excellent choice, Lydia murmured. *Be aware of how you feel about that. The grasping need, the ambition, the guilt. Now bring up that feeling of love again and put it on that awareness.*

A feeling of unconditional acceptance washed through me. But… *Is this about healing me or Lasseter?*

Bear with me. You will see. Bring up a memory of some relationship dynamics in your family or workplace. Maybe some time you've been manipulated, put upon or co-erced.

Hmm, which of so many memories? I brought up a memory of being proud at having scored a lead role in the school play only to have dad tell me that the whole family would be going on an extended trip because he had a conference to go to. I'd argued I could stay with my uncle but no, dad had vetoed that. And mum hadn't batted for me either. It was a sore memory.

Be a witness to that memory and bring up that sensation of love again. Put it on the memory. Let it do it's work.

I felt the love. And it didn't care about the what or why of the memory, it just sort of softened everything and I felt my heart expand.

Now your graduation piece. Remember there's nothing in this you have to do. You're not doing any forgiving here. You're just letting your tool do its thing.

I knew where this was going. *You want me to bring up the memory of being kicked in the corridor.*

I do. Can you do that? Be aware of how you felt. Even be aware of how pissed off you feel about it. Now put that feeling of love on it.

As I did just that my inner mind morphed to white and I became part of some limitless whole. The love exploded and washed over me, through me and out of me. I had a moment's presence of mind to direct at least some of it into Lasseter.

I heard Wellard gasp at the same time as I heard the patient take a deep breath. Driven by curiosity I opened my eyes. "Did anything happen?"

Jim laughed, somewhat nervously, "Did anything happen?' she

asks. Hell, I'd be amazed if the whole ship hadn't felt that."

"What was that?" Wellard asked, bewildered. "It felt like some explosion went off, though not an unpleasant one. I think I'll carry the memory of that feeling with me for some time to come. Though I'm curious now." He went over to the injured man, taking his stethoscope with him.

Lasseter, who was now well and truly awake, was staring at us all, "I'm not dead?"

"Apparently not," Jim agreed.

"Breathe in for me, would you? Wellard asked, his stethoscope to the man's chest. "And out. Again." He straightened and smiled. "You're one very lucky man Lasseter. I think you're well on your way to making a full and complete recovery."

"Might leave the bandages on for a couple of days, though," I suggested. There'd be less questions that way.

Wellard looked at me, then seemed to understand. "Good thinking."

Lasseter frowned, "You came to see me Jackson?"

"Nah, just helped carry you in on the gurney." I lied.

"Oh, thanks."

I grabbed Jim by the hand and yanked him to the door. We made a strategic exit before the man could ask any more awkward questions.

But I had one question for Lyd. *I didn't actually heal him, did I?*

Source did, whatever you want to call it, you were just its vehicle. But it could never have used you unless you opened to it and you did that by doing the soul work I guided you through.

Hmm. But what is source?

Lydia groaned. *I'm not a philosopher Ry. Find your own answer to that through your inner experience. You don't need an external authority to explain such things to you. You felt it. What's your sense of it?*

I searched through the memory of what I'd felt, *Sort of like it was me but unlimited by what I am in this life, or the scars I carry. Maybe more than that. Some unlimited aspect of, I don't know, everything.*

Lydia seemed pleased, or at least I felt her pleasure in my mind. *That's about as close as any of us get to explaining it.*

But it doesn't care, does it? Nothing stops it being love.

No, nothing. It doesn't judge us. Only we, at this level of existence, do that.

But what does it want from us?

Difficult. My guess, and it is only a guess, is that it wants us to learn to love ourselves and to expand our concept of self to include everything.

Shit! *Lot to think about. Anyway, thanks. Sorry if I got in the way of your day.*

Glad to help. Now go and check out what your camera footage looks like, and with that she was gone.

Jim nudged me, reminding me he was there, "I think we need to get you back down to earth. Look you're safe now, what with DeSilva locked up. How about I grab us a snack from the mess and I'll meet you back at your cabin. You alright with the gear?"

I heaved the equipment bag over my good shoulder and tested the weight. "Yeah, I'll be fine with this. What about the tripod?"

"I'll stow it in my cabin. It's on the way to the mess."

"Excellent, catch you shortly."

27

The experimental footage had been pleasing. Jim and I had picked out a thirty second piece of an albatross soaring high above the boat. We'd used that to head up the blog entry. I made a brief mention of the hassles of stowaways, without naming names, and the fact that we were trying to dodge a storm that kept trying to get in the way of our homeward trip.

But the storm was clearly hunting us. Humidity engulfed the ship, leaving us all in pools of sweat. By the time I made it to the bridge a steady chop on the surface of the ocean was noticeably starting to move the ship from side to side. I held onto the hand railing and banged on the bridge door with my foot.

Pertwie let me in, "You know you can use the code to get in."

"Not when I'm hanging on for dear life."

The chief officer clearly saw my dilemma, "No, I suppose not." He held the door open for me and took hold of my good arm, leading me inside. "How you feeling anyway? Any seasickness?"

Surprisingly no, "Not yet."

"Good. Because of the commotion during the last shift the Captain's already given me a condensed handover and he's gone down to help O'Reilly with the interrogation of our captive. Merryman's on lookout. Get me an update on this bloody storm front. Forget the coffee, you'll find some bottled drinks from the fridge. Get us one each when you have a moment."

"Yes sir."

As I made my readings and studied the available online warning sites I started to worry. "Sir, the barometric pressure is dropping like a stone."

"Let me see," Pertwie studied the figures and frowned. "The temperature's plummeting too. Merryweather!" He yelled at his other offsider who was out on viewing platforming.

Merryman poked his head in, "Sir?"

"Clouds?"

"A wall of black sir."

"I didn't want to hear that Merryman."

"Sorry sir," though he looked as worried as us.

Pertwie hit the intercom, "Attention, everyone, we are on the edge of a storm. A big one. Make sure all equipment and personal belongings are safely stowed. Secure all furniture. Secure all outer doors. Seaman Patel to Cargo Control. Manual override on cargo tilt if necessary. Engine room, engines at full power. Let's see if we can get ahead of this thing. Over and out."

My eyes must have looked huge as Pertwie felt the need to pat me on the shoulder. "Don't fret Jackson, done this before. Where's that drink?"

I found him a water bottle from the fridge and passed it to him."Is there anything we can do?"

"Try and get out of its path, but we've already been trying to do that. This thing seems intent on us. Get on the radio, Jackson, and call Port Louis in Mauritius. Let them know we're heading into trouble. And give them your latest readings, they might want a heads up on what's heading their way although they likely already know. Highly unusual to get a storm this big in this area, this time of year. They'll be tracking it but they won't mind the extra information."

The container port was indeed aware of the low pressure system. They wished us good luck and promised to keep an ear out for us. There was little else they could do. They couldn't risk aircraft flying into the storm or indeed watercraft smaller than us. They were monitoring the storm on their satellite feed and would keep us apprised.

While I briefed Pertwie on the update I caught a movement out of the corner of my eye. Hell, now was not a good time.

Pertwie noticed the glance "What is it, Jackson?"

"Our spider's back. Permission to feed himself. Won't take a second."

"Bloody hell," The chief officer swore uncharacteristically. "Hope the bastard doesn't get seasick. Yeah, feed it."

"Yes sir." I rummaged at the back of the fridge where I knew Bosun had stashed a fresh container of crickets. We'd both known the escapee Horatio might head back here. *It's going to get rough,* I warned the spider, sending him mental pictures of the dark ominous clouds and the now boiling sea. *Watch over him Aranya,* I whispered to Horatio's protective spirit. Then I went back to my work.

I studied the satellite footage Port Louis had sent through, called Pertwie over.

"Damn, it's growing. The captain better see this."

I went over to comms console, "Captain to the bridge."

Both Wilcher and O'Reilly came to the bridge, both looking harried. No doubt the interrogation hadn't been pleasant business.

No it wasn't. Reilly murmured in my mind. *We'll hand him over to the authorities when we get to Fremantle.*

If we get to Fremantle.

It's just a storm Ry. He was trying to reassure me but I caught his thought that we wouldn't have called the captain to the bridge for a mere storm.

The captain wasn't making any happy sounds as he studied the satellite picture. He hit the comms unit for another all points bulletin. "This is the captain speaking. If you have sea sickness pills, take them now. This is going to get rough. Current information has this storm growing into a category 4 cyclone. All normal shift changes are hereby cancelled. Stay at your post until we're out of this. Those on rest break report to your supervisor for task assignment. Expecting conditions to deteriorate within the next twenty minutes.

And they did.

Reilly had left to take charge of a crew, securing what they could on one side of the ship while Bosun headed up a team doing the same on the other side. While I worried about any of the people I cared about being washed overboard.

"Get everyone inside now, Reilly, Bosun. Whatever's not secure now we'll write off on the insurance." The captain gave the reluctant order. The cargo was important but so were the lives of the crew. I knew my friend Deman wouldn't have it any other way. Which reminded me.

Deman, I reached out with my mind.

I know, came the prompt answer. Lydia appraised me of your situation. *Rachel and Valdimir have gone into the akashic to try and plead your case with the storm spirits.*

Good call, though I doubted I could reassure the captain with that information.

You're in good hands Ry, Deman tried to reassure. *Wilcher's the best. That's why I gave him charge of my premier vessel.*

Thanks Deman, his words had made me feel better. *Wish us luck.*

I'll do better than that Ry, I'll manifest the outcome I want. It would help if you did too. Release your fear and trust.

"Jackson," Pertwie yelled at me, rousing me from my telepathic communication. "Weather readings. Update. Now."

Pertwie seemed to have decided that I needed to be kept busy to keep me from worry. Though truth be told there wasn't much further readings could tell us that the evidence of our eyes and ears couldn't.

Merryweather had come inside from the viewing deck and secured the door to it. Waves were starting to lash the windows. Really big waves that rose up like skyscrapers. It was like riding some evil fairground ride that thrust us downward with a bang as we fell into every wave trough. Horizontal rain pelted the bridge, accompanied by an almost demonic howling wind. Nothing of my land-bound life had ever prepared me for this. Hell, why didn't I have my camera with me now? No-one would believe the ferocity of what we were riding.

Reilly heard my thought and whispered in the captain's ear. Wilcher nodded. "Jackson you have my permission to film this monster if that's what you wish. Reilly will relieve you. Merryweather, help her to her cabin. Go get your camera. And, I shouldn't have to tell you, no going out on the deck. That's an order. Merryweather. Make sure to bring her back here."

"Yes sir."

Sheesh, did the captain really think I'd risk my own life to get video footage.

Not half, Reilly growled in my mind.

Okay, okay, and thanks.

Watch out for any unsecured doors. A wave could come through, pick you up and wash you back out with it.

Now there was a lovely thought, *I'll take care, I promise.*

Merryweather and I fought our way to my cabin and back, my gear in tow. He didn't complain but he was curious, "I thought you'd be in fear of your life, not thinking about filming."

How did I explain, "Merryweather, have you ever had a hobby or interest, one so compelling, so enlivening, that you couldn't resist it's call?"

He thought about that, "Yeah, I suppose being at sea does that for me, even in this."

"Well capturing a moment on film, something that shows others something they never thought to see, appreciate or understand, that's what does it for me."

Merryweather understood now, "You're driven."

"A bit." Well more than a bit. "Let's check on Patel in the Cargo Control room."

"I have express instructions to return you to the bridge," he groaned.

"And we will, via the Cargo Control room. Only take a moment. Just think, how many people have seen how vital the work there is to keeping a cargo ship's load during a storm like this? We're going to open the general public's eyes to that."

Merryweather swore, "Two minutes, that's all." He caught hold of me as I was nearly thrown against the corridor wall.

Patel didn't look up as we entered. His eyes were glued to the gauges. Though he must have seen us out of his periphery. "Come to help?"

"Jackson wants thirty seconds of footage of what you're doing. The pressure you're working under. The importance of the job or some such thing."

"Thirty seconds!" It was my turn to swear.

"Thirty seconds and then I'm bodily removing you, Jackson. Be quick about it."

I didn't bother with the tripod then. Merryweather held onto the back of my shirt, ready to grab me more if I fell. The room swayed as the ocean heaved. Patel rode the manual controls, hands clenched.

Merryweather gave me a gentle kick on the back of my legs, "That's it, Jackson. Leave him to it. Patel, give me a yell if you need anything brought down to you, a drink."

"Yeah, one of those caffeine boosting drinks."

"As soon as I deliver Jackson back to the bridge." He pushed me out the door. The sea was getting rougher. We both struggled to remain vertical as we hurried along the corridor.

"I guess this means there's no chance of filming engineering."

"And what could you possibly hope to film there?"

"The sweat and girme. The focus. The urgency. Capture the vibe."

"We'll both capture more than a vibe if we don't get back to the damned bridge. Move it."

The captain looked up as we returned, "What took you so long."

Reilly quietly snickered. "Thanks for bringing her safely back Merryweather."

Merryweather gave him a look and there was a wealth of understanding in it. A tribulation survived. "Sirs, I promised to take Patel a booster to keep him going."

"Good man," the captain acknowledged. "Go and give him a five minute break then come back here."

"Yes sir." Merryweather seemed more than glad to leave. Possibly fearing he'd be given charge of me again.

"Now, Jackson," the captain turned his attention to me. "Care to tell me why Merryweather knew that Patel needed a break."

Hell, "Sir, I intend to make you and the rest of the crew into heroes. The rest of the world is oblivious to the dangers of the high seas. It's not just about piracy and illegal fishing is it? It's the status of everyone who works out here." A particularly vicious wave near rolled the ship, as if emphasising my point.

The captain didn't look at me, he was too busy holding the wheel firm, "Well get to it then. If you can hang on to something while you do it. I don't need that damned camera landing on you and causing concussion. Reilly, update. Any more news on this storm?"

While Reilly and Wilcher discussed that I got international tv worthy footage of the waves crashing against the windows.

Ry, Deman's voice reverberated in my head, demanding attention. *Vladimir and Rachel are back. The forces they've conferred with won't abate the storm. Apparently it's all a matter of balance and a recent solar flare disturbed the upper ionosphere, leading to pent up energy that needs to be released.*

Does it have to be here though?

Pretty much, but if you can get the captain to steer thirty degrees to the South East you should bounce out of it. Or so we're told.

The storm spirits, even with all I'd seen and done it took a bit more belief. And how was I about to tell the captain I'd just had a message from the ship's owner.

"Sir," I yelled over the increasingly deafening roar of the ocean. "Steer thirty degrees to the South East."

"What the hell are you talking about Jackson?"

"Sir, I just spoke with Deman. I have it on his word that that will get us out of harm's way."

"The satellite link is down Jackson. Spin me another fairytale and you're out of here."

Damn it. "Sir, I'm telepathic. Ask O'Reilly, Northey, even Takemoto. Any of them will confirm it."

"O'Reilly, what the hell's she talking about?"

"It's true, sir. I heard her side of the conversation with him."

"Bugger it," The captain swore and turned. "Take the wheel." He yelled at Reilly then held onto the console as he managed to get to the comms unit. "Captain to Engineer. Put Takemoto on."

"Right away."

"Sir?" Takemoto's voice came back.

"Tell me honestly, is Jackson telepathic?"

There was a pause and then,"Yes sir, I'm afraid so sir."

"That's all."

Wilcher muttered to himself as he worked his way to the navigation console and made the adjustments, shaking his head as if disbelieving what he was doing.

Merryweather came back in and gasped at what he was seeing.

We all turned our heads to what he was looking at. A giant wave roaring towards the ship, towering what seemed almost twice it's height. But unbelievably the wave didn't send us to the bottom of the sea. Instead it picked us up as if we were rubbish in its way. The huge cargo ship actually surfed the wave until we crashed back onto the normal height of the sea with an earth shattering thud. Or should that be ship shattering thud?

"Damage report," Wilcher yelled down to engineering.

"Engines are fine sir," Takemoto replied. "All gauges in the green. We don't seem to be taking on any water. Check with cargo control."

"Patel? You still with us?"

"Yes sir, my life might have flashed before my eyes but, yeah, me and the cargo are still here. Don't think we lost any containers sir.

Weight's still the same. Can't say anything about the condition of any fragiles we're carrying though?"

The captain grunted, "We'll let the assessors worry about that later when we get to port." He peered out the windows of the bridge, staring out into the boiling mass of the ocean but the wave seemed to have carried us away from the worst of us. "Pertwie, keep us on Jackson's heading. We might yet survive this."

"Yes sir," Petwie gave me an affectionate pat on the shoulder as he passed me, "Good call. Unscientific but still a good call."

Takemoto called up on the comms, "Captain, in view of the fact that we can't be a hundred percent sure the hull didn't sustain any microfractures can I suggest we keep the engines just off full and make a beeline to Fremantle. We'll use more fuel but..." She left it for the captain to decide.

Wilcher turned to me, "Internet's acting up. So you're it Jackson. Call Deman for me?"

Um. What was I? A phone now?

Ry! Reilly growled in my head.

He had a point. *Deman, we seem to be out of the worst of us but the last wave bounced us a bit. The captain and the engineer both want to err on the side of caution in case there's any hull damage.*

Understood. Get to Western Australia as soon as can. Well done.

I didn't do anything. I just had to convince the captain I was telepathic.

Deman chuckled in my head, *yeah and I bet that was no mean feat. Get some rest.*

Soon. As soon as I finished my shift.

"What's he say, Jackson?" the captain was still waiting.

"He said do it and get some rest."

"Hmm," he gave the order for Takemoto to proceed as planned then he turned to Reilly, "She's right. The roster's thrown out the window. Jackson, you've held up well but you're looking pale. Go get some rest.

That's an order," he added before I could argue. "Merryweather, you still holding up?"

"Yes sir."

"Good, you and Pertwie finish this shift. At last report Lasseter was stable and under guard so Wellard can take over from you. I'll find someone who's not green to the gills to offside him. Reilly, you and me back here at four am if you're up to it. I know you're already into your rest break."

"I'll be fine sir, see you at four."

The sea was still wild so I wondered how I'd ever sleep. Reilly helped me to my cabin, leaving me at its door. But once inside I found Adeela spewing her guts up.

"S'sorry," Adeela looked up apologetically from the bathroom floor where she near hugged the toilet bowl.

"Er, do I need to get Wellard?"

"No, it's easing. But you might want to be somewhere else tonight."

"Uh, I don't like leaving you like this."

"Go," she ordered, then chucked up again.

I closed the cabin door and thought.

I found Cook's quarter's and knocked. The huge, towering Zulu answered, "Jackson?"

"Adeela's been really badly seasick. I think she's through the worst of it but I thought you should know as I don't think she'll be in a fit state for work in the morning. She wants to be on her own right now."

"Hell she will. Key?" he demanded.

"Here."

"You can use my cabin if you need somewhere to sleep tonight." He offered.

"I don't think that would keep me in the good books with the captain but thanks for the offer. I'll find a hidey hole somewhere."

Cook nodded, understanding, "Probably wise. Stay safe Jackson." He closed his cabin door and went to see Adeela.

That just left me the choice of using DeSilva's hidey hole or… I found myself outside Jim's door.

I didn't have to knock. Sensing me Jim opened the door and pulled me in, finger to his mouth, prompting me to stay silent. The reason was clear. Somewhere in his shopping in the Seychelles Jim must have found a roll out futon. Reilly was currently crashed out on it, face flat to the mattress, arms outspread, snoring, oblivious to the abating storm. Why he'd come here and not his own cabin was a mystery but decidedly opportune?

Jim motioned me to a small table where he had a couple of salad rolls on plates on his finest bone china. What was obviously mine was already cut up into small bite sized pieces. The aroma of lemon scented green tea wafted to my nose. *You knew I was coming.* I whispered in his mind.

I trusted my gut. As for Reilly, I felt his need for connection after the danger we'd just come through.

I guess you give him a sense of home, you're the nearest thing to true family he has.

Jim looked me in the eye, *you too.*

I smiled at that and enjoyed a mouthful of tea and salad roll. *So you know I'm homeless tonight.*

Jim looked at the body on the floor, assessing. *I wouldn't wake him. He's only got a few hours until he's on shift again. You're going to have to snuggle up against me.*

Like I'm really going to struggle with that, I commented sarcastically. I used the serviette he'd laid on the table to brush the crumbs from my mouth. *You alright with being woken at 7?*

Suits me. Being a one man show I can work as I see fit. I'll get up with you and we can go to breakfast together.

Now wouldn't that have the tongues wagging. *I'll ruin your reputation as a gentleman's man.*

Jim wrinkled his nose in disgust, *I'm no person's man except my own. I'll be what I choose. They can lump it. What about your reputation?*

Hell, I'm one of only three women on the ship. I'm guessing there's already speculation about my sexual preferences, whether I did anyone while on sure leave and so on. I'm the veritable stuff of gossip. I'll just aim to confuse them. Neither confirm nor deny. It works in journalism.

Jim laughed at that. He nodded to the bathroom. *Go freshen up. I've a spare toothbrush laid out for you. And I raided the laundry when Williams wasn't looking. I've got some of your clean clothes in the cupboard for the morning.*

You did follow your gut, I acknowledged, appreciating all he'd done to make me comfortable.

I tippy toed past the sleeping comatose man and edged my way into the tiny cubicle of a 'bathroom'. There was just enough space to fit a sink, a loo and a shower, all crammed into together. But it was private. I don't think I'd have liked to have been on a ship with shared facilities.

I ditched my dirty, sweat drenched clothes and threw them in the laundry basket under the sink. As I stood back up I gasped.

You alright in there? Jim inquired.

I have what appears to be a large tattoo on the back of my right shoulder. Come to think of it, Aranya said she'd marked me as hers. I guess I should be grateful she hadn't tattooed a dirty great tarantula or something equally fearsome, no disrespect to Horatio, or indeed Aranya, I added quickly to my thoughts in case either was listening in.

A tattoo of what? Jim's curiosity washed over me.

I needed a moment to digest it though. And I desperately needed a shower. *Wait a moment.* I wasn't sure if that was a plea or an order.

Once refreshed I studied it again. It was no small thing. A bright red and black flowery design. But what did it mean?

Jim was waiting in anticipation when I stepped out, *turn around. Ooh, very nice. Red and black, the colour of some dangerous spiders. I think the flowers might be peonies. I've seen pictures of some*

Japanese tattoos that looked a lot like this. He grabbed his computer tablet and did a search. *Ah here we are. The design is thought to have protective qualities.*

Protecting me from what?

From spirits. It doesn't give any more details than that.

Hmm. Given I travel through the akashic on occasion that could be handy. *But why Peonies particularly. Is it a girly thing?*

Apparently not. They symbolise masculine yang energy as well as nobility. I guess Horatio's guardian angel thinks you have some of those qualities.

Reilly groaned, rolled and glanced up briefly at my back then resettled, "Yeah, very nice. Now go to sleep, both of you."

Jim and I looked at each other and both rolled our eyes, we'd been told. He patted the edge of the bed. He'd already backed himself as hard up against the cabin wall as he could. I guessed we'd both have to tell our subconscious not to toss and turn tonight. Shit, would he want sex? Was I comfortable having sex with Jim while Reilly lay out to it on the floor?

Jim rolled his eyes again. *Set that busy mind of yours to rest. It's been a hard day for us all. Reilly's right, go to sleep.*

The ship still rocked and swayed to the rhythm of the dregs of the storm we'd escaped but somehow it no longer troubled me as I drifted to sleep in Jim's arms.

Epilogue

The aftermath of the storm had many of the crew out and about, checking to make sure containers were secure, checking the hull for leaks, checking fuel and reserves. At a pinch we could have steered towards Mauritius but the captain listened to the reports of his senior staff and decided it wasn't necessary. We'd make a run for the ship's homeport of Fremantle. There it would spend a few weeks getting checked in minute detail, ensuring there were no weak spots in the ship's structure.

The captain had also decided that it wasn't worth fighting the bridge's resident mascot. He had Bosun and Merryweather building Horatio an enclosure that would fit under the communications console. The outside of the enclosure had an electrically operated shutter system which could conceal it, using a remote control, if quarantine came onto the bridge. Jim was helping by fitting a microparticulate air filtration system that would ensure that if the ship was ever sprayed with insecticide when we were in port Horatio would be safe. He'd just have to be locked into his enclosure for the duration. I'd explained this as best I could to Horatio with mental pictures and emotions of concern about possible consequences. The spider had agreed to the terms as long as he was free to range when the ship was at sea. Horatio seemed to think he had equal rights in the negotiation which I didn't bother explaining to Wilcher. Anyway, I kind've saw Horatio's point as despite his size he was still a being.

Reilly continued to do his best not to acknowledge my existence outside of work, except when we were safely in the gym. Jim however, made no secret that we were buddies of a kind, often taking his meals with me. Our secret life started off the clock, when using my ability to project, I'd check to make sure the coast was clear. I'd always manage to end up in Jim's room which became our kind've home. Reilly's quarters would have been bigger but his cabin was up on the officer level so I had less reason to be up there if I was sighted.

Adeela? Well Cook had decided, be damned, he'd told the captain, Adeela and he were an item and if anyone had a problem with that they could take it up with him. No one gave the giant of a man any grief. And Adeela moved in with him.

Wilcher grumbled a bit. Something about his world was going to pot.

Surprisingly the crew accepted Adeela's new status and treated her as hands off. If they guessed anything about me and my men they didn't show it or say anything. There were whispers I had spooky powers and that seemed to be enough to keep me in the category of 'hands off' too. If, as I suspected, Lasseter had started the rumours, I was grateful.

As for DeSilva, he was in the ship's brig and there he'd stay until we handed him over to the authorities at the next port. Even if lawyers, by some fluke, got him off the charges, he'd have a hard time ever finding another job in the merchant navy. Deman and Wilcher would make sure of that.

As we neared Australia I rang my mum, via the internet, but it turned out I wouldn't be ending up in her garage anytime soon. Some virus was doing the rounds and as a consequence some states and territories had closed their borders. Which reminded me of the quarantine checks Deman had had to get through visiting the Seychelles. Apparently things had gotten worse in recent days.

Me and the guys sat around Jim's small table, in his cabin.

"So you told your mum about your injury?" Reilly inquired.

"She'd seen the news piece Adeela and I put together before we got out of that hellhole. She just wanted to know I was coping. I told her about my new job and our possible work with the Seychelles authorities. She got excited. But it was when I told her about you two she got really excited. I have to take some video of you both, sorry, and send it back to her."

"Maybe we could just sneak in on your next video call to her," Jim suggested.

"Excellent suggestion."

"Have you thought about what you want to do during your shore leave?" Reilly asked, somewhat too innocently.

"Don't know. Don't fancy going into the city and catching that bug. Might be safest to stay out of built up areas."

"Yeah, Wilcher's none too happy about the prospects of any of his crew not being in a fit state to leave when we next leave port." Jim commented.

Reilly got a gleam in his eye and produced a map which he flattened out on the table, what there was of the table. I moved a few cups and saucers to make room for it. "See this green line here. It's a fairly well used truck route that goes up to Port Hedland, from there to North of Broome to Beagle Bay, then across and down to Alice Springs. The route conveniently bypasses the flooded areas that are currently affecting the area south of Roxby Downs."

"The flood that happens to be cutting off the route from Adelaide to Alice Springs at the moment," I assumed. "What are you thinking, Reilly? You're thinking about taking a shipment through?" I'd picked that much from his mind. "And why go so far north before heading across? The roads up that way are little more than tracks in the sand."

"There's a couple of containers in Alice Springs that need to be picked up for our next sailing. We also have a buyer in Alice wanting a load of persian carpets we bought back. Something about a closing down sale."

"Let me guess, " Jim chuckled, "He's opening a business just to close it down."

"And you'd be right," Reilly readily agreed, "but he'd be paying for our inbound load. Then we'd pick up the containers to bring back.

"Where are we getting the truck?" Jim wondered.

"Deman's got one on standby, through some company that recently rebadged itself as Sutton Innovation. It has its base in mid north New South Wales. They're more famous for their software, a tracking system that's installed on many trucks to check arrival times of loads and locating any trucks in difficulties. But they do own a few trucks as well. They're prototype vehicles they're testing, looking for new fuel alternatives.

"And we get a prototype to test? What's so special about it?" My curiosity was starting to rise. Might there be a news worthy story in this?

Reilly caught my thought and laughed, "We have to agree to sign a confidentiality agreement before they'll give us more details. All they'd let me know for now is that it's powered by some new fangled electromagnetic technologies that taps into the telluric fields of the Earth and the magnetic flux that surrounds the planet."

I frowned, "Ley lines?"

"What are they?" Reilly genuinely didn't know.

"The earth's nervous system," Jim put simply. "Electromagnetic pathways around the earth that are suspected, by some, as having been the main means of transport by some cultures on earth, long lost to history."

"Bollocks, it's a lot of hearsay," my journalistic scepticism in full force.

"Actually," Jim countered, unfazed, "a lot of the science is still out there, encoded by the ancients in the geometry they used."

"Well they made it too vague because no one's been using it."

"Because we weren't ready. The knowledge was hidden in plain sight for a reason. After the demise of Atlantis the knowledge became dangerous, both to have and to use. Magic, as some viewed the science of the time, was seen to have caused the destruction of the global civilization of that era. In effect magic, aka science, got a bad name. Everyone went back to living off the land in small tribal communities. Cities and so called civilization didn't start to arise again until just before the Sumerians."

"So where's this knowledge now?" I wanted the facts.

"The Templars found some of it when they were in Jerusalem. They passed it on to various secret societies that eventually birthed organisations strong enough to stand up to the church and other vested interests. What they knew ran dangerously counter to the doctrine of the time. Heresy that could get you tortured and killed. Finally we got the mathematics of Isaac Newton and the birth of 17th century science."

"You still haven't answered my question. Where's the knowledge now?"

Reilly watched the to and fro keenly but he had his own thoughts on where that sort of knowledge might be, "If such knowledge exists the elites of the world would have some of it. In private collections. Museums. Even in some not so secret societies. But let's just for one minute guess that someone's managed to rediscover the technology independent of them. Those who have been holding on to the knowledge are going to be pissed."

I had an aha moment and leaned back in my chair musing on it, "Free energy. The holy grail, okay let's not use that term. But I can see that a lot of energy companies would be pissed. Probably wanting to make all they could out of non-renewables before they ran out."

"There's that," Jim agreed, "but it's more. It may have been a system that allowed the spiritually advanced to take physical form in any timeline their souls had ever lived in. Or might live in."

"Time travel? Shit, Jim!"

He held up his arms in surrender, "I'm only reporting what I've read. Being an electrical engineer with a healthy curiosity I couldn't help but sniff out what I could about it. Don't shoot the messenger. The premise is we are beings that exist in multiple dimensions and timelines simultaneously. It all has something to do with resonant frequencies. Even the great Pyramid of Giza might have tapped into it to do just that, send the spiritually skilled anywhere they wanted to go."

Which, given my astral travel abilities, shouldn't have been too hard an idea to swallow. "Okay, more than time travel then. Anytime, anywhere in the universe."

Jim shrugged his shoulders, "That's the theory. I'm not saying it's true. But if they want us to head up towards Beagle Bay there may be a reason, it's at the North-West edge of a major energy line that's speculated to run from there down to Bairnsdale in Victoria."

"And let me guess," the cynic in me asked, "it goes through Uluru. Right bang smack next to our destination in Alice Springs."

"Bingo."

"Well all that's just speculation until they tell us more," Reilly interrupted. "What they want to know for now is are we interested? They want me and Jim for our respective engineerin' knowledge. So that we can evaluate the prototype, give them a report and fix any problems along the way."

"And me?" I wondered.

"You can be the navigator and document the testing, with their permission. Jim and I will share the driving or whatever it is we're expected to do."

"Risks?" I'd just escaped from a war zone, survived a pirate attack, been beaten up, nearly run off a cliff and survived a major storm. Adventure wasn't exactly on my priority list right now.

Reilly sensed my reticence. "There'd be a sat phone and internet for communication anywhere and the truck would be fitted with one of their trackers so they'd know where we were at all times." Reilly was keen on testing the prototype truck so he laid out the sweeteners he'd been holding back. "We'd get a couple of days in a luxury resort in Broome, snorkellin', tropical cuisine and a look at a pearl farm. There'd be opportunities for filmin' wildlife and scenery. And at Uluru, we'll have a hire car waitin' for us. We'll have an all permits paid trip out to the rock, a chance to walk some of their canyons and then there's the market in Alice Springs itself. In between destinations we'd have a luxury class sleeper cab on the truck with microwave, fridge, air conditioner. A tent if we want to sleep outside. Everything we'd need to camp more than comfortably."

"And then?"

"Back the way we came. Back to Fremantle in time for the Merkwood II's next sailing."

Sounded simple enough. "What about me getting my new Australian passport?"

"We'll sort something out. But you can be in Australia on your Seychelles passport and visa for now."

There had to be a catch but I couldn't see one. Something niggled but my gut said this trip would be important, not just for the three of us, out to have a change as good as a holiday, but also for the sake of a scientific breakthrough. "Why not, let's do it."

References

- Wikipedia: Spiral Dynamics;
  https://en.wikipedia.org/wiki/Spiral_Dynamics
- The Art of Egyptian High Alchemy
  https://tomkenyon.com/the-art-of-egyptian-high-alchemy
- The Nine Energy bodies:
  http://www.spiritmythos.org/TM/9energybodies.html
- Sychellois Prase Book:
  https://wikitravel.org/en/Seychellois_Creole_phrasebook

Books by the author

Non fiction:

- A Simple Nuts and Bolts Guide to Yogic Meditation and Relaxation

- A Short Introduction to the Sattvic Diet (aka "Simon's Cookbook")

Left hand adventures series:

Heart of Stone - Tyra discovers she's the inheritor of an ancient human-sized stone. As she takes over its guardianship she finds herself thrown into a world of legend where her greatest ally is more than he seems. To be who she was meant to be she becomes his student in the ways of tantric sex.

A Lick of Immortality - Strange things start to happen to Sally Wilson after Simon's rescue cat licks a cut on her hand. In the meantime 'The Major' who saved the day at the end of the last novel has had some unwelcome news. To solve his problems he must travel the Bardo, life after death.

Trust and Destiny - Living out in the vast expanses of the Australian Outback Sarah happens to spy a UFO. Now she's in trouble. Meanwhile

Sergeant Michael Wilson is perplexed by recent events. He's even more startled when he starts hearing a woman's voice in her head.

Don't call me kitten! - Helena and her sister owe a debt to the Russian Mafia and now they must pay. What she's never spoken of is the ethereal condor she sometimes sees watching her, in her mirror. Just what is she willing to do so that her younger sister might continue to pursue her dreams and not be forced into prostitution?

Guardians of the Rasselas (a novella) - Eleni escapes the annual Christmas get-together, setting out to camp at her favourite lake, only to find it's mostly dried up. There are strange crystalline rocks lying on the bottom of the lakebed and they look like body parts.

Don't label me! - George was finishing his engineering degree. Sathi wanted to work in business. Hideo was a happily married teacher. When tragedy upends their lives they seek refuge on the underside of the planet. Along the way they must overcome grief and the circumstances they've been thrown into. In a world where nothing is black and white boundaries will be crossed.

The Vampire President and the Headmistress - Adelaide's on a mission from the Sentient Species Alliance. No one gets into Karpathia unless they're invited but the president of the country has sent his own plane to collect her. Her welcoming party includes the president's right-hand man, Colonial Lupei. But there are those that don't want this alliance to go ahead.

My Inner Alien - Phoenix, or Red to her friends, is in denial. She's definitely not bonded with the Arcturian whispering in her head. But going to Karpathia to film a news piece for Boswell's Alternate New Service she's thrown back into the past, to Lemuria and the beginning of Earth's problems.

Rewriting the Dream - Simon's been keeping a secret, a big one, waiting for the right time to tell Tyra, Arion and Thex. When the secret is finally revealed a mission is put together to save Atlantis, which is caught in a time dilation field, between dimensions.

The Martian Vampire Chronicles:

An open connection of the heart. - Callan's day is going really badly, then an uber powerful being turns up with a job offer. His best friend Harry's not impressed with the turn of events at their work either and decides to sell all and ride off into the wind but his sister turns up at his door, distressed and also needing a new life. Their new start might be somewhere they didn't plan for, another planet.

Beyond body, place and time - Emily's husband and daughter passed away long ago. Her grand-daughter is somewhere secret, and her divorced grandson only wants her for free childcare. So Emily is spending her twilight years travelling, learning from spiritual masters, until, that is, the plane she's on crashes into the South American jungle. The only survivors? Emily and her fellow passengers Aston and Steve.

Ideally Imperfect - Gratia has issues and she knows it. She's divorced and riddled with self doubt, mood swings and a father she can't seem to please. Standing on her deck one day she stares at the stars and decides it's up to her to change. Her first steps take her into volunteer work as a numeracy tutor and that's where she meets Tess. Nothing will ever be the same as Gratia and her grump of a father race to save Tess from her criminal family.

Oh No You Don't! - Thallon's surprised and delighted when his off-planet conversation is hacked by a human. But will she agree to go out with him? Terri's workplace supervisor's just found out you don't mess with her but will he get his revenge? Dan's having to deal with hostile competitors who want his system, but to what purpose? A lot could go wrong but no-one's on their own as friends unite to deal with everything that's coming their way.

The Transformation Solution - Mars's core is still rumbling with earthquakes but the planet's facilitator Naira has more than that on her plate of worries. What to do with the old guard of Lyreans who still sleep in stasis in the bowels of the city, one of them her own father? Octopuses have colonised the Martian ocean but no-one except Emily knows much about them. And then there's the dealing with the disharmony in the galaxy that is being broadcast from a source close to the galaxy's centre.

Across Dimensions

In the Unknown Everything Awaits - Frontline journalist Rylee Jackson faces her greatest challenge as her life is changed in a moment. Fleeing danger Ry and Adeela find an uncertain rescue aboard a cargo ship. Not everyone welcomes their passengers. Both must work hard to gain the respect of the crew. But Ry's strange new abilities thrust her into a multidimensional world where boundaries aren't quite what they seem and at least one new ally requires she shed an old fear.

Short Stories:

Finding Eden (a prequel to In the Unknown Everything Awaits) - Work comes in bits and pieces for remote viewer and psychic private detective Rachael Bashandi. When the local Protectors ring asking for help with a case she leaps at the chance. But not everyone in the Protectors Office approves of magick users. Fighting prejudice and her nebulous relationship with the Protectors she sets out to find one Eden Esme James who's disappeared without a trace.